Murder on the West Highland Way

Jo Johannesson

ISBN 987-1-84914-665-4

To my wife Anne for her love, support and advice, and to David, Karen, Emma, Stella, Sandy, Jay, Murray, Andrew, Kirsty, and Susie.

Chapter 1

Inspector Jonathan Slighman's morning routine was simple enough: get up at 6.00, breakfast by 6.30 and in the office before 7.00. Very occasionally the demands of his rank meant disruptions like all-nighters and all-dayers, but by and large he could operate restfully on auto-pilot for the first hour or so of the day.

This morning, as well as the pleasing reassurance of the consumption of tea and toast, he could preen a little at the memory of yesterday's press coverage of his off-the-cuff comments on crime-prevention given at the end of a brief statement regarding a rash of petty crime in the area .

He had pointed out, in essence, that people were all too often the victim of crime because of their own stupidity, an argument which had to be expressed with a certain delicacy if one didn't want a barrage of negative headlines along the lines of *"Local Inspector -we're all thickos"* or *"Top Cop blasts victims of crime"*. He had handled it perfectly, really, considering that it was unrehearsed and that he'd been warned against making such potentially inflammatory comments. The message was straightforward and he'd hammered it home - Don't be silly - Be alert! Don't let people into your house without proper identification. Don't be daft! Be alert! Don't respond to emails asking for your bank details or offering you easy money. Don't be foolish! Be alert! Always lock up. Don't be stupid! Be alert! Don't leave valuables on view. Don't be crazy! Be alert! Don't put your wallet or mobile phone down anywhere in public.

All simple 'don't fall for old scams' stuff really but it had generated lots of positive headlines in the local tabloid editions *"Top Cop – be alert and beat crime!" "Local Copper – don't be daft - be alert". "Cop Boss – be alert – not a victim."* It had clearly been a quiet news day as a couple of the broadsheets had rather surprisingly given it some coverage. He'd even made the early evening news on local TV. He was well pleased. Delighted even. Realistically, Slighman had climbed as high as he could after five years in this, albeit geographically huge, police backwater of mountains, lochs and wee towns, and this skillful oiling of the press would do his application for the post of Chief Inspector in the deep Midlands of England no harm whatsoever. He had, of course, passed all the relevant exams, and sailed through the initial interviews and was close to nailing it. He was a Wolverhampton man himself so knew the area well and he knew what they now wanted - a good communicator who could put an effortlessly positive spin on things with the media boys and girls. This would have provided them with a perfect example of his abilities in communicating with the public. They would have noticed, and nodded their approval. They liked men of ambition too, and he had that in spades - and in the other three suits as well. He'd taken a risk – it had paid off.

He wasn't popular with the men, that he was well aware of, but nary a toss did he give on that score. Quite a fair few coppers would dearly love to see Jonathan Slighman trip and fall, but such was the price of advancement. He wouldn't lose sleep over it. Just into his forties, he knew where he wanted to go and pretty much how he was going to get there. Where his career, and, it has to be said, his private life was concerned, he was ruthless, single-minded, and happy to manipulate or evade the rule-book. Where maintaining peace and order and upholding the law were concerned, he was perhaps somewhat less assiduous. Justice certainly wasn't his concern – he left that to the judiciary. He had energy, and as an administrator, a bureaucrat and string-puller he wasn't half bad, so his advancements had at least some merit. There were few in the force, however, who didn't regard him as a nasty arrogant prat.

He smiled an insufferably self-satisfied smile to himself as he stirred his tea and recalled the reaction of Carla, his still sleeping wife, when he suddenly appeared on the Six O'Clock last night. "Good man Jonathan!" she had enthused. "Well done you!" This was rare praise indeed and was to be savoured at length.

Carla had ambition too. Lots and lots of it. Where Jonathan was hungry for advancement, Carla was ravenous. They had a fifteen year old son at school down in Edinburgh but her real baby was her market research business. She had given birth to it, nurtured it and protected it. She had watched it grow and she loved it as she loved nothing else in life.

Her great business talent was networking – truly she was a wiz at it. She could interact with any group anywhere with consummate ease, floating effortlessly around a room unerringly picking-out anyone who might at some point in the future be utilisable, and enveloping them in an irresistible miasma of charm, thereby imprinting herself indelibly on their memory. She had built her business almost entirely on the strength of this and it was doing very nicely thank you...except...except...after five years, she too had reached the limits dictated by the surrounding area. Too much scenery, too few people. Especially people of the calibre she considered worth networking with. She too pined for a return to the packed and grimy streets of the Midlands where her pinioned ambitions could take flight. Jonathan's imminent promotion to the post of Chief Inspector back down south was coming not a moment too soon.

Jonathan tidied away the butter and marmalade, went into the hall, picked up his jacket, his hat and his car keys and opened the front door. The phone rang. He rushed into the lounge and grabbed the phone before it woke Carla who wasn't due to get up for another half hour. Missing out on even a minute's sleep made her very angry and the anger manifested itself all day.

"Hello."

"Hello, er...sorry to phone so early...em...can I speak to Adam please?"

"No Adam here my friend, wrong number I'm afraid."

"Oh, sorry."

He replaced the receiver and listened with an anxious twist to his mouth. No noise from the bedroom. Right, where were we? Ah yes. Leaving the house.

He quietly closed the door and got the car out of the garage. The drive from their home in the village of Lochain to area headquarters in Auchtergarry early on a glorious morning like this through some of the land's most stunning scenery would have moved some to poetry, but J Slighman Esq. had a career to plot, moves to plan, schemes to scheme. Lochs, glens and soaring mountains, to say nothing of a distant eagle spiraling majestically upwards on a rising thermal, went unnoticed, unversified. The expensive detached houses lining the half mile into Auchtergarry were passed unseen. The Perth/Glasgow/Fort

William roundabout, the two sets of traffic lights, the automatic barrier at the entrance to the police car park – all negotiated without a moment's awareness. His head was in the Midlands. His body made its way into the police station.

"Morning Sir," ventured the desk clerk and was rewarded with a half-glance conveying indifference mixed with a dash of sneer.

Up the stairs past a couple of constables who offered morning greetings to receive a well-practised miles-away-thinking-of-something-much-more-important kind of quarter-nod in return. Not for nothing was he disliked.

Onward. Constable Wrigley passed him without offering compliments of the day. But she was young and she was pretty.

"Morning young Janice! Nice new blouse," dripped the Inspector with as gross a leer as he could muster. Her obvious contempt bothered him not at all. How, she wondered, could any woman fall for such an odious ogling creep. Tall and handsome maybe, but he gave her the heebie jeebies. At least today he let her pass without endeavouring to brush against her.

And into the open-plan office.

"Morning Sir," attempted some.

Today wasn't a bad day so he responded with a nice grunt.

Over to the coffee machine, pour a coffee, return to desk, switch on computer, gaze at machine booting-up. Check emails

Sender D. Watts, Strathclyde : *Hey Jonny – made the front pages eh? You'll be out of the sticks in no time!* Delete.

Sender S Short, Office: *Community Group meeting for 7/7 cancelled due to 4 of us being on annual leave. Re-scheduled for 3/8.*

Sender G Hogston, Birmingham: *Christ Jonny yer in the Telegraph! And you just a humble Inspector.* Delete

Sender Dep CC Crowsboll, Leeds: *Good to see you making so many lucid points on such a platform Inspector Slighman. The force always welcomes the reiteration of Crime Prevention strategies. Keep up the good work.*

Sender Harriet Inkster, Clapham: *Ooh Jonny – me Ma saw you on telly in Dunlochan last night. Gorgeous she said. She likes a uniform does me Ma. All you lack now is a sense of humour and an ounce of integrity innit? See ya. Love (actually – dig a hole) – Harri.* Delete

Sender Trip Advisor: *Are You An American Express Cardmember? G...* Delete

Sender T Greenside, Midlands Division: *Post of Chief Inspector; Final interview set for 1st July at 10.00 Room 4b Divisional HQ. A decision will be announced by 17th August latest. Please confirm receipt of message.*

Sender R Holmley, Enfield: *You've just ruined my morning Jonny lad. Please don't appear in my Times again.* Delete

Sender Ch Insp T Hodges, Office: *When you've a minute Jonathan - I want to discuss/clarify our outreach policies for disaffected youth and ethnic minorities with you in advance of next month's Essex Conference. A pest I know but I'd better be up to speed. Maybe an hour or two next week sometime?*

Sender Amazon Local*: Top Travel Deals. Perthshire Dining Break at..* Delete

Sender D Wragg, Shetland: *What's this I hear Jonny boy? Been sliming your oleaginous way into the nation's consciousness? Do I smell a move afoot? Which poor bastards are going to get stuck with you now? Somehow, I feel nicely safe up here on the fringes of the Arctic Circle. Keep batting for the devious, the lecherous, and the underhanded. Scumbag.* Delete

Sender W. Mathewson, Strathclyde: *Impressive stuff yesterday. Good luck down south.*

Slighman nodded and narrowed his eyes. Not bad responses. Not bad at all. Even an acknowledgement from a Deputy Chief Constable. And that final interview should really be little more than a formality. As for Harri and Donna...well, what is it they say about a woman scorned...?

Dr Alistair Probe, the forensic pathologist, entered the room.

"Jonathan – you well looked the part on telly last night old son. The very picture and model of the upright copper. Be alert!...indeed! A fine message for Joe Public in this neck of the woods. Most of them wouldn't know how to lock a bloody door if you handed them a key and showed them the hole. Expecting a collapse in the crime figures now are we?"

"Heavy sarcasm Alistair, heavy sarcasm. "

Exit Alistair Probe. Laughing.

His desk phone rang.

"Inspector Slighman."

"Sir, a Superintendent Locke Midlands Division on the line for you."

"Put him through," said Slighman with a little flush of anticipation. Locke was one of Carla's most treasured and carefully cultivated networking contacts. She had met his wife at a marketing conference in London and had managed to swing her a tasty bit of business – and that was before she discovered she was a Super's wife. Fortuosity. He wasn't directly involved with Slighman's application but he had links to officers who were and had promised to keep an ear to the ground for him.

"Hi Jonathan, how are you? Well I trust?"

"Indeed I am Sir. And you?"

"Fine. Just a quick word. Can't be 100% certain of course but the mood music emanating from along the corridor suggests you're a kick-in-the-arse away from….ah… a new post. There are four others going for it but …erm…I've been told…none up to your standard Jonathan. Just keep a steady hand on the tiller eh…and Bob's your uncle."

"Right Sir. Thank you very much indeed Sir."

"You're welcome. Doubtless see you soon. Bye now."

"Goodbye Sir. Thank you Sir."

Today was a good day. Jonathan was suffused with a warming glow of self-satisfaction. Time for another coffee.

His desk phone rang again.

"Slighman here."

"Your wife's on the line Sir."

"My wife?" This was unheard of.

"Yes Sir."

"Er…put her through."

"Yes Sir." Click.

"Jonathan?" She sounded a long way from pleased.

"Erm…yes dear."

"What in the name of hell have you done with the toaster?"

"The toaster?"

"Yes, the bloody toaster!"

"It was working perfectly this morning dear."

"Well where the hell is it?"

"It's on the work-surface — between the food-mixer and the coffee machine."

"No Jonathan, there's an empty space between the food mixer and the coffee machine. A gap. A nothingness. It's gone Jonathan. Completely gone."

The world swam a little before Jonathan's eyes. Something was wrong here. Forebodings trickled in.

"Er…gone?"

"Yes Jonathan, you've grasped it. It's gone."

"Er…really…bit strange…erm..right…eh…I'll be right back dear. I'll sort it out. Ahh…don't worry..erm…be home directly.."

The phone was slammed down with a particularly venomous slam.

Slighman leapt into inaction. *What the hell? Jesus! Holy Moly.* He stood up and sat down again. Time to gather thoughts. Action. Get home…get home fast…and take a detective with him. Detection had never been his forte.

Detective Sergeant Bob Silver, as the only detective in the building free at that moment, was immediately pressed into service. Apart from telling him in as few words as possible that something appeared to be missing from their kitchen, the journey back to Lochain passed in silence. DS Silver was much older, much shorter, much balder, much fatter, much nicer, and much longer in the police tooth, than the Inspector. Better just wait and get the facts. Lovely drive though.

Carla was waiting for them. Demeanor black.

"This is DS Silver…" began the Inspector.

"DS!? Dee bloody Ess!? Wasn't there anyone more senior?"

"Er…it's only a toaster darling, not a murder investigation."

"Somebody has been in this house! While I was sleeping! And you bring back a fucking sergeant!"

DS Silver was happy to note a marriage forged in heaven.

"D'you mind if I ask a few questions?" This in a calming tone.

"Oh fire away."

"Erm…may I see the kitchen?"

Carla led the way and pointed at the toaster-less space on the worktop with a stiletto-like finger.

"So, it was definitely here when you left this morning Sir?"

"Yes."

"Did you notice anyone around the place when you left this morning sir?"

"No."

"God Almighty I could have asked that. He's a real Morse isn't he."

"Carla love, that's not helpful."

"Anything unusual at all happen this morning Sir?"

Inspector Slighman had, of course, been dreading this question, and accordingly felt his bowels soften somewhat.

"Er…well…em…after I…er…opened the front door to leave, the phone rang, so I…er…went back to the front room and answered it."

"Er…leaving the door open Sir?"

"Em. Ah…yes."

Short silence.

"Wrong number, was it Sir?"

"Yes it was a bloody wrong number!" The Inspector's voice jumped an octave.

The look on Carla's face spoke of an eon of suffering and reprisals ahead for her Jonathan.

"You damned idiot! I could have been murdered in my sleep!"

"My love...it was a petty thief. He stole a toaster."

"Moron."

"What time would this have been sir?

"Half past six...give or take a minute or two."

"Right. Expensive toaster was it?"

"No it wasn't an expensive bloody toaster, it was the oldest damned thing in the house. If you discount that useless jerk there," said Carla staring fixedly at her husband who no longer looked six foot two.

"So, why the toaster, one wonders?" mused the sergeant quietly. "Have you touched anything here Mrs Slighman?"

"No I have not."

"Right, well, we'll get the place finger printed. Don't suppose you've got CCTV out there?"

"Er...no...hadn't quite got round to that yet."

"Sergeant − he has two middle names − ineptitude and procrastination," interjected Carla.

"Er...yes I was going to..."

"Fool. You make damned sure we've got CCTV in by tonight − and security lighting."

"Yes dear."

Carla raised her eyes to the ceiling. "Be aware? Be bloody aware? My arse! Tosser. "

The 'be aware' arrow punctured poor Jonathan badly.

"Have you noticed if anything else has been stolen Mrs Slighman?"

"No."

"Sir...have you?"

"No, I haven't," said Slighman, absent-mindedly lifting the lid of the bread-bin.

"Good, but have a thorough check over the day just in case..."

"Eh...oh Jesus...erm...oh bloody hell. The loaf of bread..."

"The loaf of bread?"

"Erm...seems to have gone."

"A loaf of bread? Are you sure?"

"There was a full loaf in there – with two slices taken out."

"And it's gone?"

"Yes sergeant, as you so rightly say, it's gone."

For once Carla was rendered utterly speechless. She looked at her husband in way that suggested he was nearing the end of his useful life.

"A toaster"... long deep breath..."and a loaf of bread." The sergeant scratched his head. "Bit weird, that."

"A bit weird?" Carla had recovered her powers of speech. "*A bit weird?* Too damned right it's a bit weird. What kind of nutter breaks into someone's house and steals a loaf of bread and a toaster? My purse, my mobile phone, my car keys...all on the hall table. None of them touched. That coffee maker sitting there cost well over a grand. I'll say it's a bit bloody weird."

The sergeant nodded.

"Right," Inspector Slighman rose to his full six foot two. He had had enough of this, time to show a bit of leadership. "Nobody knows about this apart from the three of us. We have to keep it like that. Okay? This goes no further until this petty pilferer is safely banged up in the slammer or the whole force will be a laughing stock. A complete laughing stock. Right?"

"Fair enough Sir, I can keep schtum with the best of them. A SOCO will have to come for finger-printing but they don't have to be told the details. "

"Carla?"

"You really think I'm going to broadcast the fact I'm married to a complete dork? Nah. And I think what you really mean is that you, and you alone, are going to be a complete laughing stock. Be aware? Be aware!? Holy fucking Moly."

"Right then, we're agreed...Mum's the word for now..."

The phone rang intrusively and was snatched from its cradle.

"Hello, Inspector Slighman here."

"Inspector! How the devil are you?" The unmistakable rasp of Billy Bootle. Tabloid man. All-round shithouse.

"What the hell do you want Bootle?"

"Inspector...old pal. So you're down a toaster and a loaf of bread eh? "

"What! Who the hell told you about that?"

"Ah, so it's true then. Thanks for the confirmation old bean. You know we simply never print uncorroborated stories. Bye."

Jonathan Slighman, Inspector of this parish, sat down with a face registering intense bewilderment and making a noise like a rapidly deflating tyre.

Headlines proclaiming *Be Alert Cop's Toaster Nicked* or *Be Alert Cop Taken for Mug* swam before his eyes. The Midlands were suddenly in a galaxy far away.

Chapter 2

That very same morning, over in Tyndrum, James Shand and Kate Dalrymple stumbled happily along to their hotel dining room. They had intended to be up at the very crack of dawn but had had far too pleasant a night to stick to such an unforgiving schedule so rose instead at a still respectable eight o'clock. They were now on the third day of their pilgrimage along the West Highland Way and the world was a grand place. A hearty breakfast of porridge, poached eggs, smoked salmon, toast and marmalade ensued, setting them up nicely for the day. They had fallen on good fortune. Not only had the weather been perfect, but ever since Rowardennan, where they had chosen to commence their trek, they had had a wonderful time walking together. As colleagues working for a biggish organisation in London they hadn't really had that much to do with each other and had known each other only vaguely. There had originally been four in the office who had been going to do the walk, but the other two had dropped out due to lack of funds. This had almost persuaded Kate and James to call off themselves but they were both now delighted that they had persevered and made it up to this majestic wilderness. They had fallen instantly in love with the Scottish Highlands, and their feelings for each other were developing in a similar direction.

Both in their early thirties, both Londoners, and both somewhat short of an exciting history, this was whirlwind, was utterly outside any previous experience, and was most certainly adding colour to their chronicles. And, what was about to happen to them on this fine morning's walk would add further to their newly enhanced legend by giving them a tale to tell which was well worthy of a free drink or two back in the bars and restaurants of their great city, and could be related to entranced children and grandchildren etc., for years to come.

They left their accommodation in Tyndrum, light of heart and free of spirit, and headed off at a brisk march in the direction of Glen Orchy. Already they had much to reminisce about in their short relationship, and went happily over the previous day's highlights from the early morning mobbing of a buzzard by some crows till it dropped what looked like a dead rabbit for their delectation, through to the evening in the bar with a wonderfully boisterous impromptu jam session by some of the more musically gifted walkers.

The air was thick with the smell of heather and mountain thyme and they paused now and then to pick and savour blaeberries, a delicacy they had been introduced to by a fellow walker on day one. Barely a mile up the track, his overindulgence in breakfast tea was having a high-pressured effect on James's bladder which demanded action. The main road at this point was running more or less alongside their track and they were near a lay-by. The lay-by was empty and there was no-one else around but, in the interests of decorum, he un-zippingly pioneered a short way into some heavy bushes and heather.

"Oh Jesus Christ! Oh bloody hell!" - his voice carrying easily to Kate, a mere ten yards away.
"What is it?"

"Oh my God! I don't bloody believe it!"

"What?"

"Did you bring your kit with you?"

"Eh…my kit?"

"I've just found a fucking corpse."

"Oh dear God! You have got to be joking!"

"I certainly am not joking."

"Description?" asked Kate as she made her way towards him.

"Male, probably in his fifties. Big guy… huge in fact. Dressed in leathers. Bloodied. I think he's been bumped-off."

Kate made her way over to the corpse in question. "Oh my God. Bloody hell. Better call the police – and fast!"

They both reached for their mobiles.

"Got a signal?"

"Nope."

"Me neither."

"Damn. You happy to stay here Kate? I'll go and get the police."

"Yes of course. There's a couple of lorries coming. Flag 'em down."

James did accordingly and was back in Tyndrum ten minutes later.

Chapter 3

Detective Inspector Bonnie Blackthorn sat impassively as Detective Sergeant Benjamin Munro fumed volcanically about the traffic.

"Christ Almighty - cars, bikes, motor-bikes, motor-homes, caravans, buses, mini-buses, delivery vans, lorries, artics."

"That's an impressive list Ben. Did you memorise it earlier?"

The Detective Inspector was a straightforward person, clear-sighted, logical, and calm. Tallish, dark haired and brown-eyed, she was also a bit of a smasher, with a ready smile which occasionally turned radiant. Approaching forty, and with almost twenty years service behind her, she had risen to the rank of detective inspector through an understated but undeniable ability.

"Aw Jesus now what?"

Her sergeant came in at a rather gangly six foot four. Thirty four years old, with a permanently gaping mouth and puzzled expression, he looked, but wasn't, gormless. He too had achieved his ranking progression through ability. In fact he found that looking gormless was a great help to an investigative policeman.

"Looks rather like a tractor."

"We'll never get there at this rate."

"Calm down Benny Boy, that corpse isn't about to leave the scene you know."

"Look at this nutter – you'd think the screaming siren and the flashing blue-light would give him some kind of clue. Move over ya diddy!" Foot down, screech of tyres, swerve, swerve, swerve again.

Bonnie looked at her sergeant, looked at the road ahead, closed her eyes, exhaled slowly, and gently shook her head.

"Ben, do try not to kill us both. Won't you?"

Her phone played its 'Copshop' ringtone.

"Hi – any news?"

"Bonnie…the body… seems to be a middle-aged man. Maybe in his fifties. Dressed for biking. Probably doing the West Highland Way. "

"The West Highland Way…on a motor bike?"

"Oh. I thought he was a cyclist."

"Who said he was dressed for biking?"

"The guy who found him I think. He also said he thought he'd been murdered."

"Oh he did did he? Found next to the A82?"

"Seemingly."

"Well, he's probably a motor-biker. Middle aged guys and their toys. Bloody fatal. Have the SOCO team been informed?"

"Yes, they should get there within the hour."

"Right. We'll be there in ten minutes or so.

"Hi. I'm Detective Inspector Blackthorn, this is Detective Sergeant Munro."

"Kate Dalrymple."

"James Shand."

"Which of you found him?"

"I did," replied James, making his way to the corpse with the trio in tow.

"You've touched nothing?" asked DI Blackthorn peering at body."

"Nothing."

"At what time did you find him?"

"Nine fifty-two," responded Kate.

The DI gave her a raised-eyebrow look. "Right. Was there anybody else around?"

Kate shook her head. "Not a soul."

"Why did you leave the track Mr Shand?"

"Bladder."

"Hmm. You didn't see a motor-bike anywhere?"

"No."

"I believe you said you thought he might have been murdered. Why's that?"

"Well...he's pretty bloodied about the head. He's too far from the road to have been a road traffic accident. There's no cliffs or anything, and I don't think he could have just fallen over and made that much damage to himself...I wouldn't think."

"Perhaps not."

"And suicide's not an option," put in Kate.

"Really Ms Dalrymple?" enquired the DI. "May I ask why you think that?"

"Well the injury's to the back of the head. Impossible to hit yourself that hard on the back of your head...I should have thought."

"You seem to have had a pretty close look."

"It's okay, I didn't trample over your crime scene. I didn't approach closer than a couple of yards."

"Can I ask how far you've come this morning?"

"Just up from Tyndrum."

"Camping?"

"Hotel"

"What time did you leave your hotel?"

"About quarter to nine...wasn't it Kate?"

"About that, yeah."

"People there can confirm that?"

Kate smiled. "Indeed they can Inspector."

DI Blackthorn breathed deeply and looked from one to the other. "If you don't mind my saying so, you both seem singularly un-fazed at finding a bloodied corpse in amongst the heather."

"Well, we're both embalmers Inspector. We work for one of the biggest firms of undertakers in London. A veritable production-line of dead bodies," said James.

"Ah."

"No, we're not about to swoon at the sight of a corpse," added Kate.

"Okay, point taken," smiled DI Blackthorn.

As DI Blackthorn was asking these questions, DS Munro was manoeuvering himself into a position to better see the face of the dead man.

"Jesus Christ Almighty it's Big Bruno!"

DI Blackthorn looked shocked. "Never."

"I kid you not. Big Bruno as I live and breathe."

"Well I'll be damned."

"Who's Big Bruno?" asked Kate and James in unison.

"A gangster. A nasty gangster. A horrible man. "

"Local?"

"England…north England…Midlands…which is probably why you've never heard of him. Don't know of any Scottish connection though. What the hell is he doing up here?"

"Good question," replied DS Munro, "but one thing's for sure, this'll be all over every paper in the country tomorrow. The tabloids will go into orbit."

"Won't they just. Makes a change from mountain accidents and RTAs though." She turned to James and Kate. "Any idea where you'll be staying tonight?"

"Well…we had hoped to make Inveroran…" began James looking at his new amour and then his watch, "… but looks like it'll be Bridge of Orchy now."

"Where are you finishing?"

"Fort William."

"When's that likely to be?"

"Another three or four days. Depends on the terrain – we're new to this, but we're certainly in no hurry."

"Well folks, the sergeant here will take your official statements, intended stops, contact numbers etcetera, then you can go" said Inspector Blackthorn. Then, raising her eyebrows in warning, "but wherever you spend the night be prepared to be besieged by journalists and camera crews. Tonight and every night. And if you take my advice, you'll tell them to bugger off."

"Bugger off it is Ma'am!" said Kate smiling.

"Well well," mused James as they finally took their leave, "Big Bruno eh? Truly remarkable."

"It's all kind of hard to take in…" said Kate shaking her head, "…what an incredible holiday this is, is it not James?"

And with those final observations, they strode off up the glen.

The SOCO team duly arrived and set about their painstaking business. Alistair Probe, the forensic pathologist, was peering at Big Bruno's wounds. DI Blackthorn and DS Munro approached him.

"We're just leaving Alistair, anything you can say at this stage?"

"Must have happened this morning Bonnie, sometime between five and seven. I'll phone you once we have him on the slab. Be late in the evening before we can say much — maybe even tomorrow. Be a bit more accurate then of course. I don't think his body's been moved at all. Looks like he died where he fell. Something a wee bit odd though...he's certainly received a massive blow to the back of his skull, but he also has five incisions on the back of his head. In parallel lines about a centimetre apart. "

"Really. That's a bit weird isn't it?"

"Might be nothing much, but I've never seen anything quite like it."

Chapter 4

Inspector Slighman's day had been one of the worst ever. One minute he'd been riding high on a wave of compliments and congratulations, a half-inch away from a promoted post in an area he was desperate to return to, and the next he was being reviled by his wife, which, admittedly, was not that unusual, and on the cusp of national exposure as a complete bonehead. He'd be a laughing stock the length of Scotland...and the bastards in this division would laugh loudest. Who the hell had stolen the bloody toaster?...and then phoned Billy Bootle? Bootle of all people - the uber-shit of the Daily Post. If he ever got his hands on the swine who'd stolen it he'd...

His mobile rang.

"Hello, Inspector Slighman."

"Inspector, old plum..."

"Fuck off Bootle!"

"Aw, Inspector...I'm phoning to help you. Don't be nasty to me."

"You're going to have me plastered all over your front page in the morning aren't you? Doesn't sound very bloody helpful to me."

"Oh dear, such language. I may have a wee deal for you though, Inspector. An eensy weensy deal."

Slighman saw a straw float past his mind's eye and made a grasp for it.

"What kind of a deal? Not that I trust you."

"Well, inspector, you've suddenly become a minor story today. A very minor story indeed. And if you play your cards right your story might shrink even further. Could possibly jump from page two to page eight or nine – under the car adverts. If you play your cards right."

"Really? Something big's happened I take it then?"

"Surely you've heard, Jonny me brave boyo, Big Bruno was found dead smack in the middle of your patch. "

"Oh that."

"Yes indeed, that."

Inspector Slighman had indeed heard about the murder of Big Bruno but it had barely registered next to the magnitude of the theft of his toaster.

"That'll push me down a bit will it? Off the front page?"

"Jonny my friend, the murder of Big Bruno will practically fill the first four pages. Your story was just a nice space filler – this is news. The papers will fly off the shelves tomorrow."

"You mentioned a deal?"

"Oh I did Jonny, I certainly did. If you're a good chap…well…maybe we could cut you from a double column of cruel ridicule, to a paragraph or two of gentle joshing…might even miss out your name. How does that sound to you Jonny?"

"If I'm a good chap? What the hell do you mean by that?"

"Well Jonners, we know the Big Man was found dead believed murdered, but hey, that's not much to give our loyal readership now is it? We need a little tit-bit or two Jonny, and, well, you're perfectly placed to feed us them."

"Me? I know nothing about it. That's Bonnie Blackthorn's baby."

"Ah come on Jonny, just think what you've heard today. What's being said around the station? You may not think it important but just tell me what they're saying."

"What they're saying? Not a lot. Well, actually nobody's talking about anything else, but I haven't really been listening."

"You're some man Inspector Slighman. You're some man. Now tell me what you know."

"Well he was found with his head bashed in, I remember that much. Definitely murder."

"What else?"

"Dressed in biking leathers."

"Biking leathers? Right, that's good Jonny, that's very good. What else?"

"Can't think of anything else."

"Try."

"Oh yes, quite interesting really, there were five incisions on the back of his head. Nobody knows why yet."

"Gold-dust Jonny! I knew we could work together! Five incisions eh? Now that *is* interesting."

"I suppose it is quite interesting. God knows what it's all about. It almost looks like a rite of some sort. Who knows."

"A *rite*...Jonny, you're a star. We'll be as kind to you as we can – page ten maybe."

"Right. Okay."

Jonathan Slighman felt a huge and oppressive weight lift from off his chest. He might survive reasonably intact after all. Hope had returned to his life. The toaster, he trusted, was about to slip quietly into obscurity.

...

At 5.30 next morning Police Constable Davey Jackson kissed his sleeping wife goodbye, picked up his uniform hat and his keys, stepped out of his house into the soft dawn light, took a deep breath and looked appreciatively around. So majestic. So awesome. The view from their cottage was still refreshingly new to him as they had only lived there for fifteen years. It looked different every day. The loch, the mountains, the rough patches of stunted silver birch, the reeds, the heathers, the grasses, the scattering of houses, the faraway church – a fine blend of people and wilderness. The air as clear as only mountain air can be. As he neared his car his eyebrows drew together in a somewhat exaggerated frown of surprise. What the hell was that on his windscreen?...looked like a parking ticket. The fact there was anything there at all was baffling – their house was two hundred and fifty metres away from a not very busy road up a roughish track – so surely not a flier for the nearest Pizza restaurant or whatever. The look of puzzlement increased dramatically when he realised what it was. A slice of toast.

What in the name of...? Who the hell would come all the way up here to put a slice of toast on his windscreen? Some passing hikers with an infantile sense of humour and some spare breakfast perhaps?

Who knows? Some silly bugger. He climbed into his car and by the time he'd reached area headquarters in Auchtergarry he'd long forgotten it.

Two hours later he sat down to a second breakfast with Constables Michael Beech and Frederick Wyre.

"Big Bruno eh? Imagine choosing this neck of the woods to get bumped off in."

"Belinda in the public office says the phones have been red-hot since yesterday tea-time. Hacks arriving in their droves - can't get accommodation for love nor money. Poor bastards."

"Should've recommended a tent. Bunch of shites. Probably offering her wads of cash for a wee nugget here and there."

"I wish they'd offer me wads of cash. I'm skint at the moment – I'd porkie-pie my arse off for some readies – no sweat."

"I'm sure you would Fred. I'm sure you would."

"I believe every newspaper in the country's got Big Bruno on the front page. Every single bloody one from Land's End to John O'Groats. You'd think he was royalty or something. All over the internet of course "

"Yep, the papers are going to be interesting reading today all right."

"A right nasty piece of work by all accounts. Whoever bumped him off should get a knighthood...and a pension."

"Yeah but we get the job of catching whoever it was and incarcerating the poor sod."

"Hm. Maybe Bonnie'll let this one go out of compassion."

"Probably a professional contract job. She hasn't a chance. They'll be back in Newcastle or Manchester by now."

"Or Poland...Russia...Romania..."

"Found with his head stoved in and five cuts on the back of his skull I heard. Pretty wacky stuff when you think about it."

The conversation lulled as they considered the five cuts.

The sight of a rack of toast jogged Constable Jackson's memory. "You'll never guess what some nutter had shoved under my wiper-blade this morning."

"Nah, give us a clue."

"A slice of toast."

The reaction of his colleagues was not the vaguely amused half-interested one he had expected. Constable Beech gave him a truly bewildered gape, and Constable Wyre let his jaw fall open and stared disbelievingly.

"You jest," said Constable Beech.

"You're havin' a bloody laugh," said Constable Wyre.

"No. Absolutely serious. Why the shock-horror?"

"There was one on my windscreen too."

"Mine too."

"Jesus."

"What the hell's going on? Some kind of joke?"

"I didn't think anything of it," said Constable Beech, "I just thought it was some kid on the street."

"I thought my daughter had done it – she left just before me this morning."

"Christ I live about thirty miles from you Fred – and Mike's another ten miles on. Something damn funny going on here."

"Going on where?" Sergeant Thomas Grey joined them at their table.

"Somebody's put slices of toast under our wiper blades last night and we're miles..."

"...What?!" The sergeant's reaction mirrored that of Beech and Wyre.

"Aw don't tell us you got...!

"Too bloody right I did - and I live at least twenty miles away from any of you."

"Bizarre, man," Constable Jackson almost whispered.

"You said it," whispered the sergeant in response. "We'd better report this. Pronto. "

...

"Are you telling me, Sergeant," demanded Superintendent John Smart, "that…how many…?"

"Er… ten at the last count sir."

"…that ten members of this command had slices of toast put under their wiper-blades last night?"

"Yes sir."

"Toast?!"

"Yes sir."

"Good God. Men from as far apart as Loch Winney and Spinton Bridge you say?

"Yessir."

The Superintendent was tall, thin as the wind and aquiline of visage. His hair, what there was of it, was combed straight back and held in place with brilliantine. He looked and sounded mid-twentieth, rather than early twenty-first century. His delivery was staccato and fast.

"Damned strange isn't it? What's it all about Sergeant? Any ideas?"

"I can't begin to imagine, sir."

"And on a day when the Division's biggest ever murder case is…is...ah..."

"Soaking up our manpower sir?"

"…soaking up our manpower. Indeed."

"Your phone is ringing sir."

"I beg your pardon?"

"Your phone sir - it's ringing."

"Ah yes. Hello. Superintendent Smart. Eh? Page six of the Daily Post? No I certainly have not seen page six of the Post. Dreadful rag. Full of Big Bluto's death I don't doubt. What? Inspector Slighman's toaster? Stolen? Stolen! And a what? A loaf of bread? A loaf of bread! Good God. What an…an…erm…very…er… Sergeant have you heard any of this?"

"That Inspector Slighman's toaster's been stolen sir? No I hadn't heard. "

"Something amusing you Sergeant Grey?"

"No sir, not at all sir."

"Could be something serious here Sergeant. Especially on a day when…er…on a day...er…right. Has Inspector Slighman got in yet?"

"Yes sir, just arrived two minutes ago. "

"Right, get him in here Sergeant. Right away."

"Yes sir. Immediately sir."

The Inspector had gone home late the previous evening, and left early in the morning, in order to spend as little time in the firing-line of Carla's odium as possible. But Carla could condense a lot of vitriol and much spleen into a very short period, and he was now fully cognizant of his husbandly shortcomings. An unqualified failure he.

Having to confront the Super, after Carla, comparatively speaking, was a piece of cake.

"Right Slighman. Explain yourself."

"Explain myself sir?" The Inspector exhibited a small writhe.

"Yes. Explain yourself. What the hell's going on with all these toasters for God's sake?"

"Toasters sir? Oh…er…yes…er…nothing really sir. Trivial matter really. My..erm..my toaster was stolen yesterday morning."

"And a loaf of bread I believe."

"Er…yes. A loaf of bread was taken too sir. That's true."

"It's made page six of the Post you know."

"Has it really sir?" Slighman's relief was almost visible. "Must have been a quiet news day sir. Must have been desperate for a story."

"Doubtless. Doubtless. Not a quiet news day today though, is it?"

"Sir?"

"Papers wall to wall with Big Bluto today."

"Oh…er…Bruno sir."

"I beg your pardon?"

"Big Bruno."

"Indeed. And what about these slices of toast Slighman, what about them eh?"

"Slices of toast sir? Which slices of toast sir?" Another small writhe.

"You haven't heard?"

"Er…no sir. I don't think so."

"Ten of our officers had a slice of toast placed under their windscreen-wipers this morning."

"A slice of…under…what…but surely… oh good God." A writhe of greater dimensions.

"Can you explain this rather strange phenomenon Slighman? Eh?"

"Er must be a simple er…explanation sir."

"You think so do you? Like what then eh? Like what?"

"Er…well…er…perhaps…erm…"

"Come on then… sing up man. Give us your thoughts."

"Er…your phone's ringing sir."

"Eh?"

"Your phone sir. It's ringing."

"Oh. Superintendent Smart here. No. No. No. I have not read today's damned Post! What? On the front page?! Police think murder part of satanic rite! Where in the name of Helios did they get that rubbish from? The five incisions on the back of his head? What blithering idiot told them about that? Satanic rite? Good God it's hard to credit anybody could be so dim-witted...this is supposed to be a professional police force not the Keystone bloody Cops. A satanic rite. Honest to God...what!? All over the internet now? BBC website!... Mail website!...Guardian website!...stop stop stop. Enough. Slighman!"

"Yes sir?"

"Find out who's responsible for giving this embarrassing drivel to the press. A satanic rite for God's sake. We simply can't have this. Appalling. Absolutely appalling. Somebody will have to be disciplined for this. Severely. Get to it man. Get to it."

"Yes sir. Right away sir."

"And make damn sure not a word escapes about these accursed slices of toast. Be a laughing stock from Thurso to Truro at this rate."

"Yes sir. Not a word sir." Big writhe.

Chapter 5

"Good morning Inspector! How are you?"

"Get off my bloody phone Bootle – it's not eight o'clock in the morning yet. You've made us a complete joke…and you've certainly done me no favours."

"Of course I have Jonny boy. Of course I have. We put you in at page six didn't we? – no names – just a policeman's house in Lochain – pretty-well hidden in fact, if you don't mind me saying so."

"Hidden!? Not very well hidden if you don't mind me saying so…everyone here knows it's me. And it's all over the web for Christ's sake."

"Not my fault old plodder. Not my fault. People pick these things up and run with them. We could easily have named you….reminded   our   readers   of   your   'Be   Aware' pronouncements…you know *Be Aware Cop Falls for Old Scam* or something along those lines. But, hey, we kept it nice and impersonal…just for you."

"And what's all this utter twaddle about Big Bruno? Satanic rites! For crying out loud Bootle, I can't believe you'd print rubbish like that."

"Well it was your suggestion Jonny. Entirely your suggestion."

"What! I never said that!"

"Some sort of rite, you said. Can't deny that now can you?"

"Who mentioned satanic? Not bloody me."

"Well, you know...*a rite*...that suggests satanic doesn't it? Does to me anyhow."

"Bollocks."

"Anyroad me old son...er...anything new to report?"

"New! To report!? No I don't have anything new to report! And if I did you'd be the last person on earth I'd tell. Anyhow, what the hell do you want...what are you phoning for?"

"Just keeping you informed Inspector, just keeping you informed. You'll never guess what I found under my windscreen-wiper this morning."

Slighman felt prickles of sweat lining up to dampen his collar.

"Er...windscreen? Windscreen eh? Erm...no...can't imagine really. Windscreen. Erm..what did you...what did you ... ah...find?

"I found a slice of toast, Jonny."

"T-toast? W-well well. Never heard of such a thing. Strange eh? Hardly a reportable crime though is it? Not much of a story either...eh? One slice of toast."

"But it wasn't just a slice of toast old man."

"Oh?"

"The kindly toast donor also left me a list of policemen's names who also had a wee slice of toast tucked warmly under their wiper blades this morning."

"Oh."

"Yes."

"Really?"

"Oh yes really. And guess what a little birdie told me five minutes ago."

"I give up. What did a little birdie tell you five minutes ago?"

"Seemingly, and I'm sure you'll seek confirmation of this from the officer in attendance, the little bronze statuette of Bonnie Prince Charlie in Auchtergarry Museum has been nicked and a slice of toast left in its place."

"What!" Inspector Slighman's gasp was somewhere between a squeak and a yelp. He sank, punctured yet again, into his desk-chair.

"Yes. Well. What can it all mean I wonder Inspector? Our readers will find this fascinating, don't you think? *Who is the Toaster*!? *Will the Toaster strike again*? Bit like a Batman movie don't you think? *"The Toaster Terrifies Tyndrum!"* You have to admit it has a ring to it. And it's great fun innit?"

Inspector Slighman failed utterly to see the slightest hint of fun. In fact he would cheerfully have stuffed a rolled up copy of Billy Bootle's Daily Post up, or down, one of the horrible hack's orifices and set fire to it, but his true loathing, his boiling detestation, was reserved for this 'Toaster'. Who was the swine? What did he want? What was he building up to? Never in his entire career had he so much wanted to put anyone behind bars as he did the Toaster. His career, he felt, was on a shoogly peg.

"Fabulous story," Bootle burbled on, "it'll be right up there on page one with Big Bruno...although I must say that satanic-rite thing of yours fairly caught the public's imagination. Two wonderful stories! Oh we'll sell lots of our yellow rag tomorrow Inspector! Lots of them!"

"Look Bootle...er Billy...keep my name out of it for God's sake. I'll try and get you some snippets about Big Bruno but there has to be give and take."

"Hm. We could get a lot of mileage out of the '*Be Aware Cop Conned Something Rotten*' angle, you know."

A chasm not much bigger than the Horsehead Nebula yawned under the feet of Inspector Slighman.

"Billy – be reasonable – I'll get you something on Big Bruno – honest. An exclusive. I will."

"Right me old tarry-hat. It's a deal. We'll keep your profile low..."

"Low...?"

"Very low. Okay...non-existent...in tomorrow's edition. But if we don't get regular feeds – well my boss is a fearsome girl. She'll want yer head Jonny boy, she'll want yer head. And she'll get it too."

Ten minutes later Superintendent Smart looked in horror from Inspector Slighman to Detective Sergeant Silver.

"I don't believe it! I–do-not-believe-it! You say the press already know about these damned slices of toast?"

"I'm afraid so sir."

"And what in the name of Hades is this about our museum's wee Prince whatsisname being replaced by a...by a...slice of...."

"Toast sir."

"Yes Sergeant! I'm well aware of what it was replaced with! I'm just finding it difficult to say the word out loud!"

"Yessir."

"This is a disaster Slighman. A complete disaster. Who the hell is doing this?"

"By God I wish I knew sir."

" Sergeant Silver...any ideas? Any developments regarding this confounded toaster of Slighman's?"

"Well sir, nothing much, but we did get a good finger-print off a teaspoon lying on the Inspector's worktop. Unfortunately doesn't match anything we've got on record though."

"A finger-print? On a teaspoon? Bit careless wasn't it?"

"Not the work of a pro, certainly. Doesn't match the Inspector's prints - or his wife's sir, and nobody else has been in their kitchen for weeks seemingly. So must be the perpetrator's."

"Any trace on the call as Inspector Slighman was leaving his house?"

"Untraceable sir. Number withheld."

"Right. Which officer went to the museum?"

"I did, sir, just got back five minutes ago."

"Oh you did did you sergeant. Anything?"

"It's being finger-printed sir. No security as such round the statuette. No CCTV or anything like that anywhere in the museum — Christ it's just a big shed really — just local history and heritage really, nothing in the place worth nicking to be honest. Certainly no value attached to the statuette — not a work of art or anything like that. Was more just an illustrative kind of thing. Less than a foot high. Theft was just a walk in and pick up job. The cleaner starts at seven in the morning — she was putting some rubbish out the back when she thought she saw someone through one of the museum windows. Thought it was the curator Mrs Wilks in early, then when she came back in she noticed right away that Charlie had gone."

"Charlie? Oh, yes, Charlie. So. All this happened in the last couple of hours. Incredible. Right, thanks Sergeant."

"Sir."

Superintendent Smart groaned. "The tabloids will doubtless describe it as a priceless artefact stolen from a high security museum under the noses of the hapless police. Slighman — any thoughts on this? The theft of our bonnie wee prince?"

"Er…not really sir. Bit of mischief making."

"Mischief? We're going to look utterly ludicrous the length of the UK!"

"Yes sir."

"Right. Okay. Now. Sergeant…what about these blasted slices of toast this morning? Half the cars in the Highlands seem to have been toasted…if you'll excuse the term."

"No leads on that sir. Must've taken them all night to do it. Nobody saw anything."

"Them? You think there's more than one villain here?"

"Almost definitely sir. Probably two…maybe more. When the Inspector opened his door yesterday morning, one of them will have phoned his number while the other one sneaked in and hid…then buggered off with the toaster. And the loaf of bread of course." Slighman looked at DS Silver with eyes which said, *please don't mention that again Sergeant…and thanks a whole lot.*

"And all those slices of toast this morning, sir," continued the DS, "that's more than one person could have managed, surely."

"Well Slighman? Do you agree with that hypothesis?"

"Er…yes sir."

"Anything else Sergeant?"

"Well sir, it looks as though the perp is the one phoning the press. Although what his, or her, game is, God only knows."

"Not one of our boys then?"

"Don't think so sir."

"Let's hope your right Sergeant. Whole thing's baffling. Right you two, we need this person…or persons…nicked and we need him nicked damned soon. What's your strategy Slighman? Gimme a run down."

"Er...well... er...first...er I'd like...er...your phone sir."

"You'd like my phone?"

"Er no sir, I mean it's ringing sir. Your phone's ringing."

"Oh right. Superintendent Smart here. Ah Bonnie's arrived has she? Good. Send her in. Send her in."

He replaced the telephone carefully on its receiver, looked up, and sighed heavily.

"Okay you two, get out there and get at it. We need results. We need this ne'er-do-well apprehended and behind bars pronto. Get to it!"

They left. The Superintendent sighed heavily and looked blankly at the vista of highland grandeur out of his window. Hard to believe that a short twenty-four hours earlier he'd been enjoying breakfast in the wonderfully plush Chesterlake Hotel in London. The conference for top civil servants, junior ministers and high ranking police officers had gone incredibly well and his wife had loved the dance-finale thing on the last evening. This was a brutal return.

The Superintendent looked at DI Blackthorn as she entered his room and breathed a sigh which could have been construed as registering some relief, but not much.

"Right Bonnie, update me. What's happening with Big Blut...er...Bruno? Eh? Come on, fill me in. Fill me in."

"Well sir, I'm waiting for Alistair Probe to phone me with the lab results but it looks as though he was killed sometime between five and seven yesterday morning. It's definitely Big Bruno Sir. John Steven Bair to give him his full name. Lived in Manchester latterly but had moved all around Lancashire in his time...Liverpool, Preston, Blackburn...and had gangster influence throughout the area. He was a very big man physically – around six foot four and heavily built. A bruiser by trade. Violent. Has done time – short spells - mostly gambling offences and some drug dealing but he was never convicted of anything to put him away for a decent spell. Witness intimidation was a specialty, seemingly. And plenty minions to carry the can for him and do his dirty work. Basically he was a thug with some intelligence and management skills."

"Sounds like a fine fellow. I'd heard of him, as we all had of course, over the years, but he never ventured into any of my patches."

"No sir. No immediately obvious connection with Scotland at all."

"What's all this about ritual incisions Bonnie? Where did that come from? Eh?"

"Well sir, it looks as if the blow to the back of the head killed him, although forensics haven't confirmed that yet, but, seemingly, he also has five clear incisions on the back of his head, about a centimetre apart - but this drivel about Satanic rites is pure tabloid creativity I guess."

 "Post claims to have a police source."

"Hm. Hard to believe. "

"These incisions...they must have been administered after he'd been hit. Surely."

"Possibly sir, I wouldn't like to speculate at this stage. Certainly there were no signs of a struggle, or of him being restrained or anything. But I'll wait for Alistair Probe's report. Should be anytime now."

"Right. So...where's DS Munro at the moment...what's he doing?"

"He's gone off to Manchester sir, to question Bruno's widow, family, friends and what have you, and find out as much about him as possible from the local police. There's a fair bit about him on file but it's the stuff that's not on record we want. The sergeant's good at that sort of thing. Manages to wheedle all sorts of confidences out of people."

"Does he? Jolly good. Looks a bit gormless though. "

DI Blackthorn smiled and nodded.

"Yes, but don't let that fool you. Anyhow, we'll have to establish what exactly Big Bruno was up in this neck of the woods for. Not exactly the tourist type, you wouldn't think. Must have been business, surely. It's all a bit mysterious at the moment. He was dressed in biker's leathers but no sign of a bike. No sign of a helmet. No sign of a struggle. His body was slightly off the track but it hadn't been hidden or anything. It would almost certainly have been found at some point during the day with the number of walkers dong the Way at this time of year."

"So. Looks like he might have had a pre-arranged rendezvous with someone who then dealt him a killer blow."

"Very possibly sir. Although I suppose it could have been a chance meeting with someone from his past, or even a complete stranger...who knows?"

"Any idea when he got here?"

"I've had every hotel, bed and breakfast, guest house, bunk house, restaurant, café, filling-station, etc checked out but nobody seems to have seen him. And he's not easily missed. Would stand out a mile."

"Anything found in the vicinity?"

"Nope. Horribly difficult terrain out there sir, but nothing obvious like a murder weapon or bikers helmet or anything. The ground doesn't look trampled or anything – the grass and heather just spring back into shape anyhow. The team spent all day yesterday combing the place but found nothing."

"Damn, we could well use a lead or two."

"Yes. I'll put out an appeal for witnesses. It happened really early in the morning but you never know, somebody may have seen something."

"True. Right, better let you get on with it then."

"Yes sir, I'll keep you posted sir."

"Right Bonnie, thanks….oh…er…Bonnie…em…by the way, what do you make of this toaster baloney?"

"Yes sir, all a bit strange sir. The press are certainly going to have a field day. Couldn't have happened at a worse time really. Every tabloid journalist in the land seems to be congregating here for the Big Bruno story – a nice little bonus for them, this toaster story. I'm sure DS Silver will have the culprit – or culprits - locked up soon sir."

"God I hope so. I wish we could spare you for the case Bonnie. We're going to look ridiculous when it all gets out. We need results soon Bonnie – on both fronts, dammit. We need results."

Chapter 6

Inspector Slighman tried to be invisible as he slunk towards his desk, but to no avail.

"Morning sir!" came the happy chorus.

"Muesli for breakfast this morning was it sir?"

"Any news of your toaster, sir?"

"Eggs in a soft roll's quite nice sir."

"When did you *become aware* it'd been nicked sir?"

His aching, crawling, discomfort was a joy to behold.

He showed his teeth in a smile which would have flattened a field of corn, and after a pained eternity crossing the 10 metres of the office, he reached the sanctuary of his desk and booted up his PC. Email time.

Sender Harriet Inkster, Clapham: *Ooooohh Jonnnnny! Is that you on page 6 of the Post? Stolen from the house of a policeman in Lochain eh? Maybe you do have a sense of humour after all! From Be Aware to be a diddy in 24 hours! What you doing without yer toas...*Delete

Sender S Short, Office: *Meeting of Community Group re-scheduled for 3/8 has been cancelled due to previous commitments of 4 members. Re-scheduled for 10/8.*

Sender G Hogston, Birmingham: *Ah Jonny, our very own Lochain policeman. You didn't make the Telegraph today – but keep trying! The Daily Post sold big in our office today though! Thought you should be aware .* Delete

Sender Amazon local: *Select from our fabulous range of toasters. Toasters from £34*...Delete Delete Delete

Sender F Slighman, Edinburgh: *Dad has sombody nicked our toaster? Mum will be nicely inkandesint -no way Im coming home this weekend. Send a fat wad. Felix*

Sender R Holmley, Enfield: *You've just made my morning Jonny lad. That wee mention in the Post almost sneaked by us...but not quite. Waiting excitedly for developments.* Delete

Sender eBay Sales Team: *Toasters from*....Delete

Sender D Wragg, Shetland: *Jonny! What joyous stuff is this? The great Be Aware man gets his toaster nicked! Ha ha ha ha ha ha ha ha ha ha ha ha ha ha ha ha ha ha ha ha ha ha ha ha ha.* Delete

Sender B Aronson, Glasgow: *Hey Slighman you old shite – thought you'd like to know there's a toaster sale on in Galbraithe's at the moment. When you find the neddie boy who nicked it you'll have to grill him. He'll be toast after that!* Delete

Slighman closed down his Inbox. Shower of bastards. Not one remotely supportive email...not that he expected any. And how the hell do eBay and Amazon do it. The infuriating thing was that he had been given his orders from Carla to get a new bloody toaster anyhow. Maybe Galbraithe's really did have a sale on.

DI Blackthorn was driving pensively back to the scene of the crime for another look around in the hope of finding something, anything, to get the case moving a bit when Alistair Probe made radio contact.

"Bonnie. How are you?"

"I'm fine Alistair, how are you yourself?"

"Grand Bonnie. Grand. Right. Some facts.

"Hallelujah."

"The big man died sometime around six thirty yesterday morning. Half an hour at the most either way. He died where he lay – certainly wasn't moved in any way. Cause of death – he was hit very hard from behind with a blunt instrument."

The inspector worked her features into a puzzled grimace. A blunt instrument? She had never actually encountered these words outside of a crime novel.

"A blunt instrument Alistair?"

"Well, this particular blunt instrument was a banjo."

"A BANJO!?

"Yes. A five string banjo, to be precise Bonnie. Five steel strings. Jolly sharp. Hence the five incisions."

"Good God! That's hard to believe."

"Mmhm. Effective weapon nonetheless Bonnie."

"A banjo though...that's pretty neat isn't it?   Well well well. And the murder weapon'll certainly be a bit easier to find than a rock and a razor-blade, that's for sure. Anything else of note?"

"Well, looks like he probably arrived on a motor bike right enough – recent traces of oil on his leathers - but we can't be a hundred percent sure on that one. No tell tale blood or threads or anything whatsoever from anyone else. We might be able to ascertain what make of banjo it was – but for that we need to confer with someone from the banjo business. That's about it...oh he had a small amount of whisky in his stomach...but apart from that, that's it Bonnie I'm afraid."

"Okay Alistair, many thanks."

A banjo eh? How cool was that? The picture of Big Bruno's early morning whacking played over in front of her eyes. Must've been a pretty solid banjo – and a fearsome whack. Right, start looking for banjo players! Or at least a banjo-toting individual. What did she know about banjos? Little indeed. A stringed musical instrument resembling a long frying-pan. Perfect shape for holding and hitting with - like a baseball bat - or a table-leg. Less popular than the guitar of course. Could you kill someone with a guitar? Hm. An electric one maybe. Academic anyhow.

Not an easy weapon to hide that's for sure - but then it wouldn't look like a weapon – at least not until it was wielded as such. Somebody carrying a table leg or a baseball bat would certainly raise an eyebrow or two…but a banjo? No. There was something intrinsically innocent about a banjo – it was redolent of fun. Real ale and folk music, beards and trad jazz, cowboy hats and country music. Murder – not at all. And what the hell was a five string banjo? How many strings did a banjo normally have? Should it have had more strings? Was one missing, or broken? Like everyone else Bonnie was given a guitar when she was younger and seemed to remember it had six strings…but a banjo? Easy enough to find out about the things of course. The type of banjo which saw off Big Bruno may give them a useful lead, who knows?

But they needed to find it. If it still existed.

Superintendent Smart held his head in his hands.
"A banjo Bonnie? *A banjo*? Please tell me I misheard you."
"Sorry sir. A five-stringed banjo. "

"What is it about this damned case? About both these damned cases in fact. The press will take some delight from this, that's for sure. The focus of the entire UK is beamed in on our little force and laughing its head off. All I need to hear now is that the murderer was dressed as a clown with a flashing red nose and a whirling bow-tie. And the toast story might leak soon. Dear God." The Superintendent shook his head sadly and sighed, "Get me Slighman on your way out Bonnie. Get me Slighman". The jollies in the Chesterlake Hotel in London seemed of a different era.

Chapter 7

"Bad news Slighman, bad news."

"Sir?"

"It seems our man was dispatched with a blow from a banjo."

"A banjo?"

"A banjo. "

"A banjo?"

"Yes! A banjo! For God's sake! A banjo! Got it!?"

"Yes sir. Er, how is that bad news sir?"

The Superintendent's head returned deep into the folds of his hands. How could this man before him be an Inspector?

"How is it bad news? Right. Where to begin? Okay, let me enlighten you Inspector. When the gutter press finds this out it adds another dimension of farce to the hunt for Big Whatsisname's killer. Right? Although we didn't choose the murder weapon, it'll still reflect on us. Okay? Somehow, it'll merge in the minds of the great British public with your toaster nonsense and we'll look like a damned circus, instead of the highly efficient police force that we are. Now have you grasped that?"

"Yes sir, of course sir." Slighman found it terribly difficult not to smile. This banjo business would hit big – it would certainly deflect a lot of column inches away from his toaster nightmare. He couldn't wait to tell Billy Bootle.

"Right Slighman, your job continues to be the stoppage of leaks to the press. Been like a damned sieve these last two days."

"Yes sir."

"Get on with it." The Superintendent once more shook his head. *How is that bad news?* Good God.

Inspector Slighman was almost jaunty of demeanor when he phoned Billy Bootle.

"Bootle, I have something for you. Something I think you'll like."

"Really? Do tell, old Billy's all agog."

"Well you may be all agog Bootle, but I'm telling you nothing till I have your assurance that my name stays out of your appalling rag."

"Well, old man, if it's a really nice tit-bit then I think we can agree to that for another twenty-four hours."

"Twenty-four hours? No no no Billy, not just twenty-four hours. Permanently."

"Oh Inspector, my dear chum, I can't give guarantees like that. My leader-lady already knows who you are and she dearly wants you in for human interest...*Be Aware*...remember?"

Slighman's recently acquired bolshie demeanor started to back-pedal.

"Right, I shan't tell you what I was going to tell you then."

"Now now Jonny, let's not fall out. I'll tell you what, I'll keep your name out for forty-eight hours – how's that? The toaster story will be old hat by then. Nobody'll be interested. But if you don't tell me...well, grave consequences perhaps. And of course, you must remember Johnny, that you may be able to bribe me with something new tomorrow. Isn't that true?"

"Oh all right then, all right. Forty-eight hours..."

"So what's the big story?"

"Big Bruno..."

"Yes...?"

"He was hit on the back of the head…"

"Yes…Jonny….Yes?"

"With a banjo."

"Never!"

"Yes."

"A banjo!"

"Yep. A banjo."

"Well Glory Be. Jonny, I've said it before, and I'll say it again. You're a star."

Our Inspector gazed skywards and sighed a long silent sigh. He might yet escape relatively unscathed.

"Oh by the way Jonners old chap, maybe you haven't heard yet - someone has put make-up on the face of the statue of Desperate Dan in Dundee and placed a slice of toast in his mouth."

"What!?" His demeanor slipped a little once more.

"And they've posted the whole operation on YouTube."

"What…I don't believe it, I really do not believe it, Oh bugger bugger bugger." The Inspector's detestation of the Toaster, already total, became absolutely completely and utterly total. "But…aw come on Billy…" he said in a plaintive wheedle, "surely that's not a big enough story for the Daily Post? A bit of make-up and a slice of toast? Who's going to be interested in that?"

"Oh only the great British reading public Jonny, only them. But don't worry my friend, your name will not be found anywhere in tomorrow's Post. Nor yet in the one after. You have the word of Billy Bootle on that."

"Thanks for that Billy," said the Inspector, through teeth locked in combat.

…

The Inspector trusted the word of Billy Bootle about as far as he could throw a small car but his options were limited in the extreme. He reviewed his situation over a lunch of boiled cardboard and steamed sawdust eaten in a cafeteria well away from the police canteen. He needed some good news. He needed this case to gather momentum and to gather it quickly. Perhaps DS Silver had news...he picked up his mobile.

"Bob Silver."

"Bob, it's Inspector Slighman here,"

"Afternoon sir."

"Er...afternoon Bob, any news regarding this bloody toaster affair?"

"Yes, there is actually sir. There was a button and some threads caught on the side of the stand that the statuette of Bonnie Prince Charlie was on. Almost certain that it belonged to the thief − probably tore off as he or she leaned over to grab the thing. No prints on it but it's an unusual button − it has the name of the manufacturer in tiny letters on it. I managed to trace them easily enough − a Bristol based company - and they said it almost definitely came off a pair of top-of-the-range gent's cord trousers. The button's a sort of orangey-red, so the trousers will be the same colour. I've sent it off to them to see if they can tell us anything else."

"Excellent sergeant, absolutely excellent. Not very professional though...this Toaster... is he? Fingerprints in...er...my kitch..er... the first crime-scene, and now a button. At this rate we'll have our hands on his collar in no time."

"Well I hope so sir. Helps us quite a bit I would say − not many people under the age of forty wear trousers like that. Especially at this time of year − the material's pretty thick. So if the perp's

still wearing them...well...old or young, it doesn't really matter -
he'll stand out."

"Very true Sergeant, very true."

"Another thing sir, not such good news, I was sent a link to
YouTube earlier on, it's a video..."

"Don't tell me Sergeant...Desperate Dan."

"Yes sir, that's right. Have you seen it?"

"No I haven't."

"It just shows a close-up of Dan's face with a gloved hand
putting make-up on it, and then putting a slice of toast in his
mouth. All speeded up. Only takes about thirty seconds. Quite
funny really."

The Inspector seethed quietly into his mobile, praying to
himself that this particular video went unnoticed by the world's
YouTubing public.

Chapter 8

Detective Sergeant Ben Munro stood outside Big Bruno's door and rang the bell. The house was large, imposing, secluded, expensive, modern, and surrounded by huge well-cared for grounds, which in turn were surrounded by a nicely understated security fence. The gate, however, had been left open. He was accompanied by Detective Constable Rebecca Bickerstaff, who had been assigned to him courtesy of the local police division for the duration of his enquiries. She knew the area well, and had a pretty comprehensive knowledge of the local crime scene. Eight years in service, quite new to plain clothes, but loving it, and proving useful. Both officers were dressed smartly in quiet colours although the sergeant's dark grey suit seemed to make him look even more gangly than usual. The constable's dark green suit made her look efficient. Highly efficient.

The door was opened by a small neat blonde woman. Fiftyish, perhaps, made-up reasonably subtly, and dressed in a bright yellow cotton track-suit with fluffy pink slippers. She looked at them slowly, from one to the other, through weary, wary, eyes.

"Yes?" Her voice quiet. Guarded.

"Detective Sergeant Ben Munro. This is Detective Constable Rebecca Bickerstaff. Is Mrs Bair at home please?"

"I'm Mrs Bair."

"Mrs Sharon Bair?"

"Yes."

"I'm very sorry to trouble you at a time like this Mrs Bair but I wonder if we could ask you a few questions regarding your husband."

She nodded. "Of course. Come in."

The interior of the house was very pleasant, thought DS Munro - beige carpets throughout, light brown ceiling-to-floor curtains, the walls all painted a very pale latte and there were some nice paintings...though the sergeant laid no claims to any taste or knowledge whatsoever where art was concerned. Landscapes mostly, with one or two abstract pieces - but all colourful and accessible. The furniture was of dark glistening wood, tasteful, but fairly sparse. The seating was deeply comfortable, and the room they had been led into was huge with a stunning view of the immaculately kept grounds. Was this a typical gangster's house? He knew not.

"Please sit down."

"Thank you."

"Would you like a tea or a coffee?"

"Thank you very much...I'll have a tea please if you don't mind."

"Constable?" she gave PC Bickerstaff a pleasantly enquiring look.

"Er...yes, er...tea...tea for me too please, if that's okay."

"Of course." She rang a bell and a young woman wearing an apron appeared almost immediately.

"Olga dear, could you make us a pot of tea please – and a coffee, I think, for the constable," turning to PC Bickerstaff, "I know you said tea but I think that was for my convenience. I think coffee's your drink isn't it?" She smiled.

"Oh that's terribly kind, thank you so much – yes I do prefer coffee."

DS Munro was rather surprised at this exchange. He had expected recalcitrance, if not downright aggression.

A fairly tall, fit-looking dark haired young man dressed in jeans and a denim tee-shirt entered the room and looked at them coldly.

"Pigs? "he enquired, his blue eyes radiating the previously lacking aggression.

"I beg your pardon?"

"You're police eh? Don't have to answer — it's obvious — there's a smell in the house. What are you after?"

DS Munro returned his cold stare. "What's it to you?" he asked.

"This is my son Matt," said Mrs Bair, her voice even quieter than before.

Olga returned with drinks and biscuits which were quickly served in silence.

"Right, said DS Munro, "we're here to speak with your mother. And with you, of course, if that's okay."

"Why the hell should I speak with you. The old shit's dead. Dead and unmourned. We're all much better off without him — financially and every other way. You want to find his killer? You'll get no help from me."

"Well…maybe one thing…" said the sergeant, "…could you show Constable Bickerstaff where your father kept his bike?"

Matt casually and slowly looked Constable Bickerstaff up and down.

"Why not? Follow me," he said jerking his head at the DC.

They left and DS Munro turned back to Sharon Bair.

"Is your husband unmourned, Mrs Bair?" he asked quietly.

"Yes, I'm afraid he is."

"Why's that?"

"He was a cruel and unpleasant man. Is that reason enough? If you're looking for someone with a motive for killing him...well, there's not a shortage."

"Any idea why he went up to Scotland?"

"He had two loves in his life. Money, and motor-bikes. I suspect one or the other was the reason. Both, possibly."

"He didn't say anything about his trip?"

"He never told me anything. Ever."

"Did he phone you? Text you?"

She laughed. "He never phoned me...maybe twice a year to tell me to get him something. Text? No, not Bruno."

"Did he mention Scotland at all?"

"I think he got a couple of phone calls from Scotland...I didn't listen in, but after the call was over he would shove his mobile in his pocket, put on a daft Scottish accent and say '*och aye the noo mon, och aye the noo*'."

"Any idea what they were about...these phone calls?"

"None whatsoever."

"When did he get them, d'you remember?"

"I think he was left a voice-mail the day before he left. I remember him listening to it and coming out with the '*och aye the noo mon*' nonsense when he closed his mobile down."

"What about the land line?"

"Wouldn't use it. Wouldn't even have one in his office. Frightened of you guys listening in I guess."

"Where is his office?"

"Above the nightclub."

"Nightclub? Much staff there?"

"Don't know. I've never been. I would guess twenty or thirty maybe, but Bruno only had the one...er 'personal assistant'...shall we say."

"Who was that?"

"John Sangster. I hardly know the man. Don't like what I do know."

Matt and DC Bickerstaff came back into the room and the atmosphere went cold again.

"Time for you to go I think," said Matt gesturing to the door.

"When last did you see your husband, Mrs Bair?"

"He left here, on his bike, just before midnight - the night before he was murdered."

"I said time for you to go."

"Okay. Goodbye Mrs Bair, and thank you. If you think of anything which you think might be helpful, here's my card – phone number."

"Nobody's going to be phoning you," said Matt, taking the card out of his mother's hand and tearing it in two, then in four, "now goodbye."

The Detective Sergeant folded his long legs awkwardly under the restaurant table as they sat down to the curry he'd been looking forward to all day. This was what he missed back home. The nearest Indian restaurant to where he lived was fifty miles away in Oban. He perused the menu lovingly. He still had the company of DC Bickerstaff for which he was mighty thankful. He liked her. He'd been to the gents' and had undone his tie into an interesting undone-ness, and had ruffled up his hair into what he felt was a more attractive arrangement than the flat one he'd acquired over the course of the day. She had done something vaguely similar in the ladies.

"Well, not a popular man was he?"

"He certainly wasn't Sarge."

"His wife agreed that he would be unmourned – as Matt said."

"He was a complete shithouse Sarge. A bully. Everybody was frightened of him."

"A pity I couldn't have had a bit more time with her though. She was okay really. Matt…he was a complete arse."

"Matt's a bit dodgy himself so there was no way he was ever going to say much. And she seems to be a bit intimidated by him too."

"You think so?"

"Didn't you think? She kept looking at him sideways – and told us almost nothing we didn't know already - when he was there anyway."

"Yeah, that's why I got him to take you out to the garage…gave me a little chance to try relaxing her a bit. Mm…love these pakora."

"And…did it work?"

"A little. After I'd put on my dimmest daftest expression."

DC Bickerstaff smiled. The sergeant told her about the *och aye the noo mon* phone calls.

"Do they say that in Scotland then?"

Ben raised an eyebrow.

"Only joking Sarge. Well done. Anything else?"

"Not really."

"Couldn't you have tried looking even dimmer sarge?"

"Very funny Constable Bickerstaff, most droll."

"For God's sake Sarge, call me Rebecca…or better still…Becky."

61

"Okay. Becky. Actually his mobile phone would be a godsend if we could get our hands on it."

"Not at the scene of the crime then?"

"Nope. Nothing at the scene of the crime. Erm... what sort of stuff is Matt into anyhow?"

"Matt? He's almost thirty now – he'll probably take over the reins of his old man's less criminal business activities .He's certainly not involved in the drug scene like his old man was...as far as we can tell anyhow. Selling black-market fags and brandy and stuff, possibly. He opened a casino near the town centre three years ago and there's word of another application going before the licensing board in the not too distant future, so it must be doing pretty well. He's unpleasant – as you saw. Not violent in the way his old man was but I wouldn't cross him without back-up. His sister Sheila's about twenty seven. Looks like a younger...er...tougher version of her mother. Runs their nightclub in Manchester."

"Ah yes, she mentioned the nightclub."

"She runs a pretty tight-ship there. No nonsense. All legal and above board...allegedly. Bars, a restaurant, entertainment – and of course roulette, black-jack, poker, fruit-machines...you name it, if it makes money, they've got it. They've got a bit invested in online gambling too, I believe."

"Ah well. Glad they're nothing to do with me. I'll happily leave you lot down here to sort them out. Anyhow, what did Matt the charmer show you?"

"God he's a sleaze-ball. Took me out to the garage and practically hung over me. There were two cars in the garage itself - and three in the drive. The garage is huge - there were two other bikes in it – a scrambler thing, and an old Triumph

250. There was also a whole load of bike parts and things all neatly stowed on shelves and hanging from hooks. Matt said if anyone had ever touched one of his father's bikes they'd be sent to hospital. The bike he took to Scotland was a two year old Kawasaki 750cc - green. I don't know anything about bikes but I guess that's not a starter's machine."

"I guess not. God this jalfrezi's good. And that naan…"

"Mm. I wonder what happened to the bike…"

"Yeah."

"By the way, the big man must've travelled some to get up to your bit of Scotland if he only left here around midnight the night before."

"Yes, but it's well doable. The roads are dead at that time of night and a machine like that just eats miles. Probably under three hours to Glasgow – they live in the northern suburbs of Manchester so it's a quick getaway. That would leave you three or four hours to get up to Tyndrum. Easy peasy. In fact you could probably do it sticking to the speed limits. It explains why Bonnie couldn't find any trace of him round our area."

"Bonnie?"

"Bonnie Blackthorn, my DI."

"She okay?"

"Oh yes. Bonnie Blackthorn for First Minister I say."

"Wow. Single?"

"Nope. Got a partner. And a fifteen year old daughter."

"Right. What we doing tomorrow Sarge?"

"Digging for those with the biggest motives for bumping the scumbag off. Looking at his history from playschool to the present day. Finding more on that link with Scotland. His office is above the nightclub seemingly, so we'll start there. Should get a warrant easily enough if we need one. We'll have to speak to his side-kick John Sangster – I believe he might be there."

"I've heard of him Sarge. Another specialist in breaking fingers. And legs."

Chapter 9

The Daily Post

Satanic Rite? Nah...Big Bruno Banjoed!

New Evidence in Gangster's Murder Hunt

Billy Bootle Reporting

The Auchtergarry police's initial belief that Big Bruno died as a result of some satanic ritual was proved to be a nonsense yesterday when forensic experts indicated that he had been belted with a banjo. The five incisions on the back of his head were caused...

Inspector Slighman stopped reading. The page was liberally illustrated with photographs of the crime scene, one of DI Bonnie Blackthorn striding along fetchingly in a pleated tartan skirt, and a couple of mug-shots of Big Bruno. So far so good. He was almost frightened to look at the headline down below:

Who is The Toaster?

Highland Trail of Toast Crimes

Billy Bootle Reporting

Local police were left with jam on their faces after a mini crime wave hit the Highlands of Scotland. This followed the cheeky theft of a toaster and a loaf of bread from the home of a local police inspector. The culprit has left a trail of slices of toast wherever he has struck. First off he stole a valuable statuette of Bonnie Prince Charlie from under the noses of the local museum staff in spite of tight security. He left a slice....

Slighman breathed a sigh of relief. No mention of his name. Bootle had been true to his word. Everyone in the division knew who the inspector in question was but he could live with that. The general public would remain ignorant, and, more to the point, with a bit of luck the Recruitment Panel in the Midlands might remain unaware of his misadventures. He turned his Post to pages 2 and 3. A huge colour photograph of Desperate Dan heavily made up and with false eye-lashes almost filled page 2.

Desperate Dan Make-Over!

YouTube footage was posted yesterday showing a gloved hand applying make-up to one of Dundee's most famous landmarks and placing a slice of toast in his mouth. The statue has since been....

The roller-coaster that was Slighman's heart took a downward dip. This story could run a bit yet. He picked up his keys and made ready to leave. He was up later than usual as this should have been his day off but he had cancelled his own leave in order to devote every second available to the apprehension of the Toaster. Furthermore it would keep him out of the house and away from Carla.

"Jonathan?" Too late, she was up. She appeared in housecoat and slippers.

"Yes dear?"

"We need a toaster Jonathan. Remember?"

"Yes dear."

"Not a particularly difficult item to get hold of I shouldn't have thought."

"No dear."

"Then why haven't you bloody-well got one yet? It's how I start the day Jonathan. Two slices of toast, Jonathan. Every morning in life, Jonathan. It upsets me when I can't have my toast."

"You could grill..."

"Jonathan! Don't even mention the grill! If you seriously think I've got time to bend over waiting and watching for a fucking slice of bread to turn brown then you're very much mistaken!"

"Yes dear, sorry. I've been really busy...er...this murder hunt you know...and the hunt for the Toaster...er that's what they're calling the guy who stole our toaster...well it..."

"Jonathan, shut up, and get out, and when you come back, late in the day I hope - but before breakfast tomorrow morning, have a toaster under your arm."

"Yes dear."

Jonathan drove to Auchtergarry in something of a black mood. This Toaster guy was leading them a merry dance, and J Slighman was the one being flung mercilessly around the dance-floor. He'd left clues, certainly, they'd catch him, for sure, but how much damage would be done to J Slighman's career prospects by then? Speed. Speed was of the essence. DS Sliver reckoned there were two of them...well, yes, that probably made sense, but in his mind's eye the Toaster was just one person — a foul demon of a person, and if he could only come face to face with him...and get his hands on a banjo...well, it would be worth it.

He ran the gauntlet of taunts once more as he crossed the office floor to get to his desk. Dare he look at his emails? Well, he would have to and that was that.

Sender D Watts, Strathclyde: *Hey Jonny — who's this mystery inspector minus his toaster? Have I missed something?* Delete
Sender Harriet Inkster, Clapham: *OOOOOOHHH JONNNNY! I'd love to listen in to a quiet evening at home in Lochain with you and Carla the Snarla! She must be spitting live rounds...* Delete
Sender Amazon local: *Select from our fabulous range of banjos... Delete*
Sender S Short, Office: *Meeting of Community Group re-scheduled for 10/8 has been cancelled due to clash with Motivational Psychology Training at the Royal Hotel Auchtergarry. Re-scheduled for 29/8.*
Sender Music for You: *Banjo Tutorials from....*Delete
Sender D Wragg, Shetland: *Jonny! Isn't life...* Delete

Enough. He'd read the rest later after some coffee. DS Silver appeared at his elbow.

"Morning sir."

"Mm."

"Anything new sir?"

"No sergeant. What about you?"

"Well I'm even more certain now that there's two of them. At least two of them. "

"Why's that?"

"Well the footage on YouTube was uploaded at nine o'clock yesterday morning, but there's a clock in the background showing six o'clock – and the lack of people around would suggest that it was indeed videoed at six in the morning. That's actually before Bonnie Prince Charlie was nicked so it couldn't have been a copy-cat crime - also nothing about that really hit the news till about seven anyhow. "

"So, one felony in Auchtergarry, and one in Dundee."

"Looks like it. But the big question remains – what the hell are they playing at? Blowing up the YouTube footage shows what looks like an Omega Seamaster watch on his wrist. Not a cheap watch. Expensive cord trousers, expensive watch, they steal a toaster and a loaf of bread, they leave clues at every crime scene….what is going on?"

"I don't give a damn what's going on, I just want them behind bars. They're making us look ridiculous."

"Right," said DS Silver, suppressing a mutinous little smile. "By the way sir there's sale on at Galbraithe's – if you were looking for a…"

"Yes Sergeant, I've been informed. Thank you."

...

"Inspector, me old pumpkin! How the devil are you?"

"Listen Bootle, this story's growing legs. I dread to think where it's leading. It's ridiculous, we're definitely closing in on the perpetrator – he'll be incarcerated any minute now – it's hardly worth another feature in the Post is it? It's a dead story really...when you think about it."

"Ah Jonny boy, you could be right, you could be right. But we poor pressmen don't see things as clearly as you professionals. We just plod on with anything the public seem to be gagging for information about."

"Now look here Bootle, you know that's rubbish. You lot stir up your readers something rotten. It's you damn journalists who decide what the public interest is. You generate it – you lead them like sheep. Jesus when was the last time you consulted one of your readers on something?"

"Not at all Jonny, we are in constant thrall to them. We merely follow where our readership guides us."

"Bollocks."

"Whatever. Anyhow my fine Inspector, anything to bribe me with today?"

"No. Nothing. It's hardly worth it anyhow, we're all over every newspaper and website in the land. To say nothing of wall-to-wall radio and television coverage. We look like an absolute bunch of clowns. "

"Has your name appeared Jonny?"

"Er...well...no, I suppose not."

"Well, you'd better continue with your acts of kindness towards me, hadn't you, old chap. The lady upstairs is yanking my tether you know. She'd love to have you sacrificed on the altar of newspaper circulation. We've got eight different photographs of you by the way. Would you rather appear in uniform or civvies? Smiling or serious? Full face or profile…?"

"This is blackmail Bootle."

"Not at all. I'm doing you a favour. I'm acting as a buffer between you and her upstairs. She's vicious Jonny, vicious. I'm offering you protection. So. Got anything?"

"Very little. I heard he left Manchester on his motorbike at midnight on the night before he was killed. He was going to meet someone but we have no idea who. And that's it."

"Hm. Interesting . A mini-exclusive. That might buy her off for another wee bit – if you're lucky."

"Right, see that it does or the source dries up. I've got to go now. I'm off to the sales."

"Bargain hunting?"

"Yeah. Galbraithe's…always a good summer sale."

Galbraithe's was packed. Inspector Slighman made his way slowly through the crowds, up the escalator to the first floor where the ironmongery department was, purchased the most expensive toaster they had as a sop to Carla and returned to the downward escalator fully toastered-up. As his escalator made its way down, the Inspector glanced across to the escalator next to it, which was going up. There, calmly looking straight ahead into the middle-distance was a man wearing orangey-red corduroy trousers. The moment lasted very briefly before they both disappeared from each other's view, but Inspector Slighman just knew he had seen the Toaster. He caught his breath and turned round to try and run up his downward-progressing escalator but immediately realised there were far too many people on it to push past. He then tried to push past the people in front of him going down on the descending escalator but shouting *'police – make way'* simply caused panic as people re-secured their footing and gripped the hand-rail even tighter than before. He reached the bottom at escalator speed, transferred to the ascending staircase which was jammed with shoppers, and phoned DS Silver.

"He's here!"

"Who?"

"The Toaster!"

"Where?"

"Galbraithe's!"

"Right. Be there in five minutes."

"He's wearing his cords."

"Gottcha!"

"So," said Superintendent Smart, "you think you saw this Toaster fellow in Galbraithe's?"

"Yes sir. Definitely him. In this heat surely nobody else is wearing thick corduroy trousers. Especially bright orangey-red ones."

"Okay. But he'd vanished by the time DS Silver arrived – and you couldn't get anywhere near him on the escalator at the time."

"No sir. The place was crammed to the rafters."

"Get a good look at him?"

"Taken a bit by surprise sir but I'd certainly recognise him again. Mid fifties, average height, fairly trim and fit looking. An unusually pointed nose. Quite prosperous looking. Dark wavy hair with quite a lot of grey at the sides. Upright bearing. Wearing a light tan zip-up summer jacket and a white cotton shirt. " Slighman was rather proud of this demonstration of his powers of recall and description.

"Anything else?"

"Can't think of anything right now sir?"

"Was he carrying anything?" asked DS Silver.

"Oh yes, of course, I'd forgotten, he had one of those man-baggy whatsits. Expensive satchel...er thingy...over one shoulder. Khaki coloured."

"Well, that helps," said a somewhat exasperated Superintendent Smart, "anything else?"

"No, that's it. Nothing else."

"Glasses?" enquired the sergeant?

"Oh... yes...right enough...er...now that you mention it, he did have glasses on. Dark heavy–looking frame...not tinted or anything."

The Superintendent closed his eyes and rested his head on his hands.

"Anything else Inspector?" he asked wearily.

"No that's definitely it now."

"Was he with anyone, d'you think? asked DS Silver.

Slighman looked nonplussed. He opened his mouth to speak, and closed it again.

"That's a good point Sergeant," he said slowly, "a very good point. You know...I believe he was. Now let me think. There was definitely someone – a man – beside him. On the same step...stair thing...whatever it's called."

"Taller? Shorter?"

"Yes he was. Er...taller that is."

"Right," said the sergeant, "a taller man. Older? Younger?"

"Eh...mmm. No, don't remember. Wasn't really looking at him you see."

"Quite," said the Super.

"Notice anything else?"enquired the DS. "Clothes? Hair? Hat?"

"Ah. Right...yes. I seem to remember he was wearing a deerstalker."

The Superintendent's head sagged deep into his hands. This was intolerable. Not only did he have the world's most inept police witness before him, but he had a suspect on the loose who dressed like Sherlock Homes.

"Didn't have a pipe in his mouth by any chance did he?" asked DS Silver. "Anyhow," he went on, "we've got them stone dead. There's closed-circuit cameras all over Galbraithe's. They're sorting out the discs for us now."

"Right sergeant, get back there. This is a massive breakthrough. We'll get their descriptions circulated a.s.a.p. and with some luck....well, fingers crossed."

"Yes sir," said DS Silver swiftly making his way out.

The Superintendent took a deep breath. "Inspector."

"Yes sir?"

"How's the search for the mole going?"

"Mole sir?"

"Yes, dammit! The mole! The person who's been leaking all this guff to the press about this infernal Toaster. The Daily Post seems to have a hot-line to my office. And how did they know about the banjo for God's sake? It's not good enough, Inspector, it's really not good enough. How are your enquiries progressing?"

"Erm... it's difficult sir...could be anybody in the division really."

"Right. So you've managed to narrow it down to two hundred people then?"

"It is diff….er, sir, your pho…"

"Yes Inspector! I'm well aware my phone is ringing! Now go out there and make some bally progress."

"Yessir." Slighman made for the door.

"Hello! Superintendent Smart here. Yes. Yes. What!? Oh please no. All over the country? What!? Oh dear God. What a confounded mess. Thanks. SLIGHMAN! Come back here!"

"Sir?"

"Slighman. That was Chief Inspector Hodge from the Community Policing Unit in Glasgow. There are reports coming in from all over the UK of kids knocking on doors, running away, and leaving slices of toast behind. Some broken windows, some petty shop-lifting, local statues covered in make-up, the odd bicycle tyre deflated…and all with the calling-card of a slice of toast. The nation's children are running amok. They're clearly loving it for God's sake. The press will go volcanic about this, absolutely volcanic. God help us all. Any comment Inspector?"

Inspector Slighman groaned. Visions of the next day's tabloids swam before him.

"Er…not really sir. I suppose it's an easy crime to copycat sir."

"Indeed Inspector. Indeed it is. Right, the only way to kill this one is to catch the Toaster and his accomplice and get them behind bars post-haste Slighman. Post haste. Get on with it."

"Yes sir," said the Inspector making rapidly for the door yet again.

"Slighman?"

"Yes sir?"

"Is that box over there yours?"

"Oh, ah, yes sir, thank you sir. Almost forgot it."

"What the hell's in it anyhow Slighman?"

"Er...a toaster sir."

The Superintendent's hands once more took the weight of his head. One or two of the well oiled-down hairs on his head had sprung up with the constant rising and falling of his features. This was not a good day. Jollies like the Chesterlake Hotel soirée in far off London seemed of another life.

Chapter 10

DS Munro and DC Bickerstaff knocked on the door of Big Bruno's office and tried the door handle. The door was locked. They looked at each other.

"Damn. We need to get in here."

"Maybe this John Sangster chappie doesn't start till ten o'clock."

"Well there's nobody in the nightclub downstairs yet. Maybe they all start..."

The door jerked suddenly open and a shortish man well past the first flush of youth but clearly once built of reinforced concrete and broken glass glared at them.

"Yes?"

"John Sangster?"

"Who's askin'?"

"I'm Detective Sergeant Munro and this is Detective Constable Bickerstaff. We're making enquiries about John Bair." He waved a search-warrant under Sangster's nose.

"Oh? Really?"

"Yes – may we come in?"

Sangster looked them up and down.

He stepped back and gestured them in with extravagant sarcasm.

"Make yourselves at home."

The office, fairly bare and not very big, had clearly once been someone's sitting room. A nineteen-fifties tiled mantelpiece with the odd file on it graced one wall, and there were cupboard doors at either side of it. There were two ancient heavy office desks back-to-back in the centre of the room, one of which had a couple of stuffed cardboard boxes on it, and the other of which was bare except for a couple of pens and a note-pad. There were not very clean windows in two of the walls and a small hand basin had been plumbed into a third. An ancient round glass chandelier hung from the ceiling, carrying a decade of dust.

"Well?...how can I help you?" asked John Sangster, in a tone which suggested he wouldn't.

Rebecca looked him in the eye. "Right. We need to find out all we can about your employer...er...sorry, your ex-employer, that is."

"Is that so? Well well. Fancy that."

"Is that a problem, Mr Sangster?"

"Problem? Not at all. Why would it be a problem?"

"Oh, no reason. No reason at all."

"Not a problem for me lass, not a problem for me."

"How did you feel when you heard he'd been murdered?" asked DS Munro.

Sangster's face darkened. "He was a good man."

"He was a thug," responded DC Bickerstaff instantly.

"You watch what you're saying young lady..."

"...or what?" asked DS Munro.

The atmosphere in the room had turned from tense to nasty.

"Nobody says that about the Big Man. Nobody."

"Don't make me laugh Sangster," replied DC Bickerstaff, "Bruno's death leaves you impotent and you know it. Nobody's going to take an ageing has-been hard-man like you seriously on your own. You're finished Sangster, your days of breaking people's arms are over. It's pension time for you now. Or maybe even prison time…"

The scowl on Sangster's face was all the proof they needed that Becky's 'has-been' barb had hit the nail on the cranium. Being forced to take this from a young woman – even though she was a police officer - was clearly a new experience for him and was eating at his innards. But he kept quiet. He had no option.

"The fact is, Sangster," continued the detective constable, "now that the vicious brute is dead and safely out of the way, there's probably rather a lot of people out there who'd happily testify against you. So…I think it's well in your long-term interest to be as helpful as you can this morning…don't you? You don't want to upset us Mr Sangster, you really don't."

The scowl never wavered.

"What's in these boxes?" asked DS Munro gesturing with his head towards the nearest desk.

There was a lengthy silence as Sangster glared at his interrogators.

"Bike magazines," came the eventual reply.

"He was big on bikes – yeah?"

"You could say that. "

DS Munro leafed through some of them.

 "What was it he actually made his money at then?" enquired DS Munro, with an innocent air.

Another lengthy silence ensued.

"Oh, this and that. A bit of buying and selling."

 "Buy and selling what?"

There was a slightly shorter lengthy silence.

"Brandy, gin…you know…whatever."

"Whisky?"

"No, not whisky, never whisky." The silences were definitely getting shorter. A little more compliance was underway.

"No trade with Scotland then?"

"Not that I know of."

"You liked him…did you?"

"Like a brother."

"Everybody else hated him."

"I don't give a shit for everybody else."

"You'd like us to catch his killer?"

The scowling silence returned…a long pause…then he nodded minutely.

"Well, help us for Christ's sake. Had he been in contact with anyone from Scotland?"

Sangster was clearly a man who had had a lifelong detestation of the police - any help he gave would always be minimal even when the results were in his own favour.

"He may have had a deal of some sort in the pipeline, I know he was in touch with someone in Scotland last week."

"Really. How d'you know that?"

"I heard him on the phone. After he hung up – he put on a Scottish voice and said something daft in a Scottish accent."

"*Och aye the noo mon*?" said DS Munro in music-hall Scots.

"Could've been. Something like that."

"Any other connection with Scotland?...anything at all?"

Sangster gave a short brittle laugh.

"His only drink was whisky."

"Really? Did he drink much?

"A dram or two, I suppose."

"Any particular favourite?"

"Glen Laldy single malt. Always and only Glen Laldy."

"Glen Laldy eh?"

There was another pause.

"Cigarettes?" Did he buy and sell cigarettes?" asked DC Bickerstaff.

"Maybe - from time to time. All legal of course." His mocking smile told them they could never prove otherwise.

"Mm. Drugs?"

"Drugs? You mean medicines and things?"

"Oh come on Sangster... I was thinking more of cocaine...heroin......"

Sangster's mocking smile widened.

"Nah...not us. We're good guys."

"Good guys my arse. Violent thugs – the pair of you. His empire was built on drugs and you know it. You were his right-hand man. If man's the right word." DC Bickerstaff was repelled by Sangster and it showed.

The mocking smile stayed put.

"Any records of ...er...clients?" asked DS Munro re-directing the line of questioning, "People who owed him money perhaps? Anything like that?"

"Nah. Nothing like that."

"You're lying Sangster. Not that it matters much to us. It'll just take us a little longer to get at the truth, that's all. I'd be more helpful if I were you."

"Really Sergeant? If you were me eh? Why the hell should I be more helpful? I've managed along so far without helping pigs."

"I can think of two reasons Sangster – both of which we've hit on already, but let me remind you anyhow. Reason number one...with yer big boss man gone I should think people will be gagging to testify against you...so being seen to be a bit helpful with our enquiries might just influence his honour when you appear up front. Let's face it Sangster, two years is better than four...no? Especially at your age. And I should think there's probably quite a few inmates doin' time right now who'd love to get their knuckly hands on you...the less time spent with them the better...no?"

No response.

"And reason number two, of course, you want us to find Bruno's killer, right?"

Still no response. His stare remained aggressive and unbowed, but at least the mocking smile had gone.

"So, I ask again...any records of clients? Remember, we'll be emptying this joint when we leave so if the records are here, we'll find them for sure."

"And what about the greater empire, Sangster?" asked DC Bickerstaff, "he operated all over Lancashire and the Midlands didn't he? What about his...er tentacles...contacts...people working for him out there? Any names? Addresses?"

The silence which followed seemed interminable, but eventually Sangster stood up, walked to the back of the tidy desk, opened a drawer and extracted three ledgers. He tossed them on the desk, picked up his jacket, and walked towards the door.

"By the way Sangster," interjected DS Munro, "before you leave...if you don't mind, where were you on the morning of Monday June the fifth?"

The reply was immediate.

"I was in a hospital in Bolton having varicose veins ripped out."

He yanked up his trouser leg, waved a fresh scar at them, and was gone.

"And good riddance to Sangster the gangster," said DC Bickerstaff, glaring at the door.

"Indeed – he seems to have been a pocket version of the big man, d'you reckon?"

"Absolutely. A lesser piece of scum. Probably be on a flight to Spain tonight clutching his years of ill-gotten gains."

DS Munro gathered up the ledgers and headed back to the station, leaving DC Bickerstaff to undertake a more complete search of the office. Four hours of dusty rummaging produced little more than old receipts, power bills, biking literature, and a half-empty bottle of Glen Laldy.

They met again in the evening, as prearranged, at the Great Subcontinent Indian Bistro, both ravenous and in need of long drinks.

"God sarge, I'd love to put that scumbag behind bars. He gave me the screamers, he really did."

"Well that's for your lot down here to follow up – right now we can only concentrate on one thing - discovering which decent soul wasted his boss…"

"…and did the world a favour."

"Indeed."

"Have you had a chance to look at any of the ledgers yet Sarge?"

"Yeah, spent the whole afternoon poring over them. All in Big Bruno's handwriting – not a word written anywhere by Sangster."

"Hmm, I was a little surprised right enough when he handed them over. But if there's nothing to implicate him...then why not...he's in the clear. What's in them anyhow Sarge?

"Lists of names...with addresses fortunately, and sums of money. Most of the names repeat over and over. Presumably people either buying drugs for their own use or to sell on to others. The names go back about three decades – he must have started in his early twenties. Most of the old ones have been crossed out. He seemed to operate a code system. Almost all of the entries have a 'P' next to them, some have an 'L', some a 'W' and occasionally there's a 'B'. I noticed that some of the ones crossed out had a 'D' next to them. Possibly for 'deceased' perhaps? I reckon the 'P' is probably for 'paid', but the rest...I dunno. We'll pay some of the more recent ones a visit tomorrow, see if they can shine some light on it at all. Not that I'm expecting a major breakthrough but...hey, you never know, do you?"

"Very true. What about his empire Sarge? We know he operated in most, if not all of the cities in what...a forty...fifty mile radius perhaps? What about his little army of pushers and dealers there?"

"Well...I suspect that was Sangster's responsibility. At the back of one ledger, under the heading 'John' there's what appears to be a coded list of names – and numbers. Contacts, I should think, and I imagine the John in question is John Sangster – anyhow, I think we'll just hand that over to your lot Rebecca. I'm sure they'd love to pick it up and run with it."

"Oh wouldn't we just Sarge, wouldn't we just."

"And us? We'll concentrate on his victims – the people in these ledgers. I'm sure there's a host of potential Big Bruno murderers in these lists."

"I'm sure you're right sarge."

They concentrated on eating for a while.

"By the way Sarge, and a complete change of subject...this toasting thing's getting a bit out of hand isn't it?"

DS Munro shook his head and laughed. "It's a farce, Rebecca, an absolute farce. The Inspector in charge is a pure desk wallah. And a pain in the arse to boot. It was his toaster that was nicked in the first place. It's really odd, to be honest...I phoned Bonnie before we came out and she says they'll have the guys in custody within forty-eight hours. Not because of any brilliant detective work, although the DS is good – Bob Silver – but because the pair of perps leave clues all over the place. It's almost as if they want to be caught. I mean...according to the latest description of them, they're two middle-aged, middle-class guys with absolutely no previous – what the hell are they doing breaking into somebody's house and nicking a toaster and a loaf of bread for? It's bollocks."

"Yes, it's all a bit weird."

"Boy I enjoyed that curry. And I do believe that's the best naan bread I've ever tasted."

"Mm, they are rather good, aren't they?"

"Given me a bit of a thirst though. Fancy a quick beer?

"Oooh what a good idea Sarge. There's a lovely pub just up the road."

Chapter 11

Daily Post

Coast to Coast Toast!

The Toaster Spreads!

Billy Bootle Reporting

Yesterday the wayward youth of Britain went toast crazy by committing petty crimes and silly pranks then leaving slices of toast behind at the scenes of their misdemeanours. They were copying the now infamous Highland Toaster who has made monkeys of the local police...

Slighman groaned. Every tabloid in the land had the toast crime wave on the front page and as their main headline. Big Bruno was slipping down the agenda now to the bottom of the page or even page two or page three. Appalling toast puns were everywhere. **'Kids Raise a Toast!'** **'A Toast of Their Own Medicine!'.** And in the Independent **'Is Chivalry Brown Bread?'** Where was it all going to end? He consoled himself that the original theft of a toaster seemed to have been forgotten about, so his name was unlikely to appear anywhere now, but enough people knew about the whole 'be aware' nonsense and toaster theft to scupper his career prospects for the rest of eternity anyhow. He would have to tread very carefully.

His phone rang.

"Inspector, me old…"

"Oh do shut up Bootle. I've had just about enough of you, I really have."

"Oh well, I'd better behave myself, hadn't I? No more nice little exclusives for me!"

"Well I don't think anybody's interested now in who the owner of the original toaster was, do you?"

"Perhaps you're right Inspector, perhaps you're right. By the way, how's your new toaster? Working well?"

"Well yes it is as a matter of fa….how the hell did you know I had a new toaster?"

"Oh somebody spotted you buying it in Galbraithe's yesterday."

"Oh really, and who would that have been?"

"Our photographer."

Inspector Slighman took a deep breath. "Your photographer?"

"Our photographer."

"Are you telling me you have a photograph of me buying a new toaster?"

"I suppose I am really. Can't imagine when we'll use it though. Can you?"

Inspector Slighman could imagine only too well a full page spread of the great 'be aware' idiot buying a toaster to replace the one he had so skilfully lost. If that ever happened his career would definitely grind to an ignominious halt and he'd be the nation's favourite laughing stock.

"Okay Bootle. Okay. I guess you've got me by the short and curlies. Now, what exactly do you want this time?"

"Oh Inspector...don't for a minute imagine I was hinting at compromising you. No no, not at all. I'm your friend Inspector, I really am."

"What do you want Bootle?"

"Oh just more of the same sir, more of the same. The odd lead or two...in both the Big Bruno case, and the Toaster case now though. And soonish, Inspector, soonish. Ah, I never thought for a minute Scotland was going to be so much fun!"

The Superintendent's phone rang.

"Hello?"

"It's Detective Sergeant Silver on the line sir."

"Put him through."

"Sir?"

"Yes Sergeant, what is it?"

"Just thought I'd let you know we got a couple of good stills from the CC cameras at Galbraithe's yesterday."

"Photographs?"

"Yes sir."

"Excellent."

"We haven't issued them to the press yet sir - in case they're not the right guys - but we've issued detailed descriptions of both men. Should be in the evening editions later today. The photographs are being sent to every police division in the land — somebody somewhere will know them that's for sure. I think we're closing in sir."

"Wonderful. Excellent. Thank you Sergeant. Thank you."

The Super placed his phone back on the receiver and prayed that the sergeant was right.

His phone rang again.

"Sir, it's the Chief of Police on the line from Glasgow for you."

"Oh God. Right, put him through."

"Smartie? Is that you?"

"Yes it is Duncan. How can I help you?"

"Well for a start Smartie you can clear up this damn toaster epic, that's what you can do. What the hell's taking all the time?"

"It only happened two or three days ago Duncan. We do have a murder to deal with as well you know."

"Bugger the murder right now Smartie. Every budding delinquent in Britain's on the loose with slices of toast. We had all the fat-balls nicked from our garden bird-house and slices of toast left in their place…fair enough the birds are now eating the toast but hell's bells Smartie, it's all gone too far. I want this Toaster menace caught and incarcerated within the next twenty-four hours Smartie. The situation's getting out of hand. As I say, bugger the murder right now."

"Duncan, you know better than I do that the murder must take precedence. If the press thought for a moment that we were throwing all our resources into finding a toaster thief when there's a murderer on the loose we'd be slaughtered, and rightly so."

"Who's on the Toaster case?"

"DS Silver…a competent man Duncan."

"I'm sure he is Smartie, but why isn't Bonnie Blackthorn on it? She'd have had it put to bed by now."

"She's on the Big Bruno thing...I can't spare her."

"That's all very well Smartie, but in all honesty this Bruno guy was a sadistic brute, I doubt there's a soul in the land who doesn't hope his killer gets off with it."

"Well they have my sympathy Duncan, but we have a job to do and that's that. No doubt a lot of people hope the Toaster remains at large too but his feet won't touch the ground till they hit the back of a cell once we get our hands on his collar. He'll be locked up before..."

"Right Smartie, but please please please make it soon!"

"Yes Duncan, of course. We have photographs now you know – there's two of them."

"Really. Pair of neds are they?"

"Well funnily enough Duncan, no, they're not. They're straight middle-class, middle-aged, and prosperous looking."

"That's rather weird isn't it?"

"Yes, it is. And oddly enough, one of them looks vaguely familiar to me. I'm sure I've seen him before somewhere."

"Well, whatever Smartie, time to feel their collars. By the way how did the conference in London go?"

"Conference Duncan? Ah, yes. Ermm, very well really. Most enjoyable," said the Super wistfully.

"Bootle? Is that you?"

"Yes my friend, Bootle it is."

"I think I have something of interest."

"Wonderful Jonny, wonderful...what is it?"

"Well, you know the two...the two Toasters...the two...er men... we circulated descriptions of in our press release a couple of hours ago?"

"Yes."

"I've got a photograph, Bootle, a photograph."

"You little cherry blossom!"

"I'm risking my career phoning you like this."

"I would go to my grave rather than reveal a source, Jonny boy, and I mean that, I really do."

For once Inspector Slighman felt there might be an element of truth in what Bootle was saying.

"I'll meet you in the Holy Welly Café in thirty minutes."

"Roger Jonny boy, Roger!"

The Superintendent's phone rang once more.

"The First Minister's on the line sir."

"What!? Holy Jesus. Okay. Put her on."

Now what in God's name was the correct form of address for the First Meenester? Holy Moly Roly and Poly.

"Hello?"

"Hello, is that the First Minister?"

"Yes it is."

"Er…hello Marm…er…your Hon…"

"Hello Superintendent. I believe you're the senior officer in the Auchtergarry area."

"Er…yes I am…Marm…"

"I'm sorry to have to call you like this but my phone's red hot - I'm being contacted by every MSP, MP, and councillor in the land. It looks like this toasting baloney's gone absolutely viral. I find it hard to say this, but I'm looking out the window here, and somebody's replaced the Saltire on our flagpole with a sheet portraying a large slice of toast with a bite out of it."

Superintendent Smart sagged into a willowy slouch.

"Oh dear God...er... Lady...er...Marm...er.."

"Now you know as well as I do that this sort of nonsense could do irreparable harm to the public's perception of, and confidence in, both the police and the organs of governance...I need you to pull out all the stops Superintendent, all of them. It's gone quite far enough."

"Er yes...your Hon...ladyship...but...er...we also have a murder to solve up here, and a limited force to deploy in solving it. But take it from me Sir...er...Marm...we'll have results by this time tomorrow. The net's closing Miss..er sorry..er...Your Right...er...Honorableness...we're almost there."

"Thank you Superintendent, you have reassured me considerably."

The Superintendent put his phone down, closed his eyes, and tried a few deep-breathing exercises. That near forgotten stress-handling course four years back could prove of some value after all.

Constables Michael Beech and Frederick Wyre were cruising around Auchtergarry later that same afternoon in their police car, when Constable Beech suddenly yelled "Look!"

"What? Where?"

"Look at that kid! Walkin' down the street fine as ye like wi' a loaf o' bread under his arm!"

"What! The brazen wee shite!"

"Bold as brass! Right stop the car. I'll grab the wee bugger...
...hey you! Yes you! Come here! What's your name son?"

"Indiana, sur."

"Indiana?"

"Yes sur."

"Indiana what?"

"McDuff sur"

"Indiana McDuff?"

"Aye. Sur."

"Right Indiana, what's that under your arm?"

"A loaf sur."

"Where d'you think you're going with that then?"

"Hame, sur."

"Home?"

"Yes sur."

"And what are you going to do with it when you get home Indiana?"

"Gie it tae ma Ma sur."

"Your mother?"

"Yes sur."

"I don't believe you Indiana. I think you're going to toast it."

"No sur, honest sur, ask ma Ma if ye like sur. I widnae toast it. I'd nivver toast it sur. Honest ah widnae."

"How old are you Indiana?"

"Eight sur."

"Where do you live?"

"42 Cobbler Drive sur."

"Right, get in the car we're taking you home."

"Aw sur, ah can walk sur, nae bother."

"Get in the car."

"Aw sur – in that case it's 14 Balfour Street."

"Hello madam. Are you Indiana's mother?"

"Aye, I am."

"We found him on the High Street with this loaf of bread under his arm."

"Whit! The wee monster! Ah've bin lookin' everywhere for that loaf o'breid. Get inside you...ye little horror – ye were goannae toast it weren't ye?"

"No Ma ah wuzznae. Honest."

"Get inside."

"Aw Ma."

"Thanks constable, I'll gie him whit for, the wee scally. A pair o'ma tights has disappeared aff the washin' line an' somebody's pegged up a slice o'toast for them. Ah'll bet it was that wee bugger. He's grounded till he's ten he is. "

"Very good madam, thank you."

"Thank you constable. Bye... ...Indiana! You come here this minute!"

"Aw Ma."

"A child saved from a lifetime of crime there, Constable Beech."

"Aye, I do believe you're right, Constable Wyre, I do believe you're right."

DS Munro and DC Bickerstaff had spent a long fruitless morning trudging round some of the people still current in Big Bruno's ledgers. The few that they found at home clammed up the instant Big Bruno was mentioned or else pleaded ignorance. Almost all of them were cowed and afraid - the big man's legacy was extending well beyond the grave.

"Maybe we should try someone who's no longer current on his list," suggested DC Bickerstaff when they stopped for a sandwich and a coffee, "they've maybe managed to kick their habit so...well...you never know, they may be readier to talk."

"Worth a try Becky. Have a look at the green ledger, that's the one before the current one." She opened the ledger and ran her finger down the lists. "I'll pick some fairly local ones first. Mm...quite a few...we can try some of these...Harry Black...Martha De Deparo...Ian Whitsnade...Betty Albert...Joan Martin...Paul Minton... Andrew Smith..."

"That should be enough for a start Becky...half a dozen or so. Fine. Right then, let's go try the first one."

Harry Black, first on the list, had long left the address shown. No forwarding address. Vanished.

"Right, who's next?"

"Martha De Deparo, 23 Mary Street. Just up the road here."

Martha De Deparo was at home. A woman in her sixties who had never taken an illegal drug in her life, had never smoked a cigarette, and drank nothing but tea. Her son, however, had had a drug habit, fed and encouraged by Big Bruno. Martha had hated the man more than any other living soul, but she had paid him on time, every time, by holding down two jobs, selling everything she had of value, and almost ruining her health. Her son, she said, was now clean – had been for five years. His life, and hers, were now back in some kind of order.

"Have you ever seen these ledgers before?" asked DS Munro.

"The monster, the big brute, he always had one in his hand but I don't think I ever saw one open."

"Any idea what these letters mean...the 'Ps'...the 'Ls'...?"

"I know 'P' stood for 'paid'. He sometimes said *"that's you paid...you're a 'P' again."*

"The other letters?"

"Sorry, I've no idea."

"Any idea who might have killed him?"

"No. But I hope he gets off. Brought a little happiness into my life whoever he was."

Next on the list was Ian Whitsnade. A small woman, old and of extreme timidness, answered the door.

"Is there an Ian Whitsnade at this address?" enquired DC Bickerstaff after introducing herself.

"No, Ian died three years ago," her voice barely audible.

"Was he your husband?"

"My brother."

"Do you know anything regarding his dealings with John Bair?...er…Big Bruno?"

The old woman eyes widened, and the rest of her visibly shrank.

"No." A tiny whisper and a shake of the head.

DC Bickerstaff gave her her most reassuring smile and thanked her for her time.

"My God, she was a poor wee thing," said DS Munro.

"Wasn't she just? Sad little soul."

"Oh well, who's next?"

They spent some hours looking in vain for Betty Albert, Joan Martin, and Paul Minton. No longer at their old addresses, nobody knew where they now were, and nobody cared. On to Andrew Smith.

Yes, he was at home. No he didn't know anything about the mystery letters. No he didn't know anything else about Big Bruno, just glad to escape his clutches. But he was talkative.

"Hey, you're Scottish ahn't you?"

"Yes I am," replied the sergeant.

"Are you just down 'ere for this murder then?"

"Er…yes, I suppose I am really."

"What about all this toast business then? That all started up in your neck o' the woods didn't it?"

"Er…yeah…I suppose it did really."

"Crazy eh?"

"Yeah, Just a bit."

"Ha. Y'know what I think?"

"No…er…what do you think?"

"I think it's a reaction to all these TV chefs…eh?" A sideward tilt of the head and a wink accompanied the look of great pride which consumed Mr Smith, which said in essence - *how clever is that then?*

"TV chefs?"

"Oh yes. Wherever you look on the telly there's another bloody TV chef. Cooking wi' all that rubbish…what is it?...fennel or something, and balsamic…er…cream. All that high falutin' nonsense. I think the Toaster's starting his own revolution against all that…eh? Toast…eh? That's real food eh? Nothin' wrong wi' toast I'm telling you. Better than bloody polenta that's for sure. Mark my words…"

"Er…thank you very much Mr Smith, interesting theory. We'll..er…look into it…thanks again. Bye."

"Er…bye."

It was now eight in the evening, they were flagging and they were hungry.

"Right, let's call it a day Becky. Could you face another Indian?"

"I reckon I could manage two right now. I'm ravenous."

DC Bickerstaff drove, and DS Munro phoned his superior officer.

"Inspector Blackthorn? Sergeant Munro here."

"Hi Ben, how is it going?"

"Pretty slow really. We're having problems finding anyone who knows what the letters in the ledgers stand for – we know for certain now that a 'P' stands for 'paid' but can only guess at the others. It's possible there's nobody out there who actually does know what they stand for...I think he held them pretty close to his chest."

"Keep at it Ben. I suspect it might be important. We need something...anything. You never know, you may strike gold. Somebody might just remember something, some little key might just appear."

"Right Inspector, will do."

" And the Scottish link Ben? Any clues?"

"Not a sausage. Apart from the fact that his favourite tipple was Glen Laldy single malt whisky."

"Oh really? Now that's quite interesting that is. In fact, Ben, that's very interesting."

"Is it?"

"Oh yes. Remember that van load of whisky that was stolen a few months ago over by Grantown?"

"Don't tell me...Glen Laldy?"

"It was indeed Ben, it was indeed. Well well well, perhaps there's a link. I'll see if I can chase anything up this end. We've kind of hit a brick wall at the moment. We've combed the scene of the murder but absolutely nothing. Nobody responding to our appeal for witnesses either. Blank blank blank so far Ben."

"I must say Bonnie, er Inspector, that the more I find out about Big Bruno, the more I reckon his murder was an act of...well...decency, if that's the right word. He was nasty. Ruined lives for the sake of nothing but his pocket."

"Aye Ben, yer no wrong, but we have a job to do. Maybe we're only finding out who to thank."

"Aye, I wish. Anyhow, any news on the Toaster? He's a megastar down here."

"Yeah. Up here too Ben. We've had the First Minister on the phone already. It's all most strange Ben, most strange. I don't quite know what to make of it all, but there's something a bit funny about it.

The Superintendent's phone rang once more.

"Yes?"

"The Prime Minister is on the line from Westminster sir."

"WHAT!? Jesus and Mary McTavish! Right...er...God Almighty... put him through, put him through."

"Is that er... police Deputy Comm...sorry, what's that Murphy? A superintendent you say? Right. Is that, er, a police Superintendent?"

"Yes Prime Minister. Superintendent Smart, Auchtergarry."

"Oh good afternoon Superintendent Auchtergarry, er thanks for getting back to me...er...sorry Murphy, what's that? Oh we phoned him did we? Right. Hello Superintendent."

"Hello Prime Minister. How can I help you?"

"Ah, right, exactly. It's these toast things Superintendent. Must get it cleared up you know. Really must. Can't have this kind of thing going on all over the place you know. Eh?"

"No Prime Minister. Of course not, of course not."

"Jolly disruptive eh?...to say nothing of embarrassing."

"Indeed Prime Minister

"Reminds me of my time at Eton though...ha ha...toast eh? Ha ha...we used to do terrible things with toast...oh ha ha ha...what? Yes Murphy I know, just a minute. Ha ha...the toast

Olympics! That's what we called them. Ha ha...toast discus...ha ha...toast frisbee...oh dear...trying to frisbee toast into the Form Master's pigeon-hole...oh ha ha. Yes what is it Murphy? Yes I know it's serious, now do be quiet. Eh Superintendent? What a laugh eh?...then at Cambridge...ha ha...we'd put toast in this chap's pyjamas. Ha ha...his underpants too. Crunch crunch crunch! Oh hahaha. Wonderful wonderful. And Champagne Soldiers! God I'd forgotten about them...they were great...ha ha...strips of toast in each hand – one to dip in your boiled egg the other to dip in champagne! Ha ha what a breakfast eh? Oh all right Murphy...Right ...er...I was just going to say that...so, yes, er Superintendent Auchter...er...muchter, er...better get it sorted out eh? In your capable hands eh? Bye old chap. Nice talking to you. Oh do shut up Murphy."

"Er...yes Prime Minister."

Chapter 12

"Good morning and welcome to the Today Programme on Radio 4. The time is now seven o'clock on Friday the ninth of June and this is Harriet Green with the morning's news:

The Prime Minister's office issued a statement this morning to say that the toasting outbreak which has swept the country in the past two days is being properly and effectively dealt with by police forces and other agencies such as schools and kindergartens throughout the country. A marked diminution of toasting is anticipated over the next twenty four hours as the perpetrators of the original toasting crimes are expected to be apprehended shortly, thereby taking the momentum out of the toasting craze. It seems, however, that 'toasting' – that is the act of committing a minor felony and leaving a slice of toast at the scene – has spread from being an undertaking of the very young, to the adult world, with widespread reports of pranks in the workplace, universities, and in public areas being signed off with slices of toast. The effects on the economy of this massive 'misdemeanour-wave' - as it was described yesterday by the Home Secretary - have been surprising and unexpected. The consumption of gas and electricity have approached levels usually only seen during cold snaps in the winter months, and sales of bread this week have risen by over 17%. A police spokes...."

Inspector Slighman turned off his radio as he guided his car into the police car park. Expectations were high regarding the imminent arrest of these guys. His fingers were crossed. Superintendent Smart had summoned him and DS Silver to his office the previous evening and they had been informed in no uncertain terms what he, and the head of police in Scotland, and the First Minister, and the Prime Minister, and all right-thinking people everywhere, wanted. They wanted, nay, they craved, the head of the Toaster, and they wanted it now. He, she, it, them, or whatever, was a monumental embarrassment and had to be caught.

The Inspector slammed his car door and fairly ran up the stairs and into the office – not many people in yet so the taunts were muted. He had ordered a copy of that morning's Daily Post and it was on his desk. The front page was devoted almost entirely to a screaming headline:

The Daily Post

Inside: The Post's Toaster Poster!
Exclusive: The Toasters Revealed!

Britain's Most Wanted Men Photographed!
Only Inside Today's Daily Post.

Billy Bootle Reporting

After three days of toasting mayhem throughout the UK the Daily Post brings you actual photographs of the original 'Toasters' plus comments by leading figures on the impact of 'toasting'. Also a calendar of events leading up to these...

The Inspector opened his newspaper with some trepidation. Folded into the centre pages was the pull-out poster which he duly pulled out. The photograph he had handed over to Billy Bootle the day before had been blown up to fill three-quarters of the page, and packed around it were the promised comments by the great and the good and the promised diary of events. No mention of his name. Long exhale. His phone rang.

"Inspector Slighman."

"Morning Inspector, DS Silver here, we've just had a phone call from a Mrs Angelina Farquhar – she works a couple of days a week at the Sally Ann's charity shop on the High Street...she saw the photograph in today's Post - the two men in the photograph seemingly came into the shop yesterday with a donation of goods."

"Really? Good good good! Where is she now?"

"Well the shop doesn't open till ten but she's due in there at nine...so I said I'd meet her there at nine."

"Right – I'll meet you there too sergeant. I want to be in on this."

"Very good sir."

"Right Rebecca, better get started. Who's next on the list?"

"Darren Conroy, 144 Freggor Lane."

No Darren Conroy, and no Freggor Lane. Demolished two years previously. Now an Asda store.

"Next."

"Jennifer Oyston, 54 Stoke Street."

No Jennifer Oyston. Married and moved away without trace three years earlier. Good riddance said her erstwhile neighbours.

"Next."

"Andrew Mackenzie, 4 Albert Grove."

Andrew Mackenzie at home.

"Mr Mackenzie, did you know Big Bruno."

"Yes. Why?"

"Can you help us with these ledgers?"

"No."

"Why not?"

"I have never knowingly helped a police officer, ever, and I certainly don't intend helping anyone find the saint who wasted that malevolent bastard."

"Right."

"Next."

"Next...er...third man on today's list..okay, Henry Lime, 56 Jamaica Court."

The man was in. He was thin, wiry, tattooed, late thirties, and out in his backyard attending to his homing pigeons when the detectives arrived.

"You remember Big Bruno, by any chance?" asked DS Munro after they had introduced themselves.

"Oh yes, I remember Big Bruno all right. I remember him only too well. Piece of shit. May he rot in hell."

"Right. We're making enquiries regarding his murder on Monday."

"Oh yes. So how can I help?" He looked amiable enough.

"We were wondering if you could help us make sense of this ledger of his."

"Let's see it then," he said quietly, placing a plump pigeon back into its loft and reaching out for the book. DC Bickerstaff handed over a ledger. "Oh yes, I've seen this many times. What do you want to know?"

"What do the different letters mean? The 'Ps' and 'Bs' and what have you."

"Simple. A 'P' means 'paid'; and 'L' means 'late'; a 'W' means a 'warning'."

Ben Munro and Rebecca Bickerstaff heaved sighs of relief. Progress at last.

"And a 'B'? Any idea what that means?!

"Oh yes, I know what that means all right. A 'B' means 'banjoed".

"*Banjoed*!?" both the DS and the DC gasped simultaneously.

"Indeed it does. That was the Big Shit's pet phrase for putting someone in hospital. Usually with a collection of broken bones."

"Jesus Christ! That could explain the choice of murder weapon right enough!" said DS Munro.

"A vengeance murder... somebody from his past," added DC Bickerstaff.

Henry Lime laughed. "Well that's one hell of a lot of people. Hundreds if not thousands. And not one of them will help you...and that includes me. God...I cried tears of joy when I heard he'd been killed. Tears of joy. I cried for almost half an hour...just a release of fear, hatred and relief. And when I read he'd been whacked with a banjo... oh yes...oh yes...oh yes...one of the happiest moments of my life. Talk about poetic justice. Beautiful. Absolutely beautiful. I read it over and over again. I've kept that page – right into my souvenir box. I felt a sense of freedom I haven't felt for fifteen years. If you ever find the bastard's killer there'll be a rush of people demanding a knighthood. A sainthood even."

"How come you know about his ledger shorthand?"

Henry Lime looked grim. "That's how the scumbag used to threaten you if you were late. He'd get his book out and say "...look at this Henry...you've got a 'W' Henry....that's a warning Henry....now you don't want a 'B'...do you Henry...that's a banjoing Henry... and you don't want to be banjoed now, do you Henry? Evil bastard."

"Were you ever 'banjoed' Henry?"

Henry's face took on a dark scowl. "He once slapped my face, at the warning stage. Three times. Humiliating. Really...really humiliating. I was two days late paying for my heroin. I couldn't respond. I just let him do it. He could have pulled me apart if he'd wanted to. I've often thought about it...but even if I'd been armed I'd have been too frightened of him to do anything. I know you're police, and I shouldn't say this, but I had to steal two Rolex watches to pay the fucker. It was a long time ago, and in a way it did me a favour because that was precisely when I vowed to kick the stuff. Six months later and I was out of his clutches. I went through hell. I still waken up every morning and give up thanks."

"Did he have anyone with him? Did he do all his own dirty work?"

"All the time I was getting shit from him it was just him himself. He enjoyed it – you could see that. He ran a big organisation – he could easily have sat on his arse and have his heavies do the collecting. For him it was all a pleasure. He did his own dirty work – and anyhow, he was so intimidating he didn't need anyone to help him."

"Do you know anything about his background? Any enemies in particular."

"His background? Almost nothing. Started early...or so I've been told... beat up a kid when he was at primary school. Broke his nose, or his jaw or something, according to the legend. Start of a long career of violence and crime. As for enemies...I'll keep that to myself if you don't mind...just in case it helps you with your enquiries."

"Fair enough Mr Lime," said DS Munro, "we'll leave it at that. And thank you very much for your help...and good luck."

"Mrs Farquhar?" DS Silver enquired of the lady in the Salvation Army charity shop.

"I am." Mrs Farquhar was immaculately groomed, grey of hair, dressed in matching green jersey and skirt with a fine string of pearls around her neck. She was clearly of an age to be retired, but looked as if she had more energy than the rest of Auchtergarry put together.

"Thanks for phoning us with this very useful information Mrs Farquhar. I'm Detective Sergeant Silver and this is Inspector Slighman."

"Hello."

"Did you actually speak with either of these men Mrs Farquhar?

"Well yes sergeant, I spoke to them both. Such nice men. Very polite. Very well dressed."

"Did they say where they lived, by any chance?" asked the Inspector.

"Er...no. Just said they were here on holiday."

"Mention a hotel or anything?"

"No, Inspector.

"Give a name or anything?"

"No."

"What was it they donated?" asked DS Silver.

"Oh, er...a toaster, actually. Not very clean I have to say, so I gave it a good clean yesterday afternoon."

Inspector Slighman gave a weak smile, which became considerably more enfeebled as his eye caught sight of his recently stolen toaster sitting on a shelf. If ever there was something he never wanted to see again, this was it. Ah well. They could keep it.

"We'll have to take that as evidence of course," said the sergeant.

"Yes, of course," the Inspector's voice forced out on a light breath.

"Were they here long?" asked DS Silver.

"Yes, they were. They were here for quite a while. Looked through a lot of our stuff. Very chatty, the pair of them. Talked about this that and everything, so they did. Most amusing gentlemen. Certainly made me laugh. Generous too. Bought a replica set of the Lewis Chessmen - which had only just been donated the day before. We asked for £25 but they gave us £30. They really were awfully nice men."

"Did they pay cash?"

"Yes. They did."

"Did you happen to notice if they had a car with them?"

"Yes. In fact they got a parking ticket. Didn't seem to bother them. The tall one had it sticking out of his top pocket."

"Really? What time was this?

"About three o'clock I think."

"Do you know where were they parked by any chance?"

"Just round the corner I believe. In Monadail Avenue."

Gold dust. They left in anticipation of a very imminent arrest.

"Inspector Blackthorn?"

"Yes, hi Ben, what's new?"

"Thought you'd like to know…we've got the code Bruno used in his ledgers."

"Good good good. Let's have it."

"Right, 'P' we knew about – that's 'paid'."

"Yeah."

"'L' is for 'late'."

"Right…"

"'W' is for 'warning'."

"O..kay…"

"And 'B'…is for…" the DS couldn't resist a dramatic pause "…'banjoed'!"

"*Glory be*! Banjoed eh? Well well…poetic justice or what? What exactly happened when someone got 'banjoed' Ben?"

"They were hospitalised."

"Good work Ben, well done. That overwhelmingly suggests someone from his past…a revenge killing. Now, dig deeper Ben – right into his past. Burrow burrow burrow."

"Right you are Marm."

"How're you getting on with your new sidekick Ben?"

"DC Bickerstaff?...er Becky? Yeah she's good. I like her." DS Munro could sense a smile at the Scottish end of the line.

"Right Ben, keep up the good work. Bye."

"Right Sergeant," said Inspector Slighman as they drove back to headquarters, "we've got them now. A parking ticket...wonderful. We'll have their names and addresses within the hour."

"We should do. Providing the car's not stolen of course."

"D'you think it might be?"

"No, I don't suppose so, they seem like pretty law-abiding guys really."

Inspector Slighman gasped in horror. "*Law abiding!? Are you insane sergeant?* You mean apart from breaking and entering, theft of a toaster, theft of a statuette, disfiguring a cultural icon in Dundee, and setting in motion the country's most serious ever rash of petty criminality? That's certainly not what I call law-abiding!"

"Well, we can't really blame them for the copy-cat stuff."

"What?! What kind of long-haired wishy-washy tree-hugging sandal-wearing liberality bullshit is this sergeant? Too fucking right we can blame them for the copy-cat stuff. I'd have them beheaded for treason if I had my way. I want them locked up for a long long time. A long, long, time."

The angrier the inspector got, the harder DS Silver found it to keep a straight face.

"Mmm...yes... I believe the Superintendent feels much the same way Inspector."

"Of course he does Sergeant. He's got his head screwed on the right way. That's why he's a Superintendent, Sergeant, and you're still a bloody Sergeant, Sergeant."

DS Silver had to batten his face down tightly. The inspector was on a roll and continued with his glorious invective up to and into the police car park.

"We can't blame them for the copy cat stuff? Jesus Christ, Sergeant these guys are pure evil, believe you me, don't be fooled by nice manners and corduroy trousers sergeant. Evil. That's what they are. "

DS Silver switched off the engine, pulled up the handbrake, opened the door and stepped out of the car in one quick, smooth movement in his desperation to get out of the car before he doubled-up with hysterics. But, his nascent laugh died an instant death and his jaw sagged to his chest as he looked into the car they had parked beside. There smiling up at him, large as life, and in the flesh, were the perpetrators; the felons. One wearing a deerstalker and the other a pair of orangey-red corduroy trousers.

"Good morning," said the one with the deerstalker, "are you a policeman?"

"Er...yes I am."

"Good. I believe you're looking for us."

"Er...yes...yes....we are."

"Right, here we are."

Inspector Slighman had walked round to see what was happening and duly went through his own jaw-dropping process.

"G...g...g...good God!" was all he could manage.

"Ehm…ah…gentlemen," said the sergeant, "could you follow me please."

"Certainly," said he of the cord trousers, with a very pleasant smile.

As they entered the police station they were gaped at by everyone they passed. Since the Daily Post's exposé they were the most recognisable twosome in town. DS Silver led them into an interview room and gestured them to sit down.

"Thank you," said the corduroy-clad one.

"Thank you very much," said the one with the deerstalker, which he had removed on entry to the building.

DS Sliver introduced himself and the inspector.

"Delighted to meet you both," said the cords-wearer with a friendly smile, "I'm Peter Solent…"

"…and…" said he of the deerstalker, "…I'm George Solent. We're brothers."

This display of genteel bonhomie was too much for Inspector Slighman.

"Enough!" he barked, "we have reason to believe that on the morning of Wednesday 5th June you did break and enter into the private house situated at 4 Tarn Way Lochain and there from did steal a toaster and a loaf of bread."

"Eh? Oh no Inspector, certainly not. I was nowhere near Lochain on Wednesday," said Peter Solent.

"I was," said George, "I was definitely there, and yes, I must confess, I did remove a toaster from a house on Wednesday morning, although I don't know the address I removed it from."

"*You admit it!*" gasped the Inspector.

"Oh yes, well certainly, I always try to be helpful to the police," said George, as he absent-mindedly stuffed his deerstalker into his jacket pocket.

"Well thank you very much!" barked the Inspector. "Oh yes you've helped us! How much you've helped us! You've caused the biggest crime wave in Britain's history dammit! Thousands and thousands of law-abiding youngsters have been turned to criminality by your iniquitous, senseless acts!"

"Really? Whatever do you mean Inspector?" asked George.

"What the hell do you mean, what do I mean? I mean the nation is awash with slices of toast - people the length and breadth of the land have been copy-catting you and leaving slices of toast at their crime scenes."

"I'm sorry Inspector, but that's the first I've heard of this. I may have removed a toaster from a house, but I certainly have not left any slices of toast anywhere." The inspector clenched his jaw, rolled his eyes to the ceiling, shook his head and took a deep breath, allowing DS Silver a chance at interrogation.

"Are you seriously telling us, Mr Solent that, yes, you stole the toaster, but no, you didn't leave any slices of toast anywhere, like under policemen's windscreen-wipers for example?"

"I removed the toaster, yes. But I can assure you the slices of toast have nothing whatsoever to do with me."

"What about you, Mr Solent," asked the sergeant turning to brother Peter, "did you leave any slices of toast anywhere?"

"No, I certainly did not."

"Did either of you steal a bronze statuette from the museum here in Auchtergarry?"

"Well I, most assuredly, did not," said George.

"And I most assuredly did not," said Peter.

"So, let me get this right," said a somewhat flummoxed DS Silver. "You, George Solent, readily admit to stealing a toaster on the morning of June the 5th, but you deny leaving any slices of toast anywhere, and any further thefts?"

"Correct."

"And you, Peter Solent, deny any involvement in the theft of the toaster, you deny leaving any slices of toast, and you deny stealing a bronze statuette."

"Absolutely I do."

"What about defacing the statue of Desperate Dan in Dundee?" Both brothers looked puzzled. "Eh? Who? No, definitely not."

"Right Peter Solent, where were you on the morning of Monday June the 5th between the hours of 6.15 and 6.45?

"Oh, golly. Erm. I don't really know…er…don't remember to be honest."

"Mr Solent it was less than a week ago, surely you can remember where you were?"

"Erm…I'm trying, I really am – we've been all over the place in the past few weeks. I suspect, however, that wherever I was I was safely tucked-up in bed at that time in the morning."

"So you could have been anywhere eh? Not much of an alibi really? Is it?"

"Well no I suppose not, but one thing I do know is that I've never been to Lochain. Never been farther north than Auchtergarry actually. And I've never stolen anything in my life…give or take the odd paper-clip. Not ever. Em…George, do you remember where I was on Monday morning?"

"Sorry Peter, no I don't. You weren't with me though, I know that."

"No, I definitely wasn't with you. But where the hell was I? Sorry Sergeant, it's gone. Perhaps it'll come back."

Inspector Slighman, once again, had had enough. "What the hell is going on here?" he screamed. "I've never heard such nonsense! You're both plainly guilty as hell of breaking and entering, stealing the toaster, stealing the statuette, and dispensing toast throughout the fucking Highlands of Scotland. We've got fingerprint evidence at the scene of the toaster theft, and material evidence from the scene of the statuette theft. You're both going away for a long time."

"Thank you very much Inspector, but, as the sergeant says, yes, I readily admit to removing a toaster, but I certainly didn't break in...the door was wide open. And I flatly deny anything to do with slices of toast and statuettes. Absolute nonsense, the very idea's preposterous."

"Oh really. We'll see about that," growled Inspector Slighman, "we'll certainly see about that. Once we compare your fingerprints – oh yes, you left some nice prints in my kitchen, thank you very much - and the trouser button – which is plainly missing from your trousers Mr Peter Bloody Solent – we'll have you cold. Stone cold."

"Er...did you say 'my kitchen' just now Inspector?"

Inspector Slighman stood up, drew himself up to his full six foot two, inflated his chest slowly, stiffened his jaw and his upper lip, narrowed his eyes, and said, "yes, I did."

"Oh I'm terribly sorry sir, I had no idea it was your toaster. There was certainly no personal animosity involved in my little...er... theft exercise. I fully intended writing a letter of apology to whoever owned it...once I'd found out who it was.

With a sum of money enclosed to cover replacement and inconvenience costs, of course"

The inspector was beyond speech. Before him he saw not a man but a demon; a foul fiend.

"May I ask why you stole the toaster Mr Solent?" asked DS Silver.

"You know, I have absolutely no idea why I did it. I just saw the opportunity, and some strange force came over me…I nipped in and nabbed it. Quite exciting really. I've never done anything even remotely like it before, and shall certainly never do anything remotely like it again. "

The inspector's voice came back with a vengeance. "*Are you insane?* Do you really expect us to believe that you just happened to be outside my house at half past six in the morning of June the 5th, when some wrong number just happened to phone me, I just happened to leave the door open, and you, for no reason you can account for, just happened to pop in and swipe my fucking toaster? You really think we're going to swallow that?"

"A wrong number? Ah, I wondered why you'd gone back in. That explains it."

"Oh I don't believe it! Are you seriously telling us now that the phone call was none of your doing?"

The brothers looked at each other, puzzled. "Not either of us Inspector. Certainly not."

"Okay. May I ask you then, Mr Solent, what *were* you doing outside the Inspector's house at that time in the morning?" asked DS Silver.

"I just happened to be passing by. Early morning stroll."

"Really?"

"Yes, really."

Inspector Slighman glowered ferociously and leaned over the table until he was little more than a nose-length from George Solent's face. "You're lying! Every word is a lie! This whole thing was planned meticulously wasn't it? Every last detail thought out in advance. You deliberately set out to humiliate the whole police division didn't you...?"

"I can assure you Inspector that that is simply not the case. And I hardly think the theft of a toaster is likely to have caused the kind of crime wave you've been suggesting..."

"Oh no? You think not? We've even had the Prime Minister on the phone about it."

"The Prime Minister? About a toaster? Oh well, he's a buffoon anyhow, but yes, I suppose that is a bit of a surprise."

Inspector Slighman felt as if he were swimming in golden syrup. "And," he demanded, "which of you has been phoning the press? Every single thing has been immediately communicated to the gutter press. They knew about the theft of the toaster before I did for God's sake."

Again the brothers looked baffled. "I wouldn't speak to a tabloid journalist for all the tea in China," said George in shocked tones.

"Me neither," said Peter, "certainly not".

"I don't believe you!" The inspector's control was slipping. "You're evil, the pair of you! Sitting there coming across all fucking upright and worthy!...evil! Both of you!"

"Inspector Simon..."

"*Slighman*!"

"Sorry, Inspector Slighman," said Peter, "I have committed no crime whatsoever, my brother has stolen a toaster which he then donated, Robin Hood-like, if I may say so, to a charity shop. This hardly makes us evil."

"ROBIN HOOD!" *Robin fucking Hood*! You are both in need of treatment! You break and enter - steal something - give it to the Sally Ann - and suddenly you're good guys! What kind of planet do you two nutcases inhabit for God's sake?"

"Planet earth, Inspector, just planet earth."

"Right, the pair of you, that does it. That's enough of this nonsense. You're both plainly bonkers. It's Friday today. You are both under arrest, and you'll both be appearing in front of the Sherriff at the Sherriff Court on Monday. That means a weekend in the cells for you both...which is probably a good thing for you as you'll get some nice practice in for doing a long stretch of time! Now won't that be good?"

Both men smiled.

"Thank you Inspector," said George

"Yes, thank you very much," said Peter.

The inspector left the room in a haze of incomprehension, slamming the door behind him.

DS Silver looked at the brothers carefully. He too was truly mystified. They seemed wholly genuine in their thanks. The prospect of a weekend incarcerated in a police cell didn't seem to bother them in the very least. In fact they looked entirely sanguine about the whole thing. Peter removed his jacket, draped it over the back of his chair, smiled at the sergeant, and asked quietly if there were any chance of a cup of tea.

As DS Silver made his way back to his car his mobile rang. Unknown number.

"Hello DS Bob Silver here."

"Hello Sergeant Silver, I'm terribly sorry to bother you, it's Mrs Wilks here from the Auchtergarry Museum."

"Oh hello Mrs Wilks. How can I help you?"

"Well you said to phone if anything occurred to me, or if anything happened."

"Yes I did. Is there something?"

"Well yes, there is. The statuette's been returned."

"Really?"

"Yes, it just reappeared an hour ago."

"That's interesting. Were there any visitors in the museum at the time Mrs Wilks?"

"Yes there were quite a few actually. More than usual I suppose. Mostly from England I think. Don't know if it was a party or a special group or anything. Don't remember a coach or a minibus but then I probably wouldn't have noticed anyhow."

"Is it ok?"

"What the statuette? Well yes it is. It's fine...in fact it's been given a good clean. Looks better now than it ever did." She laughed.

Chapter 13

The weekend slipped by. The police in Edinburgh had been in touch to say the men in the Daily Post's poster had been identified many times over as the Solent brothers, Peter and George – proprietors of two of Edinburgh's most popular restaurants. Neither had ever been in trouble before, and both had in fact had many years active involvement organising events and raising funds for local charities. They were golfing friends of half a dozen police officers including a Superintendent and a Chief Inspector. In short, they were regarded as upstanding members of the community. Forensics had determined that the fingerprint found in the Slighmans' kitchen was a match for Peter Solent, and that the button found in Auchtergarry's museum had indeed come off his trousers. The advice given them by a local solicitor drafted in to defend them was that they plead guilty in order to minimise their sentences. Both men readily agreed to do this, even though Peter still denied any involvement.

"I'll plead guilty for George's sake," Peter explained to the solicitor, "if as you say the sheriff will be more lenient towards us."

"Well, the evidence against you is pretty damning Mr Solent, is it not? A fingerprint of yours at one crime scene...where it definitely should not have been, a button off your trousers at the other crime scene, turning up at a charity shop with the stolen toaster...and your brother readily admitting his guilt...well, pleading innocent would be pointless really – it would certainly increase both your sentences."

"Ah well, what must be must be, but I am an innocent man."

Even the tabloids on Saturday and Sunday went fairly quiet regarding the Toaster saga as their front pages were suddenly consumed by the nice new story of a glamorous celebrity chef photographed adulterously in the arms of an ex-captain of the English football team. Photographs of them, their partners, and their kids filled the first four pages. All in the public interest. The Toasters' arrest still got it big, but on page five, not page one. The story was starting to wither. Inspector Slighman was starting to breathe more easily. And, with one of the two big cases on his plate now coming to a close, Superintendent Smart was allowing himself a sigh or two of relief. Life in Auchtergarry was getting back to normal. Apart, of course, from the minor issue of Big Bruno's murder.

Inspector Blackthorn, meanwhile, just shook her head. This Toaster nonsense was weird. Had it been her case she would have liked to prod about a bit more before bringing it to court but, hey, it wasn't her case - nothing to do with her.

Sergeant Munro and DC Bickerstaff had spent the weekend going through Big Bruno's ledgers and trying to trace and interview everyone who had recently been either 'warned' or 'banjoed'. The sergeant calculated that at any one time over the previous decades Bruno had roughly forty to fifty 'clients' at a time – some bought every week, some every fortnight, some bought infrequently. Mostly they paid on time but every month there would be two or three 'warnings', and every two or three months someone was 'banjoed'. It was clear that if this was just Bruno's patch which he dealt with himself, then, with his alleged control through John Sangster over big chunks of Lancashire and the North West added to the mix, he was responsible for untold misery to an awful lot of people. Trying to find the one, or ones, who hated him enough to clout him with a banjo, looked more and more like an impossible task.

The few they managed to trace who had been 'warned' or 'banjoed' either clammed up completely, or else stated that they knew nothing about the murder, and even if they had known, they had no intention of helping the police find the killer. Some limped, some carried other visible scars, and some were clearly badly scarred psychologically. Any or all of them would probably have happily bumped him off given the opportunity – and the courage. The only fresh piece of information they had managed to dig up from an otherwise silent interviewee was confirmation that Bruno really had hospitalised some poor kid in his primary school...so...a fifty year history of making enemies.

Sergeant Munro passed his doubts about the outcome of their investigations on to DI Blackthorn but her response was to keep going. Keep turning the stones over to see if anything crawled out. There was certainly nothing happening up north to move the investigation on. The theft of the Glen Laldy single malt whisky was still an open case but nothing new had been learnt – and certainly nothing to help in the Bruno case. It also concerned her that Bruno may have been wasted by a competing drug-baron – unlikely, she knew, because of the apparently revengeful use of a banjo to whack him with – but a possibility nonetheless. So, a massive job, probably undoable, but continue as before. Dig dig dig.

Sheriff Abernethy Bultitude-Foss looked across his unusually crowded courtroom at the two accused and quickly re-read the Procurator Fiscal's report. The Solent brothers. A pair of Edinburgh restaurateurs of prosperous and gentlemanly appearance with a list of pillar-of-the-community friends as long as your arm - all willing to vouch for their integrity and decency. Hard to believe he was looking at the men who had triggered a nationwide epidemic of misdemeanours. Yes, they accepted the charges against them, and yes they pleaded guilty to both charges. Theft of a toaster, and theft of a statuette valued at £30 – now returned and in better condition than when removed. The ensuing mayhem could not legally be laid at their door. Not a lot to go on in terms of punishment. The police, he knew, wanted the book thrown at them, but they really did seem like such nice chaps. And, say what you will, the youngsters of the land had thoroughly enjoyed the episode while it lasted – it had certainly involved more monkey than it had malice. A conundrum, and here he was in a courtroom packed with what seemed like half the nation's press waiting agog for his verdict. Ah well. He took a slow deep breath.

"May I ask, gentlemen," he said addressing the pair, "which restaurants you own in Edinburgh?"

"Certainly my Lord," Peter responded with a willing smile, "we own La Grande Assiette in the New Town…"

"… and the Muckle Platter down at the shore, my lord…in Leith," added George.

"Ah." The sheriff leaned back in his seat. He knew, and loved, La Grande Assiette. A wonderful restaurant. Delightful service, sublime food, decor redolent of fin du siècle Paris, and a superb view of the castle. Perfect really. Exquisite. He and Mrs Bultitude-Foss dined there at least twice a year and had done so for many years. They really did seem like such nice chaps.

"May I further ask you, gentlemen, what possessed you to steal these items?"

George looked Sheriff Bultitude-Foss in the eye, tilted his head slightly, and assumed an expression of concerned intelligence before he replied.

"A very strange impulse, my lord. No explaining it in all honesty. But an absolute never-to-be-repeated one-off I can assure you."

"Right. Okay. Well…er…gentlemen, as I am sure you are aware, in the light of your guilty pleas, and the somewhat concrete evidence against you, I have, of course, no option but to find you guilty of these thefts. However in view of your previously pristine record, and in view of the fact that you have already spent three nights in police custody, I will consider that to be sufficient punishment. You now have a criminal record…but you are free to go. Thank you."

For the first and only time in his career, to his utter horror, Sheriff Bultitude-Foss's verdict was greeted by a spontaneous outburst of cheering and applause.

"FREE TO GO!?" Inspector Slighman was aghast. "*Free to fucking go*? Is the sheriff mad? I don't believe it! I-do-not-believe-it!"

"Well it was a first offence sir," DS Silver responded in a rather quieter tone. "It's amazing they even got held over the weekend to be honest. I kind of thought they'd maybe just get called in on the Monday and get off with a warning."

"WHAT!? You're in the wrong job Silver, you really are. You have absolutely no sense of just retribution, that's your problem. I thought they'd be banged up for months. Years. Bloody hell man, it's a joke. They led the whole country on a wild goose chase and…and… almost derailed my career for God's sake."

"Pardon sir?"

"Er…nothing. Nothing. They're bad buggers, that's all. Bad bad buggers. As the sheriff said…mind you it was the only sensible thing he did say…the evidence against them was incontrovertibly, undeniably, and indisputably, one hundred per cent rock-solid concrete - guilty guilty guilty. What's the problem? Bang them up. Slam the door."

"Yes sir."

"Now they're out there – a massive public threat. Un-be-fucking-lievable."

"Yes sir. But they're not really a massive pub…"

"Don't start that nonsense again sergeant! Of course they are. What are they going to cook up now eh? Ask yourself that! They've got a taste for it now. Oh believe you me they've got a taste for it now. Who knows what havoc they'll wreak. Doubt it not sergeant, doubt it not - we haven't heard the last of these men. Not by a long chalk we haven't."

"Bootle?"

"Yes…"

"It's Slighman."

"Poppet!"

"Don't *poppet* me Bootle! I am not your poppet!"

"Okay inspector...I'll try to remember that. How can I help you today?"

"Well...what did you make of that fiasco this morning then?"

"Fiasco? Which fiasco?"

"Which fiasco...? Setting that pair free...which bloody fiasco did you think I meant?"

"My dear petal...that was no fiasco...that was a master stroke. Put a smile on the entire nation that did — does wonders for circulation figures my friend — nothing like a smiling nation to sell copy."

"But they're the most hated men in the country! How could releasing them put a smile on the nation?"

"Hated...? I think you're a little out of touch with public opinion Inspector — the people of the land love them dearly."

"Rubbish Bootle, absolute rubbish. They're a dreadful duo — and I have enough faith in the great British public's moral compass to...er...to....er...well...er...to have faith in it. Of course the public hate them — they're not stupid you know."

"My very good friend, I hate to flag up a competitor newspaper, but if you cast a glance at page two of today's Gazette you'll see a table showing — in order of popularity — the people held in most affection by its readership as compiled by text-voting over the weekend. There, in sixth place, sneaking in after a royal or two and some toothy celebs, are the Toasters."

"You're lying Bootle."

"Not at all old chap. It's there in black and white. And, may I ask, how do you account for the fact that the courtroom erupted in cheering after the verdict this morning?"

"Well that's what I was phoning you about – there's clearly a lot of people out there confused about what happened in that courtroom. I mean the sheriff did insist they were stone wall guilty you know. That's what they were cheering about, not the fact they were being released. I don't think the people in the courtroom realised that they had in fact been released. They cheered as soon as they heard the guilty verdict and didn't even hear the bit about their release. They'd have been furious if they had. And it's your job now to inform the public how farcical their release was after such a damning verdict. The sheriff should be held to account by you journalists."

"My very dear inspector, you are, I am sure, a quite wonderful policeman, but for your own sake, please never turn to journalism. Your view of these men is unique in the land. Everyone loves them, and the people in the courtroom knew exactly what was happening. They were delighted, and rightly so. The Toasters kept the nation smiling for a week...and the nation is still smiling."

Inspector Slighman shook his head in exasperation. "Nonsense Bootle, let me assure you, my finger's on the pulse. I can well assess the public mood."

Bootle laughed. "Right, have it your own way, but keep me informed of any developments in the Big Bruno case, okay?"

"I may, if you promise to slag-off that idiot Bultitude-Floss in tomorrow's edition for releasing that pair."

"I'll tell you what Inspector, I'll underline the fact that it was, indeed, a clear guilty verdict, and that you personally think it's a travesty of justice that they have been released. Would you like me to mention the fact that it was your toas..."

"NO! Certainly not. Diplomacy Bootle, diplomacy. Just say that I have said that they are both unarguably guilty...red-handed...smoking-gun and all that...and perhaps the sheriff was...er...a little...er...shall we say...lenient. How's that?"

"Bonzer old chap, absolutely bonzer."

"Right. Good God – these guys think they're Robin Bloody Hood because they gave the thing to the Sally Ann. They're bonkers."

"Robin Hoo...? Ah...Inspector Slighman...I take it all back – you're a natural tabloid man! Bye for now!"

Chapter 14

The twins marched down the Devil's Staircase with relish and with gusto. This was the life. They'd done the West Highland Way south to north three times. This time, just for a change, they were doing it north to south. It was day two of their five allotted days. The sun was up and would be for the rest of the day, and, according to the BBC website, it would be up there in a clear sky tomorrow, and the next day, and the one after that. Bliss. The hills were where they always wanted to be. Back in Dundee, at home or at work, they would dream of days like this up in the mountains. Days spent marching and singing and laughing and joking…and of course fighting. They loved a fight. Yep, there was nothing like a good scrap.. but only ever with each other. They were as close as close could be as brothers, but it was a closeness which regularly manifested itself in an explosion of fisticuffs. A couple of solid punches later and they would be pals again, dabbing wounds, but with arms around each other.

Merrily they strode along, singing marching songs, boating songs, love songs, drinking songs, Scottish songs, Irish songs…in fact any song which bubbled up and into their fancy.

"I love to go a-wandering along the mountain track
And as I go I love to sing my knapsack on my back…"

They had left Kinlochleven at nine that morning and were going to meet their brother Horace at Kingshouse for a late lunch and a beer. What an appetite they would have! The air up here would have invigorated Rip Van Winkle. Already they had spotted a golden eagle, passed some mountain goats, and frightened off a small herd of deer. The views over Glen Coe as they marched along were simply stunning. Heaven.

Valderee... valderaa
Valderee...valderaa ha ha ha ha ha
Valderee...

Oh this was the life!

...Valderaa
My knapsack on my back!

The atmosphere and camaraderie amongst all the walkers on the Way this week were buzzing. Not only were conditions perfect but there was still a high hum of intrigue surrounding Big Bruno's demise. In the pub in Kinlochleven the night before there had been little else talked about. Everybody had his or her own pet theory, usually centred around drug-dealing or sex. But all was sheer speculation. The twins were especially fascinated. They themselves were fairly law-abiding characters but the criminal underworld had always captivated them. What the hell Big Bruno was doing getting bumped-off half way along the West Highland Way was a matter of endless discussion and debate between them...when they weren't singing.

With their fair, spiky hair and in their uniform of dark walking shorts and fawn-coloured shirts the pair were well kent and instantly recognisable among the brotherhood and sisterhood of Scottish walkers and climbers. They were at home in the hills. Hill people were their people. Comfort equated to a thick pair of socks, a good pair of hiking boots and a back-pack full of walking gear. Time for a new song.

I've got sixpence
Jolly jolly sixpence
I've got sixpence to last me all my life...

They had bagged every Munro at least twice, and some of their favourites...like Slioch, Schiehallion, Buachaille Etive Mor, or Ben Nevis itself...they had lost count of the number of times they'd climbed them. Mention any Scottish mountain to them and they could visualise it perfectly in three dimensions. They could tell you the easiest way up, the most interesting way up, the fastest way up, the most challenging way up, and any other way up you cared to enquire about.

I've got tuppence to lend
And tuppence to spend
And tuppence to give unto my wife...

They had also climbed and walked all over Europe, North Africa, and South America, and in a month's time they were off for their first visit to the Dolomites for their yearly trip with the Dundee Corrie Ramblers Club. Tackling the Alps. They couldna' wait!

No cares have I belie-eve me
No pretty little girls to decei-ei-ve me...

But this was living in the moment!

I'm as happy as a king belie-eve me...

Life on the edge!

As I go rolling home...

They paused in their descent for a moment as a bird flew close by.

"That wiz a dotterel!"

"Rubbish, it wizznae a dotterel, we're too low doon."

"Naw we're no!"

"Aye we are."

"It wiz definitely a dotterel – ah got a good look."

"Ah yer haverin'. Ur ye sure it wiznae a capercaille?"

"Aye very funny. Ah ken a dotterel when ah see wan."

"Aye an' I ken an erse..."

"There it goes look!"

Instantly they both shot off the path and moved into the heather toward a fast flowing stream where the bird appeared to have landed. Suddenly, they stopped and gaped. Both turned to stone. There, lying near the stream, gleaming in the sunlight, was a banjo. A broken banjo, but a banjo nonetheless.

As suddenly as they had turned to stone, they both, in the same instant, burst into a frenzy of action as they struggled with one another to get at the thing.

"Big Bruno's banjo!"

"Aye! I saw it first!"

"Naw ye didnae! I saw it first!"

"Dinnae touch it!"

"Ah'm no gonnae touch it! D'ye think ah'm daft or somethin'? Let go o' me!"

"You let go o' me!"

First twin:	Haymaker – missed
Second twin:	Right uppercut – missed
First twin:	Another haymaker – partial pow!
Second twin:	Straight left – bullseye!
First twin:	Left hook – whack!

"Orrite! That's enough!" First twin holding his eye.

"Okay, fair do's." Second twin holding his ear.

"Brilliant man! Big Bruno's banjo – it has to be!"

"Fan-tas-tik-ko! We'll be famous!"

"Right – better get the cops. You got a signal?"

"Naw."

"Me neither."

"Rightee ho. You bide, an' ah'll go doon tae Kingshoose."

"Right. Aw man...brilliant!"

DI Bonnie Blackthorn positively leapt up the Devil's Staircase after twin number one, with DS Silver making his ponderous way up behind them at waddling pace. The Devil's Staircase was not his idea of fun. A gentle game of golf was more his going. Well, nine holes maybe. DS Munro would have loved this but he was still mooching around Manchester and environs.

Bonnie was overjoyed. At last. A breakthrough. Though God only knew what the banjo was doing miles from the scene of the crime. Could it be some other banjo? No. Impossible, surely. It had to be the murder weapon. It just had to be. God this guy was fit – she was almost out of breath and he was hardly bothering to breathe.

"Much farther?"

"Two minutes hen…er..Inspector. We're nearly there."

"Good."

"Ah saw it first by the way."

"Right. Fine."

Twin number two appeared at the next bend and Bonnie did a double-take. Literally. Identical twins she hadn't expected. They made their way to the banjo. One glance told Bonnie that this was indeed the murder weapon. It was smashed at the business end – the big round bit - and dried blood and hair adhered to it in some quantity. The SOCO team was expected within the hour. She daren't touch it though her fingers itched.

"Is that exactly as you found it?"

"Aye it is hen…er officer. Ah saw it first by the way."

"Your brother just told me he saw it first."

"Naw it wiz me."

"Naw it wiznae!"

"It wiz!"

"Ah'll bend yer nose fer ye ye bammer!"

"Aye in yer dreams ye lang dreep!"

The bumps and bruises of their recent boxing-match were all too evident so Bonnie decided intervention was in order. "Right guys, calm down! It's of no importance who saw it first. Now, here comes my sergeant…he'll take a statement from both of you and get your details."

From the glowers passed between the twins Bonnie reckoned that 'who saw the banjo first' would be a nicely recurring source of pugilism between them for the rest of their lives.

"You haven't touched it then?"

"Naw. No way."

"Good. What's your name by the way?"

"Broon."

"Brown?"

"Aye, Broon."

"I take it there was nobody near the thing when you saw it?"

"Naw. Naebody."

"Right. Okay. Move a bit farther away from the banjo guys, we don't want anything disturbed. Right, here's my card if you need to contact me about anything. Sergeant, you take over here – statements – details – where they're going to be staying –etcetera etcetera – you know the score – I'm going to have a wee look round."

Chapter 15

The Daily Post

Toasters Give to the Poor!

Are the Toasters The New Merry Men of Sherwood?

Billy Bootle Reporting

> *It came to light yesterday after their trial that the Toasters had, in the manner of Robin Hood, donated their 'swag' to a charity shop in Auchtergarry. Could this have had an influence on Sheriff Bultitude-Foss's decision to release the men immediately? The nation had already fallen for the Toasting Twosome, and the revelation of their heart-warming generosity will surely now cement their place in the nation's affections.*

"Heart-warming generosity!?" Inspector Slighman was puce with fury. "Has Bootle gone stark-staring bonkers? Heart-warming...bloody hell! A place in the nation's affections! I don't fucking believe it..."

"Let me see that paper," demanded his nearest and dearest. "Jonathan..." she said, reading fast,"...it's hard to credit that you've allowed this moron to print this tosh."

"Eh? What the hell could I do about what the idiot writes?"

"You're a senior police officer Jonathan! In charge of the case he's dribbling on about! How can you let him do this? It's time you asserted yourself Jonathan, it really is! Pull him in for questioning. Charge him!"

"Carla darling…"

"Don't Carla darling me!"

"…I'm in no position to pull him in or charge him or anything else. He's perfectly…"

"Don't give me that crap! If you were half a man he'd be in Barlinnie prison right now breaking rocks and counting off the years!

"He's a journalist darling! Writing for one of the country's most powerful tabloids – he's the one that's pulling the strings – not us!"

"Good God Jonathan you're such a minnow! Why don't you man up and go and at least punch him on the nose?"

"That would be the end of my career…that's why. Now be reasonable dar…"

"Don't you darling me! You're creeping me out, you really are."

"What else does he say?" asked our inspector picking up the furiously discarded rag.

Cop's Complaint

Inspector Jonathan Slighman, the officer responsible for the Toasters' arrests, expressed the displeasure felt by the police at what they saw as the lenience of the Toasters' sentence.

"These men are unquestionably and undeniably guilty of these crimes. Their offences had immense nation-wide consequences, and we, and the Prosecution Service, believe a lengthy custodial sentence would have been more appropriate. However these decisions are in the hands..."

" That's a bit more like it. Excellent in fact. Names me as officer responsible for their arrest. That's good. And a not-bad quote too..."

"Let me see..." said Carla snatching the paper politely from her man. "Hm...yes. A bit better I suppose, though I'll still be tempted to lamp the arse if I ever meet him."

That would be nice, thought Jonathan, who could well imagine the heft of Carla's handbag.

"Hello. Is that Inspector Blackthorn?"

"Yes, speaking."

"Ah'm one o' the twins that found the banjo."

"Oh yes, hello. How are you?"

"Ah'm fine. Eh listen hen...er Inspector...we showed a photie o' the banjo tae oor brither Horace – he's a real brain-box - an' he said it wiz a Brondell and Mahlen BJ3003 Flyaway Resonator. American seemingly. Should have a serial number inside it. Thought ye might like tae ken."

"Er...thanks very much. That's very kind."

"Nae problem."

"Er…are you the one with the black-eye?"

"Naw hen, ah'm the wan wi' the thick ear."

Alistair Probe approached Bonnie's desk with some trepidation. "Bonnie?"

"Alistair! At last. This banjo…"

"Er…yes…that's what I've come to speak to you about."

"Good! Gimme something to bite on Alistair, please."

"I think you're more likely to choke on this than bite on it."

"Oh? Really?"

"Yes, really. Anyhow – the banjo – a Brondell and…"

"Let me guess…a Brondell and Mahlen BJ3003 Flyaway Resonator."

"Jesus Christ Bonnie – I'm impressed."

"Well…I'm impressive!"

Alistair Probe laughed. "Right, my turn to impress you. The blood and hair on the banjo were Big Bruno's. It is unquestionably the murder weapon. As regards fingerprints, incredibly, there are twenty-three sets of jolly banjo-playing prints on that banjo. Sixteen sets we have no match for – that's sixteen banjo-players with no previous, okay? So, we have a list of seven names Bonnie." He handed her the sheet of paper with its small list. "Have a squint at this."

Bonnie took the list and read down. Her eyes opened further than she had ever managed to open them before. She stopped breathing, and, apart from her jaw slowly descending floor-wards, she stopped moving. Unbelievable. Mind-boggling.

"Bloody hell Alistair," she said after an awful long time, "we'd better see the Super."

"Right."   ...

Superintendent Smart gazed at the sheet of paper. Thunderstruck. Rendered speechless. Eventually he let out a long slow breath and looked from Bonnie to Alistair Probe and back to Bonnie.

"Get Slighman and Silver in Bonnie. Now."

Around the Superintendent's desk sat DI Blackthorn, Inspector Slighman, DS Silver, and Alistair Probe.

"Right everyone, listen-up. This Big Bruno case has just gone from somewhat mystifying to utterly bonkers and bewildering. The banjo used as the murder weapon has been found - as you all know. What some of you don't know as yet is that two of the sets of prints found on that banjo belong to..."

He paused, almost unable to continue.

"...Peter and George Solent. The Toasters, if you like."

Inspector Slighman hardly reacted. Clearly, he said to himself, I'm dreaming. I'll waken up soon, but golly, it's such a strange twisted dream.

DS Silver sat slowly shaking his head – flabbergasted. What nonsense was this?

"Right," continued the Superintendent, "it's over to you Bonnie. You're the officer in overall charge of this...this...dog's breakfast."

Bonnie looked round the room, catching the eye of everyone in turn. Inspector Slighman hadn't returned to his body yet.

"Right folks. This rather bizarre development seems to interweave the two biggest cases – in the public eye at least - we've ever had. One case we thought we'd put to bed. Well it just woke up again with a vengeance. The other case – the Big Bruno one - had stalled. Well, for sure, it ain't stalled no more…in fact we'll need to keep a very tight rein on it to stop it galloping away from us. And…when the press get their grubby hands on this stuff, the coverage we've had in the last week or so will seem by comparison like some harmless inquisitiveness by the school magazine. Every news crew in the land will converge on our little patch. Not just a bunch of tabloid oiks as before – we'll have Sky News, Al Jazeera, Newsnight, Channel 4, NBC – you name it – this'll get them going. Jonathan…I want you to handle the press, okay?"

The inspector had almost emerged from his stupor. "Er, right Bonnie."

"And continue working as security – we don't want any leaks. We need to tighten-up in that respect – far too many leaks with the Toaster case."

"Here here!" interjected the Superintendent. "There's only the five of us here who know about the brothers' prints being on the banjo so let's keep it that way for now. Okay?"

Assent was nodded by all.

"Alistair," continued Bonnie, "we're rather short-handed – I wonder if you could do some more research on this banjo. Where and when bought etcetera – I believe there should be a serial number in it somewhere – that might help."

"Of course Bonnie. With pleasure.

"Bob, we're heading off to Edinburgh – within the hour - to rake up what we can about these brothers."

"Rightee-ho," responded DS Silver.

"DS Munro is still down south – we'll leave him there meantime – I'm sure there's a link of some kind between events up here and past events down there. A big link. Any questions meantime?"

Heads shook.

"Pumpkin! How the devil are you?""

"Don't fucking 'pumpkin' me Bootle. What are you after this time?"

"Just a courtesy call old chap. Just sniffing the wind...you know...sniffing the wind."

"Well go and sniff it elsewhere Bootle. Your stories are fading into history and you know it. Better get back to your rat-hole in Wapping and poke your malevolent little fingers into someone else's pie."

"Oh my dear old chum! What a hurtful put-down! I'm crushed!"

"You don't know the meaning of the word 'hurtful' Bootle. You're a stranger to human feelings."

"Well that makes two of us I suppose. Now, don't you have something for me? A little eensy-weensy something?"

"No. Nothing. Nix. Nada."

"Really...so what am I hearing about banjos and fingerprints? Hm? Fingerprints where they shouldn't be, they tell me. Fingerprints with crumbs of toast on them they say."

Inspector Slighman held his telephone at arm's length and stared at it in horror. "How in the name of ...how d'you get...who told...?"

"Ah wouldn'cha like to know! Actually, in all honestly, I don't know myself. A kind, anonymous source. Whatever would I do without them eh? But thanks once again for the confirmation."

The inspector felt increasingly like a kilt-pin in an eightsome reel.

"And I'll tell you this old man, this story's on steroids now and for the moment it's all mine! The demand for our jolly journal is going to smash all records tomorrow, and I'll get another nice wee pat on the back from my masters and mistresses for this. Whatever shall I spend it on this time Jonners? I was thinking of changing to a forty-footer this time…yacht, that is, Well, my old thirty foot ketch is ageing a…"

"Why don't you drop dead Bootle!" The inspector, iridescent with fury, slammed down his phone.

"Bonnie?" The Superintendent's voice was a tad ratty.

"Yes sir."

"Where are you Bonnie?"

"Just passing Stirling sir, be in Edinburgh within the hour."

"Right. Bad news Bonnie I'm afraid. I've just had Slighman on the line. The Post already knows about the Toasters' fingerprints on the banjo. God only knows where they're getting their information from but it's bloody maddening."

"Hm. Not good. But not entirely surprising."

"Really?"

"Well, yes, it's infuriating, but this is exactly what happened throughout the entire Toaster case…the press were ahead of the game the whole time."

"Yes, they were Bonnie, you're not wrong. You're definitely not wrong. I'll speak to you later."

Bonnie passed on the news to DS Silver.

"I must say…" opined the sergeant drumming his fingers on the steering wheel with mock-innocence, "…I was…er… a wee bit surprised when you asked Inspector Slighman to handle the press…and security."

"Really Bob? I'm sure he'll do a good job." Their eyes met, and the look she gave him suggested that what she really felt was that she'd put the fox in charge of the hen-house. And, that he was a singularly sly but inept fox.

The sergeant smiled. Perhaps there was method in Bonnie's madness.

Her personal mobile rang with her daughter's ringtone."

"Hi Honeybunch!"

"Mum, where are you?"

"I'm on my way to Edinburgh for a case darling. I might be there till the weekend."

"What about my ballet?"

"Your dad's taking you this week…"

"And my tennis lesson tomorrow…"

"Uncle Joe's stepped up for that…

"What about my horse-riding …"

"Yes yes Kathy, don't worry everything's taken…"

"Can I go to Judy's for a sleepover on Friday mum?"

"Eh?…who's Judy?"

"Judy McBella. I told you about her. She's just moved up from Berwick. She's really nice mum. Please."

"But I don't know her Kathy…what does her mum do…and her dad? Where does she live?"

"They live in Ben Glas Wynd…it's a huge house."

"Well you'd better ask your dad…but don't you dare tell him I said ye…"

Connection terminated.

Inspector Slighman padded as unobtrusively as possible to his desk. Not too bad a response from the handful of officers still at their desks. The odd snigger. Boot up. Email time:

Sender Harriet Inkster, Clapham: *Jonny..............you scumbag......you've escaped haven't you? Wriggled your oily way...*Delete

Sender S Short, Office: *Meeting of Community Group re-scheduled for 10/8 has been cancelled due to clash with Area Picnic Day. Re-scheduled for 3/9.*

Sender D Wragg, Shetland: *Jonny! Please be careful! Don't screw up again – I really want you to get this job in the Midlands... the farther away you are...*Delete

Sender eBay Seller Team: *Police Fancy Dress Uniforms, Sexy Halloween Party Uniforms* Delete

Sender F Slighman, Edinburgh: *Hey Dad are you realy in charge of the Toaster case? Their so cool. Ive got their poster on my wall. Im going to write to them. Could you get me theyre autographs? I'd be the envy of the school Dad. Send a fat wad too. Felix*

Chapter 16

George Solent answered the bell. His rangy frame filling the doorway.

"Ah, it's Sergeant Silver isn't it?

"Yes, good evening sir. This is Detective Inspector Blackthorn."

"Delighted to meet you Inspector."

"And I'm pleased to meet you sir."

"Do come in."

"Thank you," replied Bonnie, her eye briefly caught by Peter's deerstalker hanging on a coat-hook.

The Solent family home was very pleasant indeed. Hidden away at the back of Morningside but with open aspects east towards Arthur's Seat and south towards the Pentland Hills. A lovely old sandstone-built villa with a small secluded garden.

"We were just about to have a cup of tea...do join us."

"Er...thank you very much. That's very kind."

"Not at all, not at all. Do sit down, please."

"Thank you."

A woman, clearly George Solent's wife entered the room carrying a tray. Late forties, perhaps very early fifties, attractive, comfortable-looking, and smiling.

"Hello," she said, eyebrows set at an inquisitive angle.

George made the necessary introductions.

Mrs Solent left and quickly returned with two more cups and helped her husband pour tea and serve biscuits.

"Well now, how can I help you officers? I thought our case was very firmly closed."

"Well," said Bonnie, "there has been a strange development."

"Really?"

"Yes, we have found a banjo, and it has your fingerprints on it."

George's face lit up with delight.

"My banjo! You've found my banjo? But that's wonderful!"

This was certainly not the reaction expected by either the inspector or the sergeant. In fact they were rather dumbfounded.

"Er…sorry…had you lost…er…it?"

"Yes I had. Well, actually, it was stolen."

"Stolen?"

"Yes, must have been over a year ago…wasn't it dear?"

"Yes love, last May. We go to the Roots of the Lakes Folk Festival in Keswick every year inspector. In fact we were there again just three weeks ago."

"Yes, whole family goes. Fifteen of us this year – such a nice bunch of folk who go there. I was shocked when somebody stole my banjo."

"Did you report it stolen at the time sir?" asked DS Silver.

"Oh yes. Certainly. I was quite upset really. I loved that banjo."

"Do you remember what make it was?"

"Yes of course – a Brondell and Mahlen Resonator. Beautiful instrument it was. Played like a dream…not that I'm a great banjo-player or anything, but Peter and I both play – it's just such fun. Where was it found? Still in its case?"

"No," said Bonnie, "I'm afraid it's not still in its case sir. It's currently being held as evidence in the Big Bruno murder. It was the banjo which killed him."

"What!?" Both Solents rose to their feet, George filling his saucer with tea. "That's incredible," he gasped, "absolutely incredible. I wondered why two police officers had come all this was about a banjo. Well well…"

"Good God George…," said Mrs Solent "…dear me… it was a really heavy banjo, I remember that much about it. But a murder weapon…?" She busied herself mopping up tea and biscuit crumbs.

"There were a lot of other fingerprints on the banjo…does that surprise you?"

"No, inspector, not at all. Typical folk fest. Everybody has a bash at everybody else's instrument. Although it can't have been used much since if our prints are still on it"

"That's very true Mr Solent. In fact it possibly hasn't been played since it was stolen."

"There were five other sets of prints on the banjo of people with police records," said DS Silver, "does *that* surprise you?"

"Eh? Really? Oh, actually no, that makes sense…there was a group of youngsters there – late teens I think – who were part of a music therapy kind of thing for young offenders. Super kids. They probably all tried their hand at it."

"Right, er… well, thanks for that, and thanks for the tea Mrs Solent…Mr Solent. We'll leave it at that for the moment. Here's my card if you think of anything which might help us."

"Yes of course," said George, escorting them to the door.

"Lovely place you have here," said Bonnie, "have you always lived in Edinburgh Mr Solent?"

"Yes, ever since I was eight years old and Peter was six. We moved up from Salford. "

"Were you born in Salford?"

"Yes, we both were."

They made their farewells.

"Hm. What did you make of that then Bob?"

"Crazy, Ma'am, absolutely crazy. An outrageous coincidence. "

"Yes, and I'm none too keen on coincidences. Especially outrageous ones. It's getting late now and we haven't eaten for over twelve hours, so, tomorrow, get in touch with Keswick police. Check out the stolen banjo episode, these young offenders, and the folk festival thing...and get back to me as soon as poss."

"Righteeho."

"I'm going to dig into their background – these Solent brothers. Apart from the fact they're restaurateurs we don't know too much about them."

"Ever been to one of their restaurants Ma'am?"

"No Bob...have you?"

"Yeah. Miranda and I. The one in Leith...just the once...about a year ago. Very good it was too. Didn't see either of the brothers there though."

"No...I believe both brothers have a son and a daughter. The daughters pretty much run the restaurants now, seemingly...and the boys work as chefs. Good division of labour eh?"

"Seems to work. What about this...eh Salford thing?

"Yes Bob, very interesting indeed...it could be the link we're looking for. I'll phone Ben – he's pretty much on the spot."

Chapter 17

The Daily Post

Did Toaster Heroes banjo Big Bruno?

High-jinks in the Highlands

Banjo found by Walkers

Billy Bootle Reporting

There were incredible developments yesterday in the Big Bruno case, as two walkers on the West Highland Way found the banjo which crushed Big Bruno's skull. Incredibly, it was found to have the fingerprints of brothers Peter and George Solent – aka 'the Toasters' on it. Police are baffled as both the theft of the toaster, and Big Bruno's murder happened at exactly the same time - fifty miles apart. This clearly means that if they committed one of these crimes, then they couldn't have committed the

The brothers, now revered by young people throughout the land as new 'Robin Hoods', were convicted of the 'toasting' crimes, on what was described by the presiding sheriff as 'concrete evidence', and the police officer in charge said after they were convicted that they were 'unquestionably and undeniably guilty'. This makes things very difficult for the prosecution service, and any future jury...

other.

Inspector Slighman glowered darkly at his copy of the accursed Daily Post. New Robin Hoods my arse, thought he. His mind was both numb and racing at the same time. He still had not entirely emerged from the stupor induced the previous afternoon when he heard that the banjo had the brothers' fingerprints on it. Part of him was horrified that the brothers might have conned everyone and may actually be innocent of the toasting crimes, but another part of him was yelling "Yes!" because here was confirmation that these brothers were, as he, and he alone, had always said, evil. Evil enough to murder. And at least Bootle hadn't named him as the officer in charge. This case was a nightmare. Bonnie Blackthorn could catch the flak now...

He turned to page two:

The Toasters - our new Robin Hoods

Charity Shops Swamped!

Billy Bootle Reporting

Charity shops from Lands End to John O'Groats reported that they were being inundated with what may be stolen goods. One shop in Orpington reported that, among other things, a bag of cutlery with the local Royal Hotel logo on it had been left outside its door. The hotel later confirmed that the cutlery had gone missing fourteen years ago. At a charity shop in Glasgow a gent's three-piece suit, which the shop manager immediately recognised as his own, was donated anonymously. These phenomena were replicated at charity shops all over the country as thieves' consciences appeared to be getting the better of them – all part, apparently, of the new 'Robin Hood' syndrome which has swept the land since the highly publicised benevolent acts of those heroes for today - the Toaster brothers...who of course have now been linked to the timely demise of Big Bruno...a fact which will doubtlessly boost their hero status to even greater heights.

The inspector groaned. How could people be so stupid? Good God even his own son had pinned their damned picture on his wall. It was all wrong. These guys, he was now convinced, were murderers, and he wanted them banged up for many years. Evil swine. And when he thought of what they had almost done to his career...he deeply felt the loss of corporal punishment.

"Hello, is that DI Blackthorn?"
"Speaking."
"Hi Bonnie, it's Bill McKay here...remember? DCI McKay...? We met at the Equal Opps..."
"Yes of course Bill - how are you? Nice to speak to you again."
"I'm fine Bonnie, thanks. I heard you were in the building so I thought I'd give you a quick phone. I've known the Solent

brothers for many years Bonnie – if you'd like to come up to my office we can have a quick chat maybe?"

"Oh, yes, excellent Bill, thanks. I'll be right up."

Golfing pals? wondered Bonnie as she went up in the lift. She remembered Bill McKay well – a really nice guy who actually took equal opps seriously – as opposed to most cops who felt it was all just PC nonsense and a bit of a joke. This was all very intriguing – and wholly unlike any case she'd ever been involved with before. Respectability, and decency, even, seemed to bounce off her main suspects.

"Anyhow Bonnie," said DCI McKay once they'd settled themselves down, "I don't know if I can help very much with your enquiries but I felt I should at least tell you what I can."

"Fire away Bill – I'm just starting out on my enquiries into the brothers so anything you can tell me will probably be news."

"Right. I went to school with Peter – some thirty odd years ago. Just our final two years in Broadloch High School here in Edinburgh. George had already left to go to college by then – he was two years older than us. We weren't close, but we were friendly enough. I remember visiting his house once or twice to play Dungeons and Dragons. We lost touch after we left school – he went to uni in Aberdeen and I went to Strathclyde. However, when we were into our thirties, the three of us ended up as members at Craigmorton Golf Club, and we've been fairly friendly ever since. You know, we play the odd round together - there are quite a few social functions at the club - that sort of thing "

Bonnie smiled. "I take it you would vouch for their character then Bill?"

"Oh I certainly would. This whole toasting episode has me completely baffled...to say nothing of any Big Bruno involvement. I mean, bloody hell, what the hell's going on there with Peter and George? Honestly, nicer men you couldn't hope to meet."

"What about the Salford link Bill – I believe they were born there."

"Yes they were Bonnie. That's the one thing that was a bit different about them. They moved up here with their mother. Single parent. Not that common in those days. And, even more unusual I suppose, they had an older brother and sister who stayed down in Salford with their father. The brothers used to go down south to visit them regularly – and I know they've remained close as a family over the years."

"Interesting Bill. So the parents split up, and the mother came up to Edinburgh bringing the two youngest boys with her..."

"Yep."

"...and the father stayed down south with their brother and sister."

"Correct."

"How old would they have been when they came to Edinburgh?"

"Good question. Let's see...George would have been nine or ten...he's the older of the two...and Peter a couple of years younger."

"What about the ones left behind?"

"I'm afraid I don't know anything about the Salford family Bonnie – names, ages, or anything – can't help you there. But I'll tell you one thing Bonnie, I did once have the misfortune of meeting Big Bruno – I spent three years as a DS down in

Preston. He was a horrible man. He was brought in once for questioning about a serious double assault – father and son beaten to a pulp. They owed him money and he, smirking freely throughout, barely bothered to hide his guilt...safe in the knowledge that they wouldn't have the courage to testify against him, and we had no other means of nailing him. Needless to say, he walked out of there a free man."

"So, what are you saying Bill?"

"Good riddance, that's what I'm saying."

"You and the rest of the nation Bill. The tabloids have turned them into heroes. But I have a job to do...and so far we have nothing on them, apart from some fingerprints on a banjo which they claim to have lost a year ago, and a vague link to the Midlands of England. No hint of a motive anywhere. So they may well be wholly innocent."

"DI Blackthorn? DS Silver here."

"Hi Bob."

"I've been in touch with the police in Keswick Ma'am, George Solent definitely had a banjo stolen during the folk festival in May last year – a Brondell and Mahlen Resonator, to be precise."

"No real surprise there Bob – they were hardly going to lie about that. Anything else of interest?"

"Well, in this case it almost goes without saying ma'am, but the sergeant I spoke to actually knows the brothers..."

"Oh God...as you say Bob, it almost goes without saying...and let me guess, he reckons they're the salt of the earth?"

"That's about the size of it ma'am. He plays the fiddle and he's been going to the festival for donkeys' years. Spent some of the best nights of his…"

"…Yeah yeah yeah okay okay okay. We've got the picture Bob…the only suspects we've got in our murder case are both just a kick in the arse away from ascension to heaven."

"He was the one who got the group of young offenders invited to the festival. Definitely not one of them who nicked it…he was there the night it got stolen, believe it or not, and the youngsters were closely chaperoned the whole time. The brothers were genuinely upset, seemingly. A few other things went missing that night – a mandolin, and two wallets from a pile of coats and jackets lying over a table. The sergeant reckons it was someone from a mini-bus party from Newcastle – they left to go back to Newcastle just before they noticed that the banjo had disappeared."

"So, unlikely that the whole thing was engineered by the brothers then. Not that that was much of a possibility in the first place."

"No, can't see them nicking wallets ma'am."

"Nah.".

Constables Beech and Wyre were having an unusually quiet day of it. Nothing more taxing than driving around in the sun, in glorious surroundings, taking down the details of such transgressions as the theft of a mountain bike, malicious damage to a kayak, and the removal of underwear from a washing line.

They drove gently into Auchtergarry, each vaguely looking forward to pie and beans and semi-lost in his own little world, when Constable Beech hit the brakes and swerved to a halt.

"Look!" he shouted pointing excitedly.

"Good God!" responded Constable Wyre leaping out of the car.

A small pink-denim-clad beribboned girl carrying a bulging plastic bag was loitering with clear intent outside the Salvation Army charity shop.

"Hello," said Constable Beech, looking down.

Huge eyes looked up at him.

"Hello sor," said a very quiet voice.

"Well well well now," said Constable Beech, "what's your name then?"

"Hannah sor."

"Hannah?"

"Yes sor."

"And do you have a second name Hannah?"

"Yes sor."

"Okay. What is your second name Hannah?"

"McTanner sor."

"Right. And how old are you Hannah McTanner?"

"Seven sor."

Constable Beech crouched down to near parity with his diminutive interrogatee.

"And what, wee Hannah McTanner, have you got in that bag, may I ask?"

"Apples sor."

"Apples eh? And what were you going to do with those apples Hanna McTanner?"

"I thought I'd give them to the chattery shop sor."

"The chattery shop eh?"

"Yes sor."

"The Salvation Army chattery shop?"

"Yes sor."

"And where did you get the apples from wee Hannah?"

Wee Hannah assumed a worried expression.

"The big girl next door stole them sor."

"Oh, she did, did she?"

"Yes sor."

"And where did she steal them from Hannah?"

"From her mammy's apple tree sor."

"Right...er..."

"Would you like an apple sor?"

"Well...er..."

"I've got five sor. You consobles can have one each, I could have one, and there would be one each for the lady and gentleman in the chattery shop."

"Well Hannah, that sounds like a very good idea to me. Thank you very much."

"Yes, thank you very much," added Constable Wyre.

"A life-time of good-deeds lies ahead for her, Constable Beech."

"I do believe you're right, Constable Wyre."

Chapter 18

DS Munro picked up his espresso coffee and looked gormlessly at DC Bickerstaff who had been trawling records at the GRO.

"So, what do we know Becky?"

"Well sarge, no record of Solent births over the relevant period, but there was a marriage for a Mary Solent who married a James Carnthwaite in 1957 – they had four children in the next seven years –Jessica, Douglas, George and Peter."

"Sounds like our family."

"Yeah. Divorced forty years ago. The mother obviously went back to her maiden name when she took the boys up north."

"Aye, she must. Are they still alive – these parents?"

"The father died ten years ago, but there's no record of death for the mother.

"Carnthwaite eh? Is that a common name down here?"

"It's new to me sarge."

"Good. I like unusual names. Easier to trace," said the sergeant intensifying his gormless look. "Right Becky, you follow up on Jessica and Douglas, okay? And I'll keep digging around Big Bloody Bruno."

"Righteeho sarge."

"Bonnie?"

"Hi Alistair, how's it going?"

"Fine Bonnie, thanks. This banjo…"

"...Ah yes, the banjo Alistair, the dreaded banjo. Anything new?"

"Well, I believe the brothers reported it stolen, over a year ago. Is that right?"

"Yes, they did Alistair. All officially logged by the ever vigilant and efficient local constabulary."

"Well, not this banjo they didn't Bonnie, must have been some other five-stringed blunt instrument."

"Eh? Alistair? What the hell d'you mean by that?"

"What I mean Bonnie lass, is that this particular banjo – the Brondell and Mahlen BJ3003 Flyaway Resonator – has only been on the market since February of this year."

You're kidding?"

"Nope. The banjo George Solent had nicked was probably the earlier version - the BJ 3000 Flyaway Resonator. A jewel among banjos no doubt, but definitely not the one that was used to clout our corpse."

"Alistair...you've just opened a door which had been very firmly slammed shut. Time to go and see our friends the Toasters again. I think they have some questions to answer."

DS Munro was a little bit weary, and a little bit frazzled. A day in the Manchester drizzle rooting around the life of Big Bruno had turned up nothing. The few people he'd managed to speak to, either greeted him, as usual, with silence, or with a refusal to help in any way whatsoever to nail the big man's assassin. He'd even felt horribly intimidated at one house where a large family of brawny occupants encircled him in a menacing silence. Not nice.

Back in the station he ploughed once again through Bruno's police record. Hopelessly scant really, considering the magnitude of his role in the local underworld, and containing nothing resembling a clue to his murder.

"Evening sarge."

"Hi Becky. God, I hope you've had more luck today than I've had."

"Dunno really. Douglas Carnthwaite – the toasters' big brother - is a civil engineer. Has worked all over the world on big projects – harbours and dams – that sort of thing. Currently living in Blackburn and working for a road-building contractor. Married, with one son. Wife teaches modern languages at a school in Blackburn, and his son is a geologist working in Amsterdam. No police record for any of them.

Jessica Carnthwaite – big sister to them all – now Jessica Woodfile. Married Cedric Woodfile thirty years ago...marriage lasted just over ten years, then they got divorced. Five kids – a girl and four...."

"Woodfile?"

"Er...yes."

"W-o-o-d-f-i-l-e?"

"Yeah."

The DS narrowed his eyes, lowered his jaw, and assumed a look of near impenetrable gormlessness. "I'm sure I've seen that name recently...in fact, I definitely have seen it recently."

"You mean during this case?"

"Yes, I do indeed. I definitely mean during this case. Now let me think..."

"Interesting Sarge. Very interesting. Can you think and eat at the same time Sarge?"

"You bet I can think and eat at the same time, I'm starving. Let's go...fancy an Italian?"

"Oh yes. And there's a good one right across the street."

They crossed the street in question, grabbed a table, ordered food, ordered Italian beer, sipped, and waited appreciatively.

"So, Sarge, this name...?"

"Yes...I'm still thinking. We'll have to go back to the station after this Becky. I can't help thinking I must have seen it in one of those accursed great ledgers of Big Bruno's. Er...by the way...what else did you find out about Jessica?"

"Well, as I was saying, five kids – four boys and a girl – must be mostly in their twenties now. Runs a café in Longridge, near Preston – seemingly quite a popular café - and appears now to be living in Preston with another woman...a primary school teacher. Not a police record among them."

"Christ almighty...five little bits of ravioli and a sprig of salad! I won't be rushing back here anytime soon."

"Sarge, those little bits of ravioli are actually pretty damned big. And there's still a pile of garlic bread to get through."

"Hm. I'm going to leave here hungry, I know I am. What's her new partner called...any idea?"

"Hilda Booth. Whether or not they're in an actual relationship I don't know. But they do occupy the same house."

"Booth eh? Hm."

"Don't tell me you've come across Booth too?"

DS Munro touched his lower lip with his left forefinger as he extinguished the last fading glimmer of gorm from his face. "I'm not sure Becky. It's ringing a bell somewhere though."

"What's wrong sarge?...can't you finish your last piece of ravioli?"

DS Munro smiled ruefully, but the last piece of ravioli duly met its demise.

"I've remembered now," said DS Munro as they made their way back to the station, "where I saw the name 'Booth'."

DC Bickerstaff looked at him in alert anticipation. "Yes?"

"Yes. It was the name of the supermarket I got my sandwiches in at lunchtime."

George Solent smiled warmly when he answered the door.

"Inspector Blackthorn…Sergeant Silver…hello again…how nice to see you. Do come in. Peter's here, so that's a good bit of timing."

"Thank you sir."

Introductions were made between the inspector and Peter Solent.

"Nice to see you again, Sergeant Silver," said Peter as he held out his hand.

DS Silver smiled. It was impossible not to like these guys.

"Anything new been happening?" asked George.

"Well," answered DI Blackthorn, "it seems that the banjo we questioned you about yesterday wasn't actually the one you had stolen."

"Really. Oh well, maybe my one will turn up safe and sound one day after all." George's smile never faltered.

"Perhaps it will sir, but we now need an explanation for why both you and your brother's fingerprints are on the banjo which killed John Bair…er…Big Bruno."

"Ah, yes, of course Inspector," said George laughing happily, "we're banjo players! We've been to three different folk festivals in the past two or three months - there are always banjos aplenty at these things and we're a sharing brotherhood. We must have played forty or fifty different banjos in the last year."

"How many of them would have been Brondell and Mahlen Resonators though? And wouldn't you remember playing a Brondell and Mahlen Resonator?"

"How many B&Ms? I dunno – half a dozen maybe? Peter? What say you?"

"Yes, I suppose – half a dozen maybe. At least three or four anyhow. They are popular banjos...but quite pricey I suppose. I definitely remember playing one at Keswick...Bill Arnott's got one...he's had it for years though. And there was one at Perth too...but I don't remember who owned it."

"Wasn't that Katy Wilson's?"

"Oh yes, could have been."

"Well Bob, what do think this time?"

"Nothing seems to faze them ma'am. They just seem so relaxed."

"Yes, they do don't they?"

"Worth following up these other banjo owners d'you think?"

"Nah, not at this stage Bob. I'm pretty sure the whole thing revolves round our Toasters. Somehow."

"Yeah, me too."

"I'd like to have a quick chat with their kids, or at least have a look at their restaurants...more nosiness than anything else really. Let's pop in by La Grande Assiette shall we?"

"Can't do any harm Ma'am."

...

La Grande Assiette was almost empty. It was after four in the afternoon – the day's lunchers had dined and left, apart from one or two stragglers, and preparations were now being made for the evening shift. Louisa Solent, George's daughter, and Jeffrey Solent, Peter's son, were both there. Both in their early twenties and both learning the restaurant business in depth. As expected, they were both extremely pleasant and helpful. Jeffrey was a dead-ringer for his dad.

Where had they been on the morning of Monday June the 5th? They both laughed – neither of them had had any time off from the restaurant since the end of April. When the head-waiter was asked to confirm this he said that they were both there first thing every Monday morning, had been since the 'silly season' started in May, and would be until it ended late October. No exceptions. Ever.

The Muckle Platter in Leith produced the identical result from Alice Solent, daughter of Peter, and Cameron Solent, son of, and dead-ringer for, George.

"Beautiful restaurants," mused Bonnie as they drove along the shore at Newhaven.

"Yeah. Nice kids too."

"Yep. Ah well Bob, not much more for us here in Edinburgh at the moment...we could be home before midnight if we leave now...what d'ye think?"

"Let's do it."

"Yeah let's."

Chapter 19

The white van had been sitting at the far end of the car park at Crianlarich station for over a week by the time it was reported by Bargain Van Solutions in Aberdeen as overdue presumed stolen. Nobody had paid any attention to it – white vans in the Highlands, as with everywhere else, were ten a penny. Constables Beech and Wyre who used the station car park fairly regularly for a break and a fag, spotted it almost immediately once it appeared on their list of stolen vehicles.

Having identified it as a stolen vehicle they approached it as a matter of course and were somewhat surprised to see the keys still in the ignition.

"Might as well open the thing and see if there's anything in it," said PC Beech removing the keys from the ignition and walking to the back of the van.

He fumbled briefly with the lock, got the key turned, twisted the handle, opened the doors, and gaped. They both gaped.

"Well well well well well well. What d'ye know!"

"Bingo-bingo-bingo!"

There, gleaming magnificently at the back of the van was a green Kawasaki 750cc motorbike. And behind it were rows of neatly piled boxes stamped with the legend 'Glen Laldy Single Malt Whisky'.

They both took photographs with their mobile phones, touched nothing, closed the van again, radioed headquarters at Auchtergarry, lit a cigarette apiece, and radiated satisfaction.

DI Blackthorn and DS Silver had barely set off from Auchtergarry HQ, heading for Crianlarich, when her mobile went.

"Ma'am?" DS Munro enquired.

"Yes Ben, how are you?"

"Fine ma'am thanks. We've turned something up at last."

"Hallelujah Ben – things finally seem to be moving. Big Bruno's bike's just been found – in the back of a van in Crianlarich – a van stuffed with Glen Laldy whisky seemingly."

"Bloody hell!"

"Yes – I'm just on my way there now with Bob Silver. So what have you turned up Ben?"

"Right, the toasters' sister – Jessica Carnthwaite – married a guy called Cedric Woodfile and they had a daughter called Andrea. Now, I knew as soon as I heard her name that I'd seen it before, so Becky…er…DC Bickerstaff and I trawled through the ledgers again last night – and right enough – four years back there is an A. Woodfile getting stuff…cocaine?...heroin?...who knows what from the Big Arse over a two year period. And she has two warnings against her name."

DI Blackthorn took a deep breath.

"So, Ben, she's the Toasters' niece – and by all accounts they're a pretty close family. That gives us a wee bit of a motive Ben, does it not? And that's been utterly missing up till now."

"Well if she's been abused by him in any way – which seems only too bloody likely – then the temptation to do him harm might be pretty strong…but murder ma'am?.. I wouldn't have thought so."

"Well, it is a motive Ben, but I agree, I can't see guys with the Toasters' backgrounds killing for it. But…it undoubtedly helps to link things together. Keep diggin' Ben, keep diggin'"

The SOCO team had arrived on the scene some time before Detectives Blackthorn and Silver rolled up.

"Morning Alistair, what can you tell me?"

"Morning Bonnie, morning Bob. It's Bruno's bike, for sure. There's also his helmet and his gloves – definitely all his. Everything else, except one case of whisky – and one opened bottle of whisky - I would suggest, is fake."

"Fake?"

"Yes, there's one open cardboard box – from which the one opened bottle of Glen Laldy seems to have been taken. The rest of the bottles in the box are genuine enough Glen Laldy single malt but the bottles in all the other boxes seem to be filled with cold tea or something. The boxes themselves are not actual Glen Laldy boxes – they've been forged using a stencil and ink…so they ain't linked to the earlier theft from the Glen Laldy distillery."

"Right. So, ideas Alistair?"

"Well, it looks like he's been conned doesn't it? Probably thought he was going to get a huge and extremely valuable consignment of stolen whisky – rendezvoused with the van - and got himself terminally walloped."

"Yes, I would agree, something like that."

"Any whisky removed from the open bottle?" asked DS Silver.

"Yes, about two hundred mills maybe."

"So, perhaps they go into the heather a bit to finalise their deal with a dram, and…smack."

"Could be… he did have a very small amount of whisky in his stomach if you remember."

"So," mused DI Blackthorn, "our picture is…he rendezvous with van and man or men…they open the van, open a box, pick out the pre-selected bottle of Glen Laldy, perhaps taste it or smell it to confirm it's the real thing, he accepts, they hoist his bike up on the tail-lift, they go off the roadside to have a dram, maybe, and he gets treated to a solo on the five-stringed banjo."

DS Silver and Alistair Probe nodded and shrugged simultaneously.

"Something like that…maybe."

"Yeah, I'd agree."

Click…click…click.

They all turned round. Two men, one with a few grands' worth of camera equipment around his neck, and one with a notebook were smiling happily at them.

"Good morning, good morning. Billy Bootle, journalist for the Daily Post, at your service."

"And I'm Jethro Ianson, photographer for same."

Bonnie couldn't stop herself. "How the hell did you hear about this?"

"Ah," responded Bootle, "you must be the celebrated Detective Inspector Bonnie Blackthorn – and well named you are Bonnie. Unfortunately ma'am I'm afraid, we can't help you there. An anonymous source, a very fine anonymous source. Bike's in good nick eh? And did I hear the boxes are all fake?"

Bonnie glared a rare glare and slammed the doors shut, which, with hair and tartan skirt at full swing, made a fine photograph.

"Thank you officers. Bye for now." The Post's men took their leave.

Bonnie was livid. "This is absolutely ridiculous. We'll be phoning them for information at this rate. I mean, who the hell is informing them? And why?"

DS Silver shook his head and gave it a scratch. "Search me. But it is bloody annoying."

They stood for a moment in an angry but contemplative silence which was eventually broken by Alistair Probe.

"Right, can't stand here all day. We'd better get this lot back to the lab and fingerprint it. Etcetera etcetera."

Superintendent Smart gazed in weary exasperation at the form sitting in front of him. Bonnie Blackthorn had just been in to tell him about the press turning up out of the blue at Crianlarich station. Maddening. Utterly maddening. Every time they made any progress with this damned case the press were there ahead of them. And Alistair Probe had just phoned to inform him that the van and its contents were clear of all fingerprints - apart from Big Bruno's. Well, surprise surprise. This case seemed to be progressing at a pace and in a direction dictated entirely by the perpetrators. And, most infuriating of all, the duo creeping eerily into the frame as those most likely to have swatted the repugnant gangster, had already been convicted, on the strength of evidence gathered by his force, of a crime which took place at exactly the same time as Bruno's liquidation, thereby legally debarring them from having done it. And...as if all of that wasn't enough...they were being lauded throughout the land as latter-day Robin Hoods. And...everyone who ever met them thought they were such decent Johnnies. What a complete shambles.

And now this. An evaluation form for the convention at the Chesterlake Hotel in London with a three-line-whip from above to fill it in or else. Now. How in Heligoland was he supposed to concentrate on something which now seemed so ludicrously far removed from his current pickle? Did he rate the accommodation at 1, 2, 3, 4, or 5? Did the programme meet its stated objectives? Was the range of seminars appropriate to his grade? Were any training needs identified? How would he now change his working practices in the light of what he had learned? How would his new knowledge impact on his current working practices? God Almighty wasn't that the same damn question twice? Aaaaarrrrggghhh!

His phone rang.

"Sir, your wife's on the line."

Now what?

"Yes Dear?"

"Smartie, darling,…" this was a bad start. He only got 'Smartie darling' when a big request was underway.

"….I've just had Jason on the line, Smartie. He says that little Rosalind wants to start a Toaster's fan club at her school…" the Superintendent's room went slightly out of focus, "…and she wonders if you, her favourite grand-daddy, could come along…" She got no farther.

"Sorry Martha darling. Sub judice. No-can-do. Terribly busy – must rush. Bye"

"Er…bye."

The Superintendent expelled a long breath, closed his eyes, and groped unseeing for his evaluation form.

...

"Inspector! Old thing."

"Aw Bootle go away. What the hell do you want now?... I thought I'd heard the last of you."

"And lovely to hear you too Inspector. Now, as you've probably been told we were there to help when your chaps found the whisky van..."

"There to help!? You're insane Bootle, you really are."

"As I was saying, we were there to help at Crianlarich station and a wealth of fine material we got too. However...we would really like to know the result of the fingerprinting before we go to press..."

"What..? You'd like...? Are you...? ... get lost Bootle. There's absolutely no chance of that."

"Now Jonners, old pal, don't be hasty. Remember I've got a super-harridan breathing down my neck demanding results."

"That's your problem Bootle, not mine."

"Er...well...that's not entirely the case old man. She's bringing up things like 'who murdered Big Bruno?'"

"Eh? Well, her and everyone else. She'll just have to wait for the results of a trial for the answer to that one, won't she?"

"Yes but the thing is...Jonny boy...it can't be the Toasters."

"Can't be the...what? And why exactly can't it be the Toasters? They're guilty as sin."

"But Jonny, you've already stated, and have been quoted as such by every paper in the land, that the evidence against them for the theft of your toaster is incontrovertible. Absolutely 'stone wall', you said."

"And so it is...er...well...so it was."

"Ah, me old gum-shoe, do I detect a small change of mind? Can't possibly have committed both crimes now can they? Same time...different places."

"They are the murderers Bootle. And that, is a fact. Believe me."

"So they didn't steal your toaster?"

"Oh who cares about my damned toaster! It's old hat. Give it a rest Bootle."

"So, what, my old friend, shall I tell my esteemed leader? Shall I tell her you now admit to screwing up the Toaster case...?"

"What!? I did no such thing!"

"...that you've changed your mind and now believe they committed a crime fifty miles away instead?"

Inspector Slighman's face darkened and his voice dropped to a menacing growl.

"Right Bootle...now get this straight...I have not changed my mind. Okay? Got that? I don't know how they did it, but I believe these men committed both..."

His voice jumped back up to its natural high register and the dark menace returned to a wheedle.

"...er...both...well, obviously they can't have...well, it's not my case is it? I don't have to work it out...do I?"

"Okay Jonny lad. Fear not. Here's the deal. We won't remind our readership that you...what was it you said exactly?... that they were 'both unarguably guilty of nicking the toaster'...that they were 'caught red-handed...and...' with a smoking gun'. I think that was it. Because, let's face it, if you still stood by those pronouncements, then you'd have to believe them innocent of Big Bruno's murder...right?"

Slighman had a very big bullet to bite here. He paused...but he bit it.

"I sup-pose so."

"Good man. Right, and the rest of the deal is that you continue to keep us up to speed on police developments. How does that sound, me old toothbrush?"

"I can't do it Bootle."

"'Course you can old man."

"I'm the officer in charge of internal security...and this is a murder case...not petty pilfering."

"Oh that's such a shame Jonny me old son. Her highness will have you slaughtered in the morning...she's gagging to have you on our front page...you're so tall and handsome Jonny...and all in the cause of public interest of course..."

"This is downright blackmail Bootle!"

"Jonny, I'm trying to protect you!"

"Okay...okay...there were no fingerprints in the van other than Big Bruno's and there was nothing else whatsoever of any help in the case...now, are you happy?"

"Oh Jonny! Yer a broth of a boy so you are! A broth of a boy."

Chapter 20

Across the Pond

"...Good morning fellow Americans and a hearty welcome to the Hans Nelsan Hour on Sea to Sea AM – the radio station for the nation which searches and probes without trepidation. We scrutinize and analyze where others will not tread. In today's program we have a report from Whinoawa County on the latest sightings of a suspected alien in near-human form seen floating above a trailer park in downtown Whinoawa City. Also in this hour of clear-sighted investigation of the paranormal and the unexplained, we will turn our focus on the miracles being performed across the nation by faith-healing-for-u-dot-com, as visitors to the website have been able to resurrect dead goldfish and hamsters previously declared deceased by the veterinary profession. But first off we cross the Atlantic Ocean to England's Scottish county to look into the birth of the 'toasting' phenomenon which is now starting to make an appearance here in the good-old US of A. This disturbing case involves a range of crimes including homicide, police corruption, gangsterism, treason, sedition, and espionage. Now over to our woman on the spot – Joleene Geronski - for further elucidation..."

"...Hans, many thanks for that. Yes here I am deep in the Scottish Rockies where a local gangster who terrorized the entire region was gunned down by an American banjo player who left a slice of toast with maple syrup at the scene of the

crime which took place on the summit of Mount Nevis. I am at the moment jostling with reporters from dozens of the more staid and conventional news outlets such as NBC, BBC , ABC and CBBC in a very crowded news conference held by the very upright and rather handsome Commander Slighman...I'll just try and ask a quick question...er Commander!

"Yes? – the tall woman in the short green dress."

"Thank you so much Commander. Joleene Geronski - Sea to Sea AM. I wonder if you would very much mind telling my listeners back home in the United States of America which countries you believe to be implicated in this evildoing?"

"Er...Scotland and England."

"Thanks for that Commander. Well folks – you heard it here first. That's all we have time for at present so I'll hand you straight back to Hans in the studio..."

...

Hamish MacDonald Duke stood outside the police station in Auchtergarry. The joy that was deep within him permeated his entire being and his face assumed the kind of expression which would not have been out of place on a saint arriving at heaven's door. This was his moment and he savoured it intensely. This was what he had been born for. His destiny. His fate. He drew a long breath, tugged at the fraying, greying, collar of his white nylon shirt, tucked some of its tail into his black tracksuit bottoms, and, in his mind's eye, strode manfully into the police station, and up to the officer staffing the public desk.

"Aye aye Hamish, and what is it can we do for you today then?" enquired PC Flora McTodd with a gentle smile.

"Ah've come to confess Flora."

"Oh have you now Hamish. And what exactly is it that you've come to confess to?"

"Murder, Flora."

"Oh it is it? And who's murder is it that you've come to confess to Hamish?"

"Big Bruno's, Flora."

"Big Bruno's? Really Hamish?" PC McTodd kept her smile admirably under control. "Now are you sure Hamish? I wouldn't like to see you locked away for something you'd just dreamt about."

"Aye, I'm sure Flora. I hit him with a banjo, so I did."

"And you didn't just dream about it Hamish?"

"No I did not Flora."

"Well Hamish, just you tell me a bit about it then. How exactly did you go about murdering Big Bruno?"

Hamish smiled. "I lured him up to Glen Orchy with eighty-two cases of Glen Laldy whisky. That's one thousand two hundred and thirty bottles, to be precise."

The smile on PC McTodd's face froze a little and her eyes narrowed. She had been involved a little in the initial stages of the Glen Laldy whisky theft and Hamish had the figures spot on. The unusual thing about the bottling plant at Glen Laldy was that it put 15 bottles in a case, not the usual 12. Surprising enough that he knew how many cases had been stolen, but how on earth would a hopeless fantasist like Hamish Duke know that there were fifteen bottles in every case? As far as she knew, that figure had never been mentioned in the press. Certainly not in the local press or radio stations anyhow, and the bigger papers had hardly picked the story up at all.

"Really Hamish? Tell me more."

"Well, he was evil wasn't he? So I phoned him and told him to come up and meet me at quarter past six in the morning at the first lay-by in Glen Orchy and he could have the whisky for a hundred pounds a case – that's eight-thousand two-hundred pounds. I put on a Scottish voice when I did it."

PC McTodd's eyes narrowed further. "But you've already got a Scottish voice Hamish."

"Ah, but a real Scottish voice, know what I mean Flora?"

"Right – like *'och aye the noo'* you mean?"

"Yes, like that. That's it."

"Did you read about that in the paper Hamish?"

"I don't read the papers Flora."

"Did you hear it on the radio then?"

"I don't have a radio. Or a television."

"Have you got a computer Hamish?"

"No. No computer."

"Right. Okay. So Hamish, tell me, how exactly did you get from your wee flat in Braehead all the way over to Glen Orchy at that time in the morning."

Hamish fell silent and partook of some serious thinking.

"I took the bus the night before and waited."

"Did you take a tent with you Hamish?"

"No."

"A sleeping bag?"

"No."

"Did you take anything with you at all Hamish?"

"No."

"Absolutely nothing?"

"No, nothing."

"Except a banjo of course, Hamish."

"Eh? Oh yes. A banjo."

"And how did the van get there Hamish?"

"Eh…my pal took it."

"Who's your pal Hamish?"

"Tam Martin."

"Wee Tam? Now Hamish, Tam can't drive. Can he?"

Hamish studied his feet.

"It's true Flora, honest."

"Right Hamish, are you working today?"

"No it's my day off Flora."

"Right. Just you get yourself back home Hamish, we'll maybe send an officer out to take a statement from you later. Okay?"

"Okay Flora."

"Inspector Blackthorn?"

"Yes."

"It's Flora McTodd here Inspector. Front desk."

"Hi Flora. Nice to hear from you. How are things?"

"Fine ma'am. I just thought I'd better tell you – we've just had a visit from Hamish Duke – er…do you know Hamish at all ma'am?"

"Mm, no, don't think so Flora."

"He's a poor wee soul really ma'am, went to the same primary school as me in Braehead. Good at sums and things but hopeless with everything else. I've known him all my life I suppose. He's a fantasist ma'am – he's been a cowboy, a spaceman...and recently, a city banker. Lives in his own dream world. Anyhow, he's just been in to confess to the murder of Big Bruno."

Bonnie Blackthorn laughed not unkindly. "Really Flora? Well that saves me a lot of work!"

"It does indeed ma'am. However, he seemed to know a bit more about the whole thing than I would have expected."

"Oh?"

"Yes – of course he knew about the banjo and what have you, but he said he lured Big Bruno up to Glen Orchy with eighty-two cases of Glen Laldy whisky. That, he said, was one thousand two hundred and thirty bottles. Which, at fifteen bottles a case – which is very unusual, is exactly what was stolen back in January from up by Grantown."

"Right. Interesting."

"He also said he offered him the whisky at a hundred pounds a case and arranged to meet him at the lay-by in Glen Orchy at quarter to six in the morning. "

"Did he really. Well well."

"He also said he put on a Scottish voice to lure him up with. I don't know if you want to take it any further Bonnie...er ma'am, but I thought I'd better tell you anyhow."

"No, you did the right thing Flora...I wonder...I think I'll be paying Hamish a wee visit. Thank you very much indeed."

...

DS Munro and DC Bickerstaff had busied themselves most of the day trying to uncover as much information as possible about Andrea Woodfile with little success. Andrea lived in a small flat in a quiet residential street in Wigan, but according to her next door neighbour she had gone off on holiday some days earlier. Camping, she thought, as she'd seen her put some camping gear in the back of her little van. She was a gardener, seemingly. Self-employed, the neighbour thought. She was a quiet girl, late teens, early twenties . Kept herself to herself by and large. Pleasant enough. Said hello and goodbye – passed the time of day – that sort of thing. But nothing more. Her only visitors seemed to be her mum and her brothers – they dropped in quite a bit. There were three or four brothers, her neighbour thought. Nice looking lads. No, she didn't know anything about them, and no, the name Carnthwaite meant nothing to her.

A visit to the home of her mother in Preston had a similar result.

"She's gone off on holiday love," her neighbour informed them, "her and her daughter. Camping."

"Any idea where?" asked DS Munro.

 "No, don't know where they've gone pet. They go away quite a bit – usually to the Lakes, or Derbyshire or somewhere."

"Do you know her daughter well?"

"Me? No, hardly at all. She's a gardener, I know that much, but that's about it."

Of Andrea's four brothers, three of them were at their respective homes – and the other one was living in Los Angeles. Yes, Andrea had gone camping with their mother – they went every year. They could be anywhere...they loved camping and they loved walking. They never planned a route, they just followed their noses, but with a preference for the wilder regions…Wales, Scotland… the Lakes. …although they ended up on the Isle of Wight last year. This was going to be a long trip for them this year as their mother had decided to retire and Andrea had arranged for a friend to cover her gardening business for her while she took an extended break. No, their mother didn't have a mobile phone, and Andrea, although she carried one for emergencies, refused point blank to switch it on when she was on holiday…they always sent post cards every week though. As for transport…the brothers weren't sure. They knew a friend of a friend of their mother had lent them a car or a small campervan or something, but they had no idea who the friend was…she had so many friends, they said.

Sergeant Munro asked each of them if they had been to Scotland recently, and they all replied firmly in the negative, citing their work records as evidence. Each brother also reacted with shock when asked about Andrea's dealings with Big Bruno. None of them, it seemed, knew anything of her erstwhile drug problem.

"Not making much headway, are we Sarge?" said DC Bickerstaff as they sat forlornly outside the last brother's house.

"No not really Becky. Is it possible she hid her drug-taking from her brothers?...they're supposed to be a close family after all."

"Well Sarge, I've two sisters and neither of them knows I used to smoke five fags every Friday and Saturday night."

"Wow. You devil you."

"Managed to kick it though."

"Well done Becky Bickerstaff."

"Yeah, but seriously Sarge, the brothers may well have known about it. Could just be an act - it's not that difficult to put on a 'shock-horror' face."

"True. There's a lot of born actors out there. Anyhow, getting back to Andrea and her mother, if they've gone camping – which looks pretty damn certain - they might prove a tad difficult to find. Especially if, for some reason, they don't want to be found."

...

Hamish McDonald Duke sat in his Spartan little flat feeling rather pleased with himself. Clearly he had convinced Fiona McTodd that he'd murdered Big Bruno. And, more to the point, he had now fully convinced himself of it too. He had dealt well with the awkward questions Fiona had asked. He was undoubtedly the perpetrator. Who could argue? He just had to wait now for the police officers to come and arrest him. They'd put him in prison. He'd be a hero.

He didn't have to wait long for the police to arrive. Less than an hour. He would have preferred officers in uniform arriving in a police car with a flashing blue light but DI Blackthorn and DS Silver were a pretty good next best thing. He let them in.

"Well Hamish, what's all this about you bumping off Big Bruno?" asked DS Silver, who knew Hamish well enough from one or two of his previous fantasies.

"It's true Sergeant Silver. I whacked him. Ask PC Flora McTodd, she knows."

"Yes, Flora told us all about it Hamish. How many bottles of whisky was it again?"

"One thousand two hundred and thirty sir — in eighty-two cases."

"And how much was that worth Hamish?"

"A hundred pounds a case...that's eight thousand two hundred pounds."

"Right. That's a lot of money Hamish."

"Aye, it is Sergeant."

"Tell me Hamish," asked DI Blackthorn innocently, "where did you find Big Bruno's mobile telephone?"

"In the bus shelter Inspector Blackthorn," said Hamish before he could stop himself.

Bonnie smiled. "Have you still got it Hamish?"

"Yes miss. It's in the bedroom."

"I think you'd better let us have it Hamish, if you don't mind," said DS Silver, "c'mon show me where it is."

"How did she know I'd found it?" a deflated Hamish asked DS Silver when they went through to his bedroom.

"Oh she's very clever Hamish. Very very clever. You can't fool her."

"Will I get arrested?"

"No, you're a hero now Hamish. We'll need you as a witness. Very important."

Hamish brightened. "Can I leave the country?"

"Er... were you thinking of going away somewhere Hamish?"

"No Sergeant. But I thought I'd better ask."

"Better you just stay at home Hamish."

Chapter 21

"Bootle?"

"Buttercup! How lovely!"

"Don't give me that 'buttercup' crap Bootle, you'd sell me down the river as soon as look at me."

"You have a place in my heart Inspector, a place in my heart."

"Oh yes…a place in your rear is more like it. Anyhow I've got some breaking news."

"Good good good! I can't wait! Let's hear it!"

"Not so fast Bootle…not so fast. I need some assurances first…I'm risking my neck here."

"Whatever you want Jonny…you can have it. It's yours."

"Well, as usual, my name stays out of the Post…"

"Indubitably…"

"…and you must not under any circumstances quote this as coming from a police source. I am after all in charge of stopping leaks."

"Of course Jonny – goes without saying…an 'anonymous source' it shall be."

"Right Bootle, okay - but for God's sake just make sure it can't get traced back to me or I'm dead in the water. "

"Trust me Inspector, trust me. I always protect my sources."

"Right, listen carefully…"

"I'm all ears."

"…Big Bruno's mobile's been found."

"Has it indeed?"

"Yes. It's a pretty ancient handset seemingly but in spite of the techy boys crawling all over it, it's completely clean apart from his voicemail greeting which just says *'John Bair - leave a message'*...and two recorded messages. Nothing traceable. That's about it really."

There was a pause.

"Come on then old man...what about these messages?"

"Eh? Don't be insane Bootle, I can't divulge that. Good God I've told you about the phone – that'll give you an exclusive won't it?"

"Jonny, my love, if I go back and tell my boss...that's she of the razor-nails and the writhing-snake hair-do...that there's two messages on the phone but I haven't found out what they are she'll have me smeared thinly across the floor."

"Bootle if I get caught giving you any more info...well it doesn't bear thinking about."

"Oh Inspector...you mustn't give way to nasty misgivings. I can understand the odd qualm or two..."

"...These are a bit stronger than qualms Bootle! This is a murder case – not a nicked bloody toaster! I'd be trusting you with my very existence Bootle...and quite frankly I'd rather trust Uncle Joe Stalin than you."

"Ah Jonny...let me run two small things past you. Firstly, I, Billy Bootle of the Daily Post, have never revealed, and will never reveal, a source which did not wish to be revealed. Ever. And, secondly, I have been most assiduous in protecting you from my esteemed but cruel leader. She still wants yer head Jonny...she still wants yer head."

Slighman groaned.

"...she's been polishing a plate for it all week. Why, only this morning she said something I didn't fully understand, to be honest, about focusing some extra reporting on the toasting saga into the Midland's edition...she's had wind of an application there for the post of...what was it again?...er...oh I forget... was it Chief Inspector or something? Surely that can't be you can it?"

Slighman gasped in horror. "You know damn well it's me Bootle! That's sheer bloody unadulterated blackmail."

"Don't worry Jonny boy, I'll protect you..."

"O yeah...that's wonderful...that really reassures me."

"...I will, I will. You're a safe little bobby in my hands Inspector...but I need to hear these voicemail messages or we're both toas...er...sorry...history."

Slighman was confronting defeat and he knew it. "Right, okay, I'll email you the transcript but you'll have to wait till I get home – I'm certainly not sending it from headquarters."

"Okaydokay. No problem. But get it here by 7.30 old man...we do have deadlines to meet you know."

...

"So, what do we do today Sarge?"

"I think we should head for Salford Becky. See if we can find out anything more about the young Solent brothers and the family before they split up and moved to Edinburgh.

...

Bootle clicked on his email attachment. Slighman had been as good as his word:

The following is a transcript of two voicemail messages left on a mobile telephone device believed to belong to John Bair. Both messages appear to have been left by the same person who has adopted an exaggerated Scottish accent, probably to disguise his voice. The first message was recorded on 3rd June this year and the second on 4th June.

1) *Aye hello. This is a message for Mr Bair. A'thing's in place noo regarding what we talked aboot earlier. As we said there's eighty-two cases in total Mr Bair, containing 15 bottles each. That's one thousand two hundred and thirty bottles to be precise. At a hundred pounds a case as agreed. We've received yer first installment so we're happy at this end to go ahead. We suggest we do it this Monday morning – that's the 5th of June. It'll have to be early in the mornin' Mr Bair. We'll let you know exactly where and when tomorrow. G'bye the noo.*

2) *Aye, it's me again Mr Bair. Ye say in yer reply that yer comin' up on a motorbike and ask if we can accommodate that. Och michty me aye, Mr Bair. We've hired a van wi' a tail-lift so getting' yer motorbike up into it'll be nae problem at all. An' ye can just return the van to Bargain Van Solutions in Manchester when yer feenished wi' it. We'll be waiting for you at the first lay-by after Tyndrum on the road to Bridge of Orchy at half-past six tomorrow mornin'. Ah'll jist repeat that, that's the first lay-by after Tyndrum on the road to the Bridge of Orchy at six-thirty a.m. tomorrow. It's a plain white van. There'll be two of us there. I'll be wearing a deerstalker hat. We'll see you then. G'bye the noo.*

...

Bonnie's mobile rang. Unknown number.

"Hello DI Blackthorn here."

"Hello Inspector Blackthorn, this is Detective Inspector Redcar here from the Met. Sorry to bother you but we may have a murder case on our hands with some similarities to your one up north."

"Really?"

"Yes. One of our London underworld lowlife was bumped off yesterday in circumstances not entirely unlike your Big Bruno affair."

"Oh yes? In what way?"

"Whacked with a musical instrument."

"Really?"

"Well, actually, an accordion landed on his head."

"An accordion?"

"Yes. Out of a fourth-floor window."

"A big accordion was it?"

"A hundred and twenty base."

"That er...sounds big. Who was he?"

"Oh just a slimy toe-rag who did errands for some of the bigger fish. The odd knifing here and there, that sort of thing. Won't be missed."

"Right. So...er...have you found anything eh...other than the fact that he was terminated with an accordion...to link the two deaths?"

"Not a sausage...but we'll send you the case-notes...and keep you informed."

"Er...right...thanks for that Inspector Redcar."

"You're welcome. Bye."

...

Ben and Becky had had a trying day in Salford. The house, and indeed the entire neighbourhood in which the brothers had been brought up before they left with their mother for Edinburgh had been demolished decades earlier in order to build a dual-carriageway, and their school had been knocked down to make way for a new housing estate. They had managed to get hold of the school records but they only went back thirty years and there were no Carnthwaites registered. Clearly Peter and George were in Edinburgh by this time, and Jessica and Douglas had moved school. The local police station had long gone, centralised, modernised, and computerised, but with no record of Carnthwaites or Solents.

A trawl of the local shops, churches, libraries, doctors, dentists, etc, produced nothing beyond confirmation of where they had once lived. Nobody remembered them. In fact almost everybody had moved into the area since the houses and the school had been pulled down. They tried tracing teachers from the school but with little success. The only two they managed to find had no recollection of Carnthwaites and the name Solent meant nothing to them, and no, they weren't in touch with any of the rest of old staff either. Blanks everywhere.

As a last resort they tried the four pubs still in existence which would have served the area around the long gone houses and school, but again nothing but shrugs and headshakes.

"Right Becky, let's call it a day. And pretty much a wasted day at that."

"Okay Sarge. Frustrating though."

"Yep. Certainly is. D'you want to go for something to eat or shall we drive back first?"

"I think I'd better eat Sarge, I'll fall over if I don't have something soon."

"Yeah me too. We haven't done fish n'chips yet…"

"True. Let's do it. I saw one round the corner earlier – tables, chairs, all mod cons…nineteen-fifties style."

"Perfect."

Fish and chips, bread and butter, and a pot of tea each. Ordered, eaten, and thoroughly enjoyed. The café was amazing. Art-deco lighting and mirrors, formica table-tops, tall bench seats, and old film posters and photographs from the fifties covering the walls. Even the glass salt, pepper and vinegar dispensers seemed to be the originals.

"That was wonderful, thank you very much," said DS Munro when the waitress came to clear the table.

She smiled. "Glad you enjoyed it."

"It's a lovely old café isn't it?"

"That's nice of you to say so, yes we're very proud of it."

"Have you worked here long?"

"My parents started it over sixty years ago."

"Really…did you go to school here?" DS Munro put on a gormless expression as he segued seamlessly into a gentle interrogation mode.

"Yes I did…the school's long gone though."

"Well, perhaps you can help us," he said smiling as he flashed his warrant badge and introduced himself and his companion, "we're making enquiries about a family which lived here in the fifties and sixties."

"Well, I can but try. I didn't know everybody mind," she said smiling.

"No of course not. This family was called Carnthwaite."

"Carnthwaite…?" she tilted her head and narrowed her eyes. "I remember the name, certainly, two, maybe three boys I think…but…no I don't remember anything about them."

"Anything at all could help," said DC Bickerstaff encouragingly.

"No, I think they were older than me" she shook her head with unmistakable finality. "Give me a minute though, I'll ask Gerry…he's my brother. He's three years older than me."

She walked over and spoke quietly with the man who had cooked their fish and chips. He put down the bowl of batter he was about to dip a fish into, placed the fish back in its box, wiped his hands on his apron, and approached them frowning.

"Carnthwaite?"

"Yes…ring any bells."

"Yeah. Certainly does."

The eyes of the police officers brightened visibly.

"I don't remember all their names like, but Douglas was in the year above me and I seem to remember there were a couple of younger brothers too." He tapped his chin with two fingers and assumed a look of deep concentration. "I think there might have been a sister an' all. Older I think, but can't be sure."

191

"What can you tell us about them?"

"Well...there was stories..."

"Really...what kind of stories?"

"Well, one thing I know for sure is that Douglas got a right beatin' from this big kid who'd just arrived in our school the week before, and I don't remember ever seeing the big kid after that so presumably he left again... soon after like."

DI Munro and DC Bickerstaff both inhaled sharply.

"Really. You don't remember the name of this big kid by any chance?"

"No, sorry."

"You mentioned stories..."

"Yes, well, I was just a kid meself remember, and it was a long time ago...could all have been rumour for all I know..."

"Maybe so, but tell us anyhow," said DS Munro.

"Well, Douglas was off school for ...well, I dunno, seemed like ages...could've been a few weeks I suppose after the beating and he was never really the same like when he did come back. Went really quiet and...what's the word?...kind of introverted I suppose. Shied away a bit from people. Poor bugger. And there was a story going round that his father went to see the big kid's father and got a right smackin' for his trouble. I remember being told that he was...you know...er...intimidated like...by this and was frightened to take it any further - which caused a lot of problems with his wife and that. In fact they split up after that...so I believe anyhow."

Ben Munro and Becky Bickerstaff looked at each other, both immediately appreciating the potential significance of this information. At last, it seemed they were making progress. Major progress.

"Of course," continued Gerry, "in them days nothing official was done...at least as far as I know nowt was done about it. A school playground fight? Yer havin' a laugh...the police would have chucked you out of the place. And the school probably just washed their hands of it an'all. Bad news for that family mind."

"Indeed it would have been. I don't suppose the name John Bair rings any bells does it?"

"John Bair? Nah. Can't say it does."

"John Bair?" said his sister who had been listening closely throughout, "isn't he that dreadful gangster fellow who was murdered recently? Big Bruno?"

Brother Gerry gasped.

"Yes it was," responded the sergeant.

"What!? D'you really think that was him – that big kid?"

"It's possible. Needs checking out, but that's what we're good at."

"Well I never did."

"No, nor did I," said his sister.

Chapter 22

The Daily Post

Exclusive!

Big Bruno's Mobile Found!

Is 'Och Aye' the key to solving Big Bruno's murder?

Billy Bootle Reporting

Police in the Scottish Highlands have been handed yet another substantial clue in the Big Bruno murder case with the discovery deep in the heather in a remote Highland glen of Big Bruno's mobile phone. A man with a Scottish voice leaves details for a Highland rendezvous at which the Manchester gangster would collect a huge consignment of stolen whisky valued at several hundred thousand pounds. Every detail of the rendezvous is recorded on the message – so, just how many clues do these hapless plodders need in order to solve the case now being referred to by the detectives as the 'Och Aye' case due to the repeated use

of this phrase by the man who left the messages? The strong Scottish accent on the recording does not sound even remotely like the voice of either of the Toaster brothers who both have pleasantly gentle Edinburgh accents. This would suggest that in spite of initial police suspicions, these heroes for today may have nothing to do with the vile gangster's death. In an obvious attempt to implicate the Toaster brothers the man tells Big Bruno that he will be wearing a deerstalker hat at the time of the rendezvous. However, should the Toasters actually be found to be implicated in ridding the world...

Detective Inspector Blackthorn threw the Post disgustedly onto the kitchen table. What absolute tosh! This case was a nightmare. How the hell could anybody carry out a proper investigation using tried and tested police procedures when somebody was feeding the press every bit of information and every clue which came their way...and for the press then to garble everything into the most awful tabloidesque drivel which pandered utterly to sensationalism and spurned anything even faintly resembling the truth? And on top of all that the perpetrators seemed to be leading everyone by the nose and drip-feeding the police bits of evidence piecemeal when it suited their agenda...the banjo...the button...the tea-spoon...the mobile phone. They were the puppeteers and the cops were dancing on their strings.

She filled the kettle and switched it on. Who could she trust? Well DS Silver certainly; DS Munro naturally; Alistair Probe for sure; Superintendent Smart...goes without saying. Slighman? Nah...she was pretty damn sure he was the mole. That prat Bootle from the Post probably had him by the short and curlies. She had known Jonathan Slighman for five years now, and knew him fairly well. He was, she was well aware, a sleazebag, a careerist, a womaniser...but...she also knew that he wouldn't risk his career by leaking info to the press unless he was desperate. But she also knew that he would cover his tracks bloody well...so...she would simply have to work within the constraints of a leaky case and get on with it.

Better phone HQ and see if there had been any developments – she wasn't due in for another hour as she had arranged to take daughter Kathy to the dentist at 9.30. The land-line phone was dead. Damn. Battery failed to charge...yet again. Damn damn damn. Bloody useless thing. That meant she'd probably been incommunicado for the past twelve hours. Her mobile only got a signal on top of the wardrobe in the spare room. Bugger. Better get up there.

As soon as Bonnie raised her arm in the spare room she received a text and a missed-call indicator. Both from Ben. She stood on the bed and phoned him.

"Bonnie?...er...Inspector Blackthorn?"

"Yes Ben – what's happening – my landline's dead."

"Right, we'd a bit of a breakthrough last night."

"Good Ben – we desperately need some movement in this case. What have you learned?"

"Douglas Carnthwaite – i.e. the Toasters' big brother - was beaten up at school by, and I quote, *a big kid*."

"Was he indeed!"

"Yes he was. Without shadow of a doubt that big kid was Big Bruno - and we'll get that confirmed later this morning. The beating, seemingly, affected him quite badly – possibly permanently."

"Poor kid."

"Yes, but not only that, Douglas's father went to see Bruno's father and he was given a thumping for his pains, putting the fear of death into him. Put enormous strain on the family – which eventually split up...the mother and two brothers, as we know, went to Edinburgh, and the father and the other two kids stayed down south."

Bonnie was teetering somewhat on top of the bed. "Right Ben, brilliant. That, on top of the supplying of drugs to Andrea Woodfile, increases the murder motive dramatically. The evidence is pointing straight at George and Peter Solent – they must have hated Big Bruno...and no wonder. He really screwed their family up."

"He certainly did..but does it give us enough to arrest them on?"

"Hmm. The funny thing is Ben, the more evidence we gather against them the less worried they seem, and the less sure I am that they pulled the trigger... or swung the banjo or whatever. And they seem to be the ones who are controlling this case. The ringmasters. The conductors... or whatever."

"Oh there was one other thing…Becky did a trawl of the records this morning and it seems the Solents did in fact report their concerns regarding Big Bruno and Andrea to the police about three years ago…twice in fact. Didn't show up on our initial searches because whoever recorded it misspelt their name. Anyhow, nothing was ever done. No follow up."

"Brilliant."

"Yeah. So what now then Bonnie..er Inspector?"

"I'll run things past the Super…see what he says. I suspect he might want them nicked. At least for questioning."

"And down here…?"

"Well you're more or less finished there now I think Ben. The Carnthwaites and Woodfiles seem to have disappeared into the bush with tents and stoves and you've unearthed a whopper of a motive. Just get things written up and double-checked then you'd better get back home…okay?"

"Fine ma'am. Will do."

"And give DC Bickerstaff my sincere thanks Ben – sounds like she's been a great help."

"Er…well…actually, she's got some leave to take so she was thinking of coming up to Scotland…never been north of the border before. You know…give the place a once-over sort of thing…"

"Really! How nice Ben…I look forward to meeting her."

Bonnie felt she could sense the reddening of a face at the end of the line.

…

Inspector Slighman looked at his computer with considerable unease. He really ought to check his emails. He knew his Inbox would be stuffed as he hadn't checked it for days but the fear of a polite enquiry from the recruitment panel in Birmingham regarding his role in the Toaster/Big Bruno/Och Aye shambles made him a quivering jelly. He would have no option but to tell them that not only was he handling the press, he was also in

197

charge of internal security, both of which roles must look like upturned dogs-dinners even from the far away Midlands. He'd been lucky so far - of that he was well aware – but how long would his luck hold? It would just take his enemies the click or two of a mouse to drop him in it and scupper his chances of ever getting a move up and out of Auchtergarry. He clicked the email icon:

Sender Harriet Inkster, (uh-oh - enemy number 1...) Clapham: *Hey Jonny! I've just heard on the grapevine that you're applying for Ch Insp in the deep south. Have all the women in bonnie Scotland got you sussed then Jonny boy? Or is it sweet little Carla who wants a move...and a wee promotion for hubby...such an ambitious girl isn't she? (she'll dump you someday Jonny lad you mark my words). Better keep yer fingers crossed that HR in Birmingham remain blissfully unaware of yer world-class ineptitude and creepiness Jonny or yer stuck amongst the bonnie blooming heather for evermore!! I've never liked the Midlands Jonny - they deserve you – so good luck! Scumbag.*
    Phew. Bitch. Delete.

Sender F Slighman, Edinburgh: *Dad Im pateintly awaiting for the Toasters autographs. Great now their murderrers eh? What guys! And dont forget my fat wad either dad. Felix.* WHAT GUYS!? The world's gone mad. Quite mad...and all that money on school fees and they can't even din the most basic of English into them. Jesus Christ.

Sender T Greenside, Midlands Division: *Post of Chief Inspector; Thank you for confirmation of receipt of message regarding interview.* Big phew! No hint of a rocking boat there.

Sender Amazon Local: *Kindle special offers!* **'Interviews and how to Win Them'** *yours for £4.99.* **'How to Wow that**

Recruitment Panel' £3.50.   Bloody   Hell   how   do   they...?
Actually...might be worth...

Sender S Short, Office: *Please note the Community Group has now been disbanded due to organisational restructuring. New structures to be announced in due course.*   How exciting. Delete.

Sender D Wragg, Shetland: *(*uh-oh Donna - enemy number 2...*)
Whoops Jonny Jonny Jonny do please stop screwing up all over the place. I really want you to get that beautifully distant post. BTW I hear there are lots of jobs for upright polis in New Zealand. Go for it Jonny!* Bitch again. Phew again. Delete again.

Sender eBay Seller Team: *Special offer! 'A New Life for You in New Zeal....'*   Holy Moly. Delete!

Slighman drew a long slow breath, closed his eyes, and exhaled gently through pursed lips. Not too bad at all... all things considered.

...

Bonnie's mobile went off – 'Cop Shop' ringtone.
"Hi DI Blackthorn here."
"Bonnie – Belinda here. I've got a message for you from an Inspector Redcar."
"Who?...oh yeah...I remember. What does he want?"
"Something about an accordion death being just an accident or something..."
"Oh really...you don't say...what a surprise."
"Yep, some musician left his accordion on a table near an open window or something. Fell out and killed somebody. A felon. Or something. Bang. Deid."
"Amazing...and how exactly did it manage to jump out the window from the top of a table I wonder?"

"Eh?...oh, wait a minute I wrote it down here somewhere. Oh yeah...it was a tall skinny table or something. Like an aspidistra table maybe? Anyhow, the accordion was too heavy for it. A leg broke, over it toppled...and out went the accordion."

"Really? To the detriment of the poor felon?"

"Yeah."

"Belinda...?"

"Yeah?"

"What the hell's an aspidistra table?"

"It's...er...my granny had one...it's like a tall...er...skinny kind of table for a plant...you know...like an aspidistra. Victorian."

"...Okay," said Bonnie, who had never before heard of an aspidistra, "I get the picture. I have been enlightened. Many thanks Belinda."

...

Superintendent Smart felt somewhat more chipper than hitherto. At last progress was being made. A case looking fairly...well, shower-proof, if not exactly watertight...was beginning to develop. The weight of evidence now accruing against the Toaster brothers in the 'Och Aye' murder was pretty damning. He looked around the room at his team gathered there. DI Blackthorn, Inspector Slighman, DS Silver, DS Munro, and Dr Alistair Probe... a fine body...mostly. Let's see what they thought.

"Right Bonnie. Bring us up to date. Give us the facts. Let's hear it. Where are we at the moment eh?"

"Okay. The evidence is building. The Toaster brothers are looking more and more like the culprits."

"On what basis Bonnie, on what basis? Fill us in."

"Well, clearly the fact that their fingerprints are on the murder weapon is in itself fairly damning..."

"Indeed it is," interjected Inspector Slighman nodding earnestly round the table, "indeed it is".

"…and in the recorded message on Big Bruno's phone the guy says he'll be wearing a deerstalker…à la George 'the Toaster' Solent…"

"Convicted out of his own mouth," said Slighman still nodding and looking round earnestly.

"Hm…bit weak though that one, surely," opined DS Silver, earning a ferocious glower from Inspector Slighman. "I mean the voice is unrecognisable…clearly put on."

"On its own, yes, perhaps it is a tad flimsy, but in combination with everything else it could certainly help sway a jury."

"True."

"Anyhow…we come to motive. We already knew that the Solent brother's niece – Andrea Woodfile - had had a run in with Big Bruno…she was getting stuff from him over a two year period – and that she had twice got to the 'warning' stage through late payment. We don't know exactly what happened back then but he was, as we're all too aware, a very nasty and violent piece of work, and she would have been extremely vulnerable. It could all have been pretty ugly, and doubtless would have given the entire Solent, Carnthwaite and Woodfile clan good reason to despise the man. "

"Doubtless indeed," Inspector Slighman intensified his grave expression and added more vigour to his nodding.

"And now, Sergeant Munro here," said Bonnie indicating the newly returned sergeant, "has uncovered an even bigger motive for the Toasters to murder Big Bruno…"

"Really!? Excellent!" Slighman looked at DS Munro with new-found admiration. This was all going very well by his book. He now appeared to be nodding from the waist up.

"Right Ben," said Superintendent Smart, thinking that DS Munro still looked a bit gormless, "let's hear it. What's this motive you've uncovered?"

"Yes, er, well Bruno beat up their big brother – that's Douglas Carnthwaite - at school. Very badly we believe. And then Bruno's father beat up Douglas's father when he went to confront him about it. The police at the time weren't involved – a playground punch-up, however violent, wouldn't have got near their radar in those days and it's very unlikely that the Carnthwaite's even considered going to the police about the father having been beaten up by Bruno Senior. Anyhow, to cut a long story short, this all resulted in the father having...er...well we don't know...some kind of breakdown maybe, the parents splitting up, the mother taking the two youngest boys to live in Edinburgh, and the two oldest children remaining with their father in Salford. So, in effect, the family was devastated...rent asunder in fact...by John Bair and his father, and I guess when the brothers found out about Andrea's run in with the brute...they decided enough was enough and started to plan his demise."

"Seems like a strong motive to me," said Alistair Probe, "I'd have been in there swinging my banjo for sure if it had been my family."

"So," said Bonnie, "we have the fingerprints on the banjo, the deerstalker message on the mobile, a big motive...and...one rather strange but added piece of evidence which is both useful, and awkward as hell."

"What's that Bonnie?" enquired Superintendent Smart, "what on earth do you mean?"

"Well," said Bonnie inhaling deeply, "they went to incredible lengths to get themselves convicted of a crime which took place at exactly the same time as the murder, but over fifty miles away, thus giving themselves the perfect alibi."

"Hm. I guess we all swallowed their little ploy Bonnie," said Superintendent Smart drumming his fingers on his desk.

"Yes...we...er..." muttered Inspector Slighman, "...we...erm...yes...we did."

"Well," continued DI Blackthorn, "it gives us a problem."

"In what way Bonnie? In what way?" asked the Superintendent.

"In precisely the way they wanted. If they're guilty of crime A, they can't also be guilty of crime B."

"But it's pretty clear now that they are in fact guilty of crime B isn't it Bonnie? So they can't possibly have been guilty of crime A." The Superintendent was getting slightly worried.

"They were found guilty," continued Bonnie, "in a court of law on what was described at the time as incontrovertible evidence."

"Incontrovertibly, undeniably, and indisputably, one-hundred per cent rock-solid-concrete-guilty, was the verdict of some," added DS Silver quietly, earning himself a glare from Slighman which was incandescent enough to be detected from Inverness.

"So, we have a problem," Bonnie looked round the table. "Any ideas how to solve it chaps?"

"What do you mean a problem?" asked Inspector Slighman, "surely we just have the guilty decision on the Toaster case reversed...or revoked...or overturned or whatever... and have them tried for murder."

"Not so simple, I don't think," said Bonnie, "there has to be a miscarriage of justice proven, and for that there has to be an appeal."

"So?"

"So, who's going to appeal? Not the Toasters, that's for sure."

"We will of course Bonnie," said the Superintendent, "might be a little...er...embarrassing...but unavoidable. We'll have to bring the case down. Our own, once deemed to be cast-iron case."

"Well, I'm no expert, but that might prove harder than you think."

"Really?"

"Well it would have to go before the Scottish Criminal Cases Review Commission and be proven to be a case of wrongful conviction, with the brothers then being exonerated. But as far as I am aware, the brothers, or a third party acting on their behalf, would have to set the thing in motion themselves, and they ain't gonna do that, are they?"

"But surely we can place the new evidence before the court at a murder trial and have the old conviction overturned," said

Inspector Slighman, the beginnings of outrage starting to show on his face.

"But," reasoned Bonnie, "the Procurator Fiscal isn't going to bring a case to court where the accused have cast-iron alibis which the court itself has already described as such. And, of course, we have no other suspects for the theft of the toaster."

Superintendent Smart rummaged in his desk for an analgesic. This was not funny.

"I'm going to get in touch with the Crown Office later this morning and see what they can come up with," said Bonnie, "there must be a way round it. Surely."

"Right," said the Superintendent, "you do that Bonnie, and the rest of you keep up the hunt for evidence. The case against the brothers is quite strong as it is, but the more we get the stronger the case becomes, and, probably, the greater the chances of getting the whole toasting baloney booted out."

They rose and departed.

Chapter 23

Silas B Gridning had a naturally down turned mouth and eyebrows. They formed deep lines which conjoined, carved their way down his face, and merged into a seemingly bottomless delta of etched jowls. These weathered contours had been fashioned over the decades because his expression of choice - rarely altered from morning till night - was a dyspeptic glare which gathered his flesh into tight folds. But today was a bad day so he had intensified his everyday glower down a notch to a scowl. A man of business was Silas B. Gridning, who had built his enterprise over the years on a platform of rudeness, over charging, poor service and changing the company name on a regular basis.

These unwavering business principles had made him a rich man. Mail order, initially, and now internet-selling, were perfect mediums for Silas B Gridning to prosper in, and prosper he did, by the simple expedient of charging for cheap-to-middling quality, but providing junk. You want a new hose for your shower? A non slip stair mat perhaps? How's about a matching duvet cover and pillow slips adorned with a rambling rose motif? A moth trap maybe? A kiddy's harmonica or starter guitar? A garden storage box…? Well, whatever, Silas B Gridning of Gridning Supplies Ltd was yer man.

Oh…so you didn't expect the guitar to be plastic…? Or the harmonica to have only three notes…? Or the duvet cover to be too small, horribly synthetic, and flimsy enough to read through…? Oh dear. Did you read the small print? Oh deary deary me. No…sorry, we don't operate a money-back policy. Bye.

Today, however, this sure-fire money making system had hiccupped. A letter from a Gridning Supplies customer had landed on his desk thanking them for their excellent service and the fine sturdy quality of the garden storage box received. This was baffling and way beyond infuriating – for two reasons. First of all, nobody, but absolutely nobody, should ever under *any circumstances whatsoever* give out the company's mail address, and secondly...Silas knew for a fact that the garden storage box in question was made of plastic so feeble a decent yogurt pot could sneer at it. It was tat of the first order. The very idea that one of his customers could be happy enough with the blessed thing, and with the after-sales service, to go to the bother of writing a letter of praise had taken his breath away and given him palpitations. This had never happened before and was not what he had entered business for...toiled and scratched for. A satisfied customer?...this was unforgiveable. A mistake had been made. A big, big, mistake. Someone in the organisation had fouled up big style. And Silas had a damn shrewd idea who that someone was. He snatched up the letter, stomped across his office floor, threw open his door, glared across the twenty-five upturned faces crammed into the company's call centre, and yelled "Damien!"

A slightly-built young man stood up from his desk and made his way towards Silas B Gridning's office with a rather absent-minded smile on his face, raising his eyebrows and nodding a friendly nod at his fellow workers as he passed their desks. Silas followed his progress shaking his head. What a useless article. Damien approached and entered the office.

"Yes Dad?"

"Sit down."

"Thanks Dad."

Silas waved the letter under his son's nose. "Does the name Gemma Hogan mean anything to you Damien?"

"Oh yes Dad, it does. She called the day I started – a week past Monday in fact - with a complaint about her garden storage-box. So I sent her another one."

"Eh? You what? Another one? Another identical one?"

"Oh no Dad, I had one sent from John Lewis's."

"What!? Are you mad?" He gazed at this son in disbelief. Where had he and Sheila gone wrong with this one? Five kids, four of them turned out perfectly well, all hard-headed go-getting achievers working in law and banking and pulling in big bucks, and this hopeless object who floated through life with his maddening perma-smile and sickening tendency to see the best in everyone. A degree in Social Studies and Sustainable Development for Christ's sake. Whatever the hell that was.

"Are you telling me you actually spent your own money sending her this thing?"

"Well, you know Dad, she sounded so nice on the phone…and it only cost sixty quid."

"Sixty qui…oh Jesus." This was truly insufferable. If only he hadn't promised Sheila he'd take the clueless twit on over the summer – and that he wouldn't sack him regardless of what. Damn damn damn. "I can't believe you wasted your own money on a customer Damien. You really are a throwback."

"Well actually Dad, they agreed to invoice Gridning Suppl…"

"What!? I don't believe it! So I'm paying for the deranged old bat's storage box?"

"Er…well yes. Not that she's deranged…or even old…but you are a millionaire Dad, aren't you?...a few times over? You won't miss sixty quid, will you? It's peanuts."

Gridning sagged. How do you explain to an alien masquerading as your son that every penny you possessed was loved and treasured? Peanuts? Sixty quid would get him a month's worth of lunchtime sandwiches for God's sake. He took a deep breath – he was dreading the answer to his next question.

"Is..er…is she the only one you've…er…you've sorted out by any chance?"

"Oh no Dad, I've done a couple every day. The reputation of the company must have risen a fair bit by now…good eh? I expect you'll get more letters from satisfied customers in the next week or two."

The engravings on Gridning's face etched themselves ever deeper.

"Tell me Damien, when exactly is it that you leave?"

"I start my new job on Monday Dad, so this is my last day."

Silas B Gridning sighed a long sigh of relief. Thank God.

"Right Damien. Fine."

"Er...I wonder Dad...could I possibly leave a bit early today please?"

Nothing would have pleased Silas Gridning more than seeing his son leave the office early and for good, but his mood was dark and he was hard-wired to refuse all such requests.

"Eh? Why do you want to leave early?"

"I'm going to pop round by the police station."

"The police station? What the hell are you going there for?"

"Well you know I was up in Scotland last week bagging Munros?"

Silas did indeed know this. Munro bagging. Climbing up wet lumps of rock for fun. Another sign of his son's sad deficiencies.

"Yes, I know. What of it?"

"Well, it's funny really, but I was showing Colin – er he sits at the next desk to me – my holiday photos and it seems I might have inadvertently taken a photograph of a crime."

"Oh yeah. What crime would that have been?"

"Well, have a look at this and see what you think."

Damien pulled out his smart phone, walked round to his father's side of the desk and flicked through some photographs. "Just a minute, it's here somewhere."

Gridning Senior sighed and shook his head. "Is this going to take long?"

"Here it is." Damien showed his less than doting father a photograph he had taken of one of his Munro-bagging companions first thing in the morning as they climbed the lower-reaches of Ben Dorain. Filling most of the screen was his friend's head. Another soft-brained no-hoper, thought his father.

"So what am I looking at Damien? Where's the crime?"

"Well, when I showed it to Colin he immediately pointed to the little group there…way off in the background…see?"

"Yeah. What about them?"

"Well, look closely – if I zoom in. I know its faint and far away but look…there's what looks like a white van, a green motorbike, a guy wearing orangey-coloured trousers, a big bloke wearing something black from head to foot, and another bloke carrying a…"

Silas B Gridning sat up straight. Bored no more. "…a banjo!" he shouted.

"Well, the image is much too small and too far away to be certain, but yeah it looks…"

"It's Big Bruno for sure!" yelled Silas B excitedly. "Bloody hell Damien for once in your life you've done something worthwhile…well done…you're not a complete dope after all!"

"Thanks Dad," responded the smiling one, who was, and always had been, utterly impervious to his father's insults.

"And you were going to take this to the police?"

"Yes of course. It's evidence, isn't it."

"It may be evidence, Young Damien, but there's no way this is going straight to the police. They can wait their turn." So saying Silas B Gridning, no longer glowering his A-star glower, picked up the phone and dialed a number.

"Hello Daily Post news desk, can I help you?"

"Yes, you can," said the man of business, as close to jauntiness as he had been for a decade and a half, "you can put me through to Billy Bootle."

Chapter 24

Inspector Jonathan Slighman and his good wife Carla sat at home together eating a late breakfast. This was the first time in some weeks that they were actually doing something together, if sitting in a silence of Arctic frostiness can be so described. It was Saturday morning, the Inspector had a day off – his first since the Toaster nonsense had kicked-off - and Carla had not yet begun the daily, never-ending, caring, tending, and nourishing of her market research business. Carla didn't do days off. Ever. As they sat there, each with their own chilly thoughts, the sound of a key turning in the latch accompanied by the unmistakable dissonance of their son Felix's tuneless whistle reached their very surprised ears.

"What the..."

"What's he doing home?"

"Morning mater, morning pater. Surprise surprise eh?"

"Too damn right it's a surprise..." snapped his startled mother, "...what the hell are you doing home? You'd better not be in any trouble at school young man."

"On the contrary mater darling. All is hunkus dorus. In extremus."

"Well...eh...good to see you Felix..." said father Slighman in tones which strongly suggested he felt otherwise, "...but...er...why are you home? Didn't expect you back for another fortnight."

"Oh just a flying visit you know. A few things to do. That sort of thing."

"What sort of thing?" enquired mother Carla

"Oh, this and that. This and that."

"This and that!? What's that supposed to mean? I smell a fish here."

"A fish?"

"I think she means a rat…"

"…don't you dare tell me what I think I mean Jonathan. There's something fishy going on here or I'm very much mistaken. Just home for a flying visit?...I wasn't brought up yesterday you know…"

"…born yesterday darling."

"Don't 'darling' me!"

"Honestly Mum, nothing wrong. All's well. All's very well in fact."

"I don't trust you Felix. You must have had to get up at the crack of dawn to get here at this hour...that's not exactly you're style now - is it?"

"I've turned over a new leaf Mum. I'm a whole new Felix. Early to bed, early to rise and all that."

"Don't give me that rubbish - you're up to something Felix I know you are."

"I'm not. Honest I'm not. Er…Dad…you're not heading towards Tyndrum today by any chance are you?"

"Tyndrum? What d'you want to go there for? What's this all about Felix?"

"Well I want to pop into Auchtergarry later but I really need to take a photograph of the murder layby near Tyndrum and the bus doesn't go that way."

"Just a minute…" said father Slighman standing up from the breakfast table to full height and leaning manfully against the worktop "…what in hell's name d'you want a photograph of the layby for?"

"Right…eh…I'll tell you…er…hold on a second Dad…" said Felix whipping out his mobile and taking a quick photograph of his father who he caught looking nicely moronic, "…er…yes. I'm giving a talk at school and I need visual aids. Photographs."

Slighman was aghast. "Do you mean to tell me that you've just taken a photograph of me next to our worktop to help you illustrate a talk?"

"Yeah. Well that's where it all began innit? So why not."

"Why not? Why the fu…er…why bloody not!? Are you insane? An illustrated talk? This is a murder case not a fucking lecture at the Horticultural Society."

"You watch your language Jonathan!"

"I don't believe this! Here I am bursting a gut to bring two mass murderers to justice and my own son's giving pretty little illustrated talks about it."

"Mass murderers? Dad?"

"Well you know what I mean. These are bad guys Felix."

"Anyhow it's a PowerPoint presentation, not an illustrated talk."

"What's the difference? Eh? It doesn't change the fact that they're evil."

"Nah, no they're not, they're great. Everybody wants them to get off."

"Let me put you right on that score before we go any further young Felix – the nation is desperate for them to be brought to justice."

"Rubbish. You're just pissed off because they made you look a diddy."

"Felix! I agree with you absolutely but don't you dare talk to your father like that!"

"Don't talk to your….you agree with…what the hell kind of rebuke is that? Anyhow I want you to delete that photograph right now."

"You're kidding."

"I certainly am not kidding. Delete it. Now."

"Okay. No problem. I'm cool with that," said Felix deleting the offending photograph.

His father breathed a small sigh of relief. "Anyhow, who in their right mind's going to turn up to hear a kid like you talking about something you can't possibly understand?"

"Loads of people. We've already sold every ticket Dad. Could have filled the place twice over."

Slighman's jaw sagged. "Tickets? What d'ye mean tickets?"

"Tickets...you know...for moolah. Two quid a throw. Three hundred seats in the gym hall. Me and Torquil Eccles have set up our own enterprise company...part of the Teens Enterprise programme at our school. Making a bloody fortune."

Carla looked at her son with new-found admiration. "Really? That's wonderful darling...but do watch your language."

"You're making money from my murder case?"

"Too right we are. Manna from heaven this case Dad. Not only is my old man the inspector in charge of the whole thing, it was our toaster that got nicked. Perfect. Now I just need photographs of Bonnie Prince Charlie's statuette, the Sally Ann charity shop, the pig sta...er...police station in Auchtergarry, etc etc and we're set up. Everyone's falling over themselves to hear about this case. I'm booked to speak at Watson's and Heriot's next...and Torquil's going to contact Eton and Harrow later today."

"What! This has to be stopped! It's an outrage."

"Nonsense Jonathan we can't curb the boy's entrepreneurial instincts. This is an excellent opportunity for him to get a firm grounding in the arts of business practice." The inspector started to deflate slowly back on to his chair.

"But this is..."

"Jonathan! Enough!"

Slighman continued his deflation. One didn't argue with Carla, especially if money was involved. "Now, Felix, tell me..." continued mother Carla, "...such a robust product...how are you marketing your talks?"

Slighman groaned.

"Facebook mostly Mum."

Slighman groaned again.

"Ah, you're harnessing social-media strategies...excellent!"

Yet another groan.

"And I've seven thousand followers on Twitter. Increased by almost three hundred yesterday alone."

"Really? That's jolly good. I am impressed."

"Twitter? Remind me...what's that all about?"

"Oh for God's sake Jonathan you're such a dinosaur. Never mind, I'll explain it all to you later."

"I am not a dinosaur!"

"Oh for God's sake Jonathan, you're still wearing socks your mum knits for you. Of course you're a dinosaur. Now tell me Felix, moving forward, how are you going to cascade momentum once you've delivered all your presentations?"

"Torquil and me have..."

"I," interjected the inspector.

"Eh?"

"I...Torquil and I....not Torquil and me. Torquil and I. Good God."

"Whatever Dad. Anyhow, we've started on a book – 'The Tyndrum Toasters and the Och Aye Murders'"

"You've what?!" gasped his horrified father.

"A book – cool eh Dad?" Father Slighman, rendered speechless, replied not.

"Why that's wonderful Felix! I'm delighted."

"Thanks Mum."

"Yes, it's a pity in a way that you had to delete that photo of your father..."

"Eh...oh no Mum, that doesn't make any difference, I'd already sent it to Torquil."

"Oh good. So you can use it after all."

Slighman felt as if he was invisible...non-existent...perhaps observing all this from some astral plane. Very strange.

"There's just one thing..."

"Yes Mum?"

"...er...your Dad's not really the man in charge of the case you know...it's Superintendent Smart who's..."

"Ah who cares who's really in charge? If I tell them my old-man's in charge, then my old-man's in charge - they'll believe me. Entrepreneurial licence Mother dearest. No problem."

Carla's bosom swelled with maternal pride. What a boy.

The phone rang. Inspector Slighman picked it up, croaked a whispered "yes?" into the mouthpiece, thought better of it, cleared his throat and bawled "yes!?".

"Sergeant Silver here Inspector."

"Yes Sergeant," the inspector's voice was weary, "what can I do for you?"

"Er…sorry to bother you Sir…I know it's you're day off and all that, but…er…have you seen today's Daily Post by any chance?"

"No I have not seen today's Daily Post Sergeant Silver. Why?" The inspector braced himself for further debilitating trauma.

"Well Sir, incredibly, there's a photograph splashed right over the front page purporting to show the Toaster brothers and Big Bruno beside the…er…murder layby…just before the deed took place."

"Eh? Say that again?"

"Well, it seems some Munro bagger managed to capture a photograph of the whole damn shooting-match by purest chance. Orange trousers, deerstalker, banjo, motorbike, biking leathers…the lot."

The inspector's rollercoaster took a steep upward turn.

"But that's marvelous!"

"I thought you'd be pleased Sir. It's all a bit distant and the focus isn't too sharp but it looks like the real deal right enough. The report's by our old friend Billy Bootle."

"Is it indeed. I'll maybe call him – I think I…er… I may have his number around somewhere."

"Superintendent Smart has called for an impromptu meeting Sir – he was having a day off today too but he's going to come in. Meeting's planned for 12 noon…but if…"

"Oh I'll be there, don't worry. Day off or no day off. It's curtains for them this time that's for sure. See you later Sergeant."

"Yes Sir."

The inspector replaced the telephone with a grateful sigh.

"What's happening Dad? That sounded pretty damn interesting."

"Never you mind what's happening young Felix. It's a police matter."

"Nonsense Jonathan, surely you can tell your own son what's happening."

"This is a murder case Carla! Not tales from Beatrix bloody Potter."

"But he's taking his first steps in business and enterprise Jonathan...how can you be so mean?"

"Mean? He'll get by without any help from me – he's already sold all his tickets remember. Anyhow, I'm going. I have to get into the station for twelve."

"Great Dad! You'll be passing the layby...can I get a lift?...then into Auchtergarry?"

The inspector rolled his eyes to the sky, took a deep breath, and acquiesced.

Chapter 25

DI Blackthorn was already in the police HQ at Auchtergarry an hour before the scheduled meeting. She held her mobile to her ear and she glared at the front page of the Post. She was not pleased. This photograph should never have been given to the press. Especially not the Post.

"Hello, News Desk."

"Is that Billy Bootle?"

"It is indeed. At your service."

"This is Detective Inspector Blackthorn here..."

"Ah the lovely DI Blackthorn!"

The lovely DI Blackthorn smouldered silently.

"I wonder if you would be so kind, Mr Bootle, as to give me the address and phone number of Damien Gridning."

"My dear Inspector I already have. I knew you chaps would probably want them so I emailed them to you just five minutes ago. Such a nice chap he is, Damien. A pippin, an absolute pippin."

"Doubtless he is, but I do hope, Mr Bootle, that you haven't compromised our case with the drivel on your front page this morning."

"Drivel? My dear Detective Inspector, whatever can you mean?"

"You know exactly what I mean Mr Bootle. According to your nonsense, not only do you claim that everyone in the photo is clearly identifiable - as the Toaster brothers and Big Bruno - you go on to claim that the photograph was taken 30 seconds before the murder, and I quote: *the Toaster heroes caught for you on camera seconds before mercifully relieving the world of an evil monster. We invite you, our valued readers, to take a last long look at he who is about to depart by banjoing...and say 'good riddance!'* What unutterable tosh!"

"Really Inspector? What's wrong with it? Do tell."

"Right. Where to begin? First of all the photograph hasn't been authenticated..."

"...We ran it past our techy boys Inspector...they were happy."

"Get away...were they really? What a surprise. Secondly, absolutely nobody's clearly identifiable..."

"...Really Inspector? Orangey trousers...massive bloke in biking leathers...deerstalker hat...who else could they possibly be?"

"In a court of law...anyone."

"Oh hardly Bonnie...the guy wearing the deerstalker hat's carrying a banjo..."

"A banjo! The resolution on the photograph's so poor it could be a teddy bear – or a feather damn duster."

"Aw come on Bonnie...they're who we say they are...the Toasters and Big Bruno. Clear as the nose on your face."

DI Blackthorn had an aching desire to scream at him not to call her 'Bonnie'. But she refrained.

"And may I run the principle of 'innocent till proven guilty' past you. You've actually condemned the very men you're holding up as heroes as being guilty of murder."

"Ah yes, my dear D.I., but with extremely powerful mitigating circumstances. They remain heroes."

"Oh really...I presume you know there's only one possible sentence for murder in Scotland...and that's life imprisonment."

"We'll get them off Inspector, don't you worry. We're going to start a *Free the Toasters* campaign a week before the trial begins..."

"...Oh that's marvelous Mr Bootle...a campaign which you know will sell lots of papers...but will be doomed to hopeless failure."

"People power my bonnie lass! Can move mountains. You wait and see."

Bonnie boiled, but quietly.

"And, Mr Bootle, may I just mention, that any jury put together in Scotland now will undoubtedly have been influenced by your fact-free claptrap."

"Oh…hardly fact-free, my dear, and, heartbreaking to my journalistic soul as it is, the majority of the population don't actually read the Daily Post…but, having said that, I feel certain that our common-sense approach to the case could only be an influence to the good anyhow."

This was too much for DI Blackthorn.

"Yes. Well. Really. Goodbye, Mr Bootle."

"Toodle pip, my dear, toodle pip!"

The DI's demeanour was cold and darksome as she added Damien Gridning to her list of contacts and pressed 'Call'.

"Hello," said a cheerful voice, "Damien here."

"Damien Gridning?"

"Yes, that's me."

"Hello Mr Gridning, this is Detective Inspector Blackthorn from…"

"…Oh yes! I know who you are…you're working on the Och Aye murder, aren't you!"

"Yes Damien, I am."

"Jolly exciting eh?"

"Er…well, maybe a bit too exciting at times. Anyhow, Mr Gridning…"

"…Oh please call me Damien, Inspector."

"Right…Damien. Do you still have the original photograph you took on Ben Dorain?"

"Yes I do."

"Okay, we need to get that photograph from you Damien…in fact it would have been better if you had taken it straight to us instead of going to the press with it."

"Well Inspector, that was my intention, absolutely it was, but as soon as I showed the thing to my father he phoned that dreadful Bootle fellow and a deal was struck on the instant. I wasn't very pleased let me tell you...but my father...well, he's a steamroller."

Bonnie's mood was softening.

"Okay Damien, but you must take the phone you took the photograph with to your nearest police station and..."

"...Oh yes of course Inspector...I'm...er...sorry to interrupt...but I'm actually only about twenty miles from Auchtergarry right now. I start a new job on Monday so I thought I'd kill two birds with the one stone this weekend – bag another Munro or two, and hand over the photograph...and...er....answer any questions you might have. Just stopped for a quick flask of tomato soup...ha ha. So I should be with you in the next hour...is that okay?"

Okay?"

Wonderful Damien, wonderful. See you soon – and thank you very much." Bonnie's mood had lightened noticeably.

...

The meeting commenced. Superintendent Smart, Detective Inspector Blackthorn, Inspector Slighman, Detective Sergeant Silver, Detective Sergeant Munro, and Alistair Probe all in attendance.

"Right then," said Superintendent Smart placing the Daily Post on the table and prodding at its front cover, "what do we make of this little development then?"

Everyone looked at DI Blackthorn.

"Well," began the DI, "it's somewhat unexpected, I must admit. Of course the photograph will have to be authenticated by our computer geeks before we can truly regard it as evidence, and hopefully they'll be able to enhance the resolution...but it's interesting is it not? Taking it at face value – which is all we can do at the moment – it's really the first piece of evidence we've had which hasn't been drip-fed to us by the perpetrators..."

"D'you mean the Toasters Bonnie?...the Solent brothers?" asked Superintendent Smart.

"Well, they're certainly in the frame Sir...but whether they actually wielded the banjo..."

"...Oh of course they did Bonnie...how can there possibly be any doubt?" Inspector Slighman gave a hands out, palms up gesture denoting incredulity.

"Erm...with all due respect Jonathan...it's only a matter of days ago that there was no possible doubt about their theft of your toaster."

"Oh that's ridiculous Bonnie...that was just a cover...fooled us all. Each and every one of us."

DI Blackthorn raised a demurring eyebrow but took it no further.

"Well, anyhow, getting back to this photograph...and by the way, I've spoken with Damien Gridning who actually took the photograph...he'll be here in half an hour or so with the smart-phone he took the photograph with...which is mighty convenient really. Er...he's up to bag Munros again. So we'll get it to the geeks post-haste. Yes. Anyhow. It's our first piece of evidence from an independent witness. So, what does it tell us folks?" She looked around inviting contributions.

There was a brief pause as everyone looked at everyone else.

"Well," said the superintendent feeling perhaps he should kick off, "it...er...seems to tell us exactly what we need to know...er...don't you think?"

"And that is...?" enquired Bonnie.

"It's them," interjected a decisive and rather dismissive Inspector Slighman who had never for a moment doubted the Solent brother's guilt, and who strongly believed that a quick arrest and conviction would nail him his new post. "They're readily identifiable; they're exactly *where* the deed took place exactly *when* the deed took place. They're undoubtedly with the victim, and they've got the murder weapon. What more do you need? We've got them cold. End of story."

"It does look pretty...eh...pretty damning...right enough," added DS Silver, "and when you add the fingerprints on the banjo, the message on the mobile, the button…etcetera etcetera…yes…I'm afraid I'd have to agree. The evidence points one way and one way only. Guilty. No question."

"Is that definitely the right van?...motorbike?" asked DS Munro looking dim. "Everything looks authentic enough…I suppose…distant though…just wondering."

"Hopefully, Ben, we'll get some sort of confirmation on that and everything else in the photograph once the computer team's finished working on it - but I don't expect certainties."

"Nor do we need them Bonnie," said Inspector Slighman, "it's a brilliant piece of evidence as it stands. These guys are dead in the water." He could almost taste his promotion.

"Well, at this stage, to be honest, I think Ben's right to be wary – the photograph is an amazing piece of evidence…but…"

"…But what Bonnie? Come on…for God's sake…" Inspector Slighman shook his head in frustration.

"Well, Jonathan, it's just that I think that any decent defence lawyer might just point out that absolutely nobody in the picture is clear enough to identify with any certainty…and ditto for the van, motorbike, deerstalker and banjo."

"Perhaps so Bonnie…but any decent prosecutor would have a field day with it – it's a gift. No jury's going to doubt their guilt…we've got too much against them. As I say – they're dead in the water - let's stop wasting time - get them in and get them charged. They're guilty."

"I'm inclined to agree I guess," said Alistair Probe looking miserable, "but my God they had reason enough."

"Poppycock," muttered Slighman inaudibly.

"Okay Bonnie, it's your case," said Superintendent Smart, "what do you think?"

"Well…yes…the case against them looks sound, but…there's a couple of things. Firstly, they would undoubtedly have been charged already had they not got an awkward little alibi…namely a conviction for the theft of a toaster. I've spoken with the Procurator and she's of the opinion that we'll have to deal with that conviction before we can proceed with an arres…"

"Oh I don't believe it!" howled Inspector Slighman, throwing his pen across the table.

"Well, I'm afraid we're stuck with it. She said that…eh…in her opinion, because they obviously won't appeal against their sentences, that we'll have to move for a Royal Prerogative of Mercy…"

"…A what?"

"…A Royal Prerogative of Mercy…it's granted by the Queen, but on the advice of the First Minister. It would revoke their sentence."

"Good God Bonnie – how long's all this going to take?" The superintendent was aghast.

"Pass. Don't know. Weeks I would guess. Months maybe."

"Bloody hell…unbelievable."

"Well, we'll get that particular ball rolling tomorrow."

"Er…you said there were two things Bonnie…what's the second?" asked DS Munro, assuming his favourite 'for use in meetings only' dim expression.

"The second thing is that whatever we've thrown at the Solent brothers so far, they've reacted with a relaxed smile – up to now they appear to have been pulling the strings. Maybe they still are."

"No way Bonnie – this photograph changes everything," said Inspector Slighman, "we've got them where we want them now."

"Well I would still like to speak with their niece – it's rather a strange coincidence that she's disappeared on a camping holiday at the same time as all this is going on."

"Maybe just keeping her out of harm's way Bonnie," suggested Alistair Probe, "wouldn't want her disclosing things at the wrong time…so off they send her on her jolly hols."

"Hm. Maybe Alistair. Anyhow, DS Munro and I are off to Edinburgh after this to speak with the brothers – confront them with this new evidence…gauge their reaction."
Meeting ends.

Chapter 26

DI Blackthorn and DS Munro sat in a companionable silence as they passed Loch Lubnaig on their way south towards Edinburgh.

A radio call came in from Sergeant Silver to tell them Damien Gridning had delivered his smart phone, and an initial check on the photograph and the phone itself had confirmed the metadata was sound so it was almost definitely taken at 6.27 on the 5th of June and a quick run through an image verification programme had shown nothing untoward. There were no dodgy halos...all the shadows were in the right place...etc. It seemed perfectly bona-fide. It was undoubtedly the murder layby. And Damien himself was undoubtedly on Ben Dorain on the morning in question as about thirty other photographs on the phone testified. His enthusiastic description of hill conditions, companions and routes all added further verification. Additional checks would be carried out on the photograph and device in Glasgow in the morning but it was pretty safe to accept its authenticity.

The silence resumed as they churned the case over in their minds as they drove along the A84 towards Edinburgh. Ben had not yet met the Solent brothers.

"So what are they like? These brothers," he asked breaking the silence.

"Well...," replied Bonnie, expelling a long breath, "...they're about the last people on earth you'd expect to commit murder."

"So I'd heard Ma'am."

"Yes. They're just such...erm...well...they're charming really. They're open...and they have an aura of...of decency about them."

"Well if it *was* them that bumped the scumbag off...they certainly had good reason Ma'am. I've seen the results of some of his handiwork down south. Not pretty. If ever anybody got his just desserts, it's him."

The inspector's mobile rang with Kathy's ringtone.

"Hi Honeybunch."

"Mum where are you?"

"On my way to Edinburgh darling..."

"...What?...again?"

"...This is only the second time Kathy...and I'll be home tomorrow."

"But it's my piano lesson tonight Mum."

"Yes I know sweetheart...your uncle Joe's taking you."

"What about my subject choice for next year?...that has to be in for tomorrow morning."

"Eh...that's the first I've heard of it."

"Well...I forgot yesterday...and the day before..."

"Oh Kathy! Honestly...well you'll just have to ask your dad to help."

"But Mum...he doesn't know his arse from his elbow about school subjects."

"Kathy! Watch your language."

"Well, it's true Mum."

Sergeant Munro tried, with little success, to hide a grin.

"Oh for heaven's sake Kathy. Well I'll phone you about them later this evening."

"Okay Mum. Bye."

"Bye Darling."

DS Munro jammed the car into third gear as they caught up with a wayfaring caravan on a series of S-bends. His mobile rang. Becky. It was on loudspeaker and lodged safely on the dashboard so he prodded to receive call.

"Hi Becky."

"Hi there sexy squirrel."

"Errrm…" squeaked Ben as the car veered to within an inch of the ditch, "I'm in the car with DI Blackthorn Becky…"

"Oops. Sorry Ben…er…Sergeant…oh dear…" Suppressed giggle.

Ben glanced red-faced at DI Blackthorn whose turn it now was to try hiding a grin.

"Er…what do you want Becky?"

"Right…sorry Ben…mrmmg." Her giggle-stifling was poor. "Sorry…it's actually police business Sarge."

"Really?"

"Yes…" continued Becky getting herself under control, "…it could be something or nothing, but I drove up this morning and arrived at a campsite a couple of hours ago at Loch Gaurley…"

"…Yes I know the one."

"Well, as I was entering the site some cars were leaving…and I just happened to glance at the last one which was crammed with gear and I noticed a 'Coblinson Bakery' carrier bag in the back window…"

"Yes?"

"Well, it rang a bell Sarge. I knew I'd seen a shop quite recently called that but I couldn't place it for the life of me. So, after I'd pitched my wee tent I went for a drive to get a signal so I could Google it…and guess what…there are only three Coblinson Bakery branches and one of them is just round the corner from where Jessica Woodfile lives."

DI Blackthorn and DS Munro looked at each other. Serious now.

"Really?"

"Yes, so I shot back to the campsite and asked about them at reception. The man there could remember absolutely nothing about them – it's a big campsite and busy as hell this time of year.

"How did they pay?"

"Almost everybody pays cash – they're mostly one-nighters — and he couldn't even say which receipts were theirs. But no Woodfiles or Carnthwaites. And all I noticed as I passed them was that they turned north as they were leaving the campsite.

There were three or four cars but whether or not they were travelling together – or even had anything to do with each other - I haven't a clue. The last car…the one with the carrier bag… was red, but that's as much as I can tell you."

Ben looked at his superior officer and gestured enquiringly towards the mobile phone.

"Hi Becky…DI Blackthorn here. Nice to talk to you."

"Hello Ma'am…yes nice to talk to you too."

"Good work there Becky. Excellent in fact – I'd love to have a word with the Andrea Woodfile– if it's her. If they turned north then they're heading into our neck of the woods. I'll get on to it right away. Thanks again Becky. I'll say goodbye…d'you want to speak to the squirrel again?"

"Errggm…no thanks Ma'am."

Bonnie picked up the radio, made contact with DS Silver and passed on the news from Becky.

"Let's have a good look for her Bob, I'd really like to speak with her. Check every campsite in the area – must be dozens. Not much to go on I know…two English women and a red car…but could be well worth the effort. How many patrol cars out at the moment?"

"Er…just a second Ma'am….six I think."

"Right, get them the details in case they come across the car…and we can afford to get one of them to check campsites. See if Mike Beech and…what's his name…Fred Wyre are out there – they've been involved with the case already – it was them that found the motorbike."

"I'll get on to it right away Ma'am."

...

PC Wyre picked up the radio handset.

"Car 105."

"Is that Copper Beech?"

Sigh. "Nope, it's Copper Wyre."

"Hi Fred – Bob Silver here…where are you?"

"Just approaching Ballachulish from Glen Coe."

"Right, I've got a job I want you to do."

"Okay Sarge…shoot."

"Right, the niece and aunt of the Toaster brothers may be camping in the neighbourhood – Jessica and Andrea Woodfile - but they might not be using those names. We think they're driving a red car with a 'Coblinson Bakery' carrier bag in the rear window…if it's still there. We don't know what they look like unfortunately…Andrea's in her early twenties…that's about all we can say. Bonnie's going to try and drum up a photograph of them from one of her brothers down in England…till then that's all we've got to go on. Have a look round some campsites anyhow. If you think you've found them, tread very lightly. Don't approach them – don't show any interest - but let me know immediately okay?"

"Okay Sarge."

PC Wyre replaced the handset.

"Well, that should be easy enough. Scour sixteen hundred square miles of the Scottish Highlands looking surreptitiously for a baker's bag in a red car."

"Yep, like looking for a needle in a haystack without letting the haystack know what you're up to."

"Easy-peasy. What a joke."

"Yup. Eh…?...bloody Nora! That car we just passed parked by the Tourist Information Office…that's it!"

"You jest."

"I jest you not. Red car, Coblinson Bakery bag. We've found them…I even got the number."

"Clever boy. Better call Bob."

Bob Silver approached the red car, which had been followed to Fort William and was now the only car parked in the car park at Old Inverlochy Castle. The occupants, two women, were just getting out.

"Good afternoon, I'm Sergeant Bob Silver from Auchtergarry Police...may I have a quick word please?"

They answered warily, but in the affirmative.

"Are you by any chance Jessica and Andrea Woodfile?"

"Yes, we are. Nothing wrong is there?" answered Jessica.

"No no, not at all, but we're investigating the murder of John Bair...er...Big Bruno...and we believe that you, Andrea, have had dealings with him in the past."

She took a deep breath. "Yes, I did. He supplied me with drugs...cocaine mostly...but that was well over three years ago. I haven't touched anything stronger than coffee since then...thanks to family support and an excellent psychotherapist."

"Erm...this may be quite a sensitive question Andrea...was he threatening, violent or abusive towards you?"

Andrea took another deep breath and looked Sergeant Silver straight in the eye.

"Yes he was. I was late paying him twice. He was very threatening. Very threatening indeed. Left me in no doubt as to my fate if I didn't pay up. He grabbed me by my hair the first time. Very painful...and very, very frightening. I was petrified. But the second time he not only grabbed me by the hair...he hit my head against a door. He permanently damaged my left eye...I can see fairly well enough with it but, as you can see, I still can't open it properly. I'm glad he's dead. He was a brute. He also beat up a close and lovely friend of mine who was late with her money. Thankfully she's clean too now...but she has a limp now, thanks to him. I've no idea who killed him, but I wish him, or her, well."

"Me too," added her mother, "he damaged so many lives...so many families. Good riddance to him. Evil man."

Chapter 27

George Solent answered the door.

"Inspector Blackthorn! How nice to see you..." His broad smile was spontaneous and natural. "...Please come in. What a pleasant surprise."

"Er thank you Mr Solent...this is Sergeant Munro."

"Hello Sergeant – good to meet you...come in...come in."

He led them through their wonderfully comfortable front-room and out into their back garden with its panoramic views of Edinburgh.

"Peter's here...we've just been playing golf...and having a small glass of wine. The women-folk are away for the weekend so it's just the two of us."

Peter stood up and was introduced in turn to Sergeant Munro.

"Do sit down..."

"...Thank you."

"...would you care for a small glass...?"

"No...no thanks. Strictly business I'm afraid."

"Oh well...how can we help you today then Inspector?"

"Well, I presume you've seen the photograph on the front page of today's Post..."

"Oh yes indeed, we have. It's what we were talking about before you rang the doorbell..." said George "...it's...um...a bit strange isn't it?"

"Er...in what way is it strange Mr Solent?"

"Well, disregarding all the utter hogwash that idiot has written about us being heroes...it almost looks as if we really were there doesn't it? They certainly look a bit like us from a distance...but of course, as you know, we were nowhere near the place. Is the photograph genuine...d'you think?"

"We believe it is Mr Solent…" said Sergeant Munro, "…and to be honest, such is the weight of evidence against you now, that if you hadn't been convicted in the Toasting case you'd be under arrest by now and charged with the murder of John Bair."

"Weight of evidence? Murder?"

"Well, sir," said Bonnie, "we now know that John Bair…'Big Bruno' if you like…had an utterly devastating effect upon your family. He severely beat your brother Douglas – to his lasting detriment. His father also beat up your father. Your parents…and indeed the whole family…split up because of it…and, as if that wasn't enough, your niece Andrea became badly caught in his sticky web. These are fairly strong motives for murder gentlemen." The brothers looked seriously at each other but remained silent.

"To say nothing of your fingerprints being on the murder weapon," added DS Munro.

"Oh dear," Peter smiled sadly, "with all that going against us then, it's just as well we have that Toasting conviction."

"You may not have that conviction for much longer Mr Solent," said the sergeant, "we're looking to have it overturned…by using the Royal Prerogative of Mercy."

"By using what?"

"The Royal Prerogative of Mercy – it's rarely used – but in a case where new evidence is available…and where the person or persons convicted clearly won't appeal against their sentences…because they give them alibis for a much more serious crime…namely murder…then it's our only option."

"I'm a bit confused here," said George, "I can see why you might think we have murdered Big Bruno…which, let me assure you, we most certainly did not…but explain again about this 'Royal Mercy' thing."

"Well," explained DI Blackthorn, "clearly you won't appeal against your Toasting sentences…because they give you an alibi…but the evidence we now have suggests you were actually elsewhere when Inspector Slighman's toaster was stolen…so we have to find another way to have those sentences of petty theft overturned so you can be tried for killing John Bair."

"But surely this 'Royal Prerogative' thing is going to take forever," said Peter.

"It certainly won't be quick."

There was a moment's silence as they all took breath. The evening sun glowing orange on Blackford Hill and Arthur's Seat went unnoticed.

"Look," said George, "this is ridiculous…we obviously need to speed this nonsense up – if you believe we should be tried for murder then we are certainly not going to stand in your way. We, more than anyone, need the truth to emerge. Let's get to trial I say…the sooner the better – what about you Peter?...do you agree?"

"Absolutely George. Of course I agree. Let's get our names cleared."

"Right," continued George, "I have a suggestion…Peter had nothing whatsoever to do with the theft of Inspector Slighman's toaster. As he told you when we were first arrested, he was elsewhere…but…er…well, unfortunately he can't remember where. He simply agreed to a confession in order to help minimise our sentences. So he'll be perfectly willing to appeal against the sentence. As for me…well I clearly don't want to appeal against a crime which I readily admit to having carried out…but to show good faith and to get things moving for you and dispense with this 'Royal Mercy' nonsense…I'd be more than willing to appeal against my conviction on the grounds that because of my exemplary record I should have been acquitted with just a warning. How's that? Peter? Would you agree to that?"

"Of course I would. I know absolutely that we're innocent of Big Bruno's murder…and as I've said all along, I had nothing to do with the theft of the toaster…or the statuette…or anything else for that matter.. As far as I'm concerned, if it helps the police in any way to get to the bottom of all this then I'm more than willing to cooperate – to appeal...and even stand trial for murder if we must. Let's go for it."

DI Blackthorn and DS Munro were briefly rendered speechless.

"Well, gentlemen," said DI Blackthorn in a state of some shock, "thank you very much for that, but I must repeat that the evidence against you is overwhelming. You're staring life-imprisonment in the face."

"Surely not Inspector..." said George "...surely not. I have great faith in our system of justice. The truth will prevail in the end."

"I couldn't agree more..." added his brother ...I couldn't agree more."

"Well...I'll phone you as soon as I can to let you know what's happening regarding this."

"Fine," said George, "better phone my land line, I can't find my mobile anywhere."

"Okay, and thanks again gentlemen."

The sun was setting as DI Blackthorn and DS Munro drove over Braid Hills Road. Bonnie, driving for once, stopped the car, switched off the engine, and took a breather while enjoying the panorama of low sunlight dappling a darkening Edinburgh.

"What an incredible pair of guys," said DS Munro shaking his head, "absolutely incredible."

"Well I did warn you they were very likeable...but even I can hardly believe they're willing to appeal. Simplifies things so much."

"So, what kind of time-scale are we looking at now Ma'am?"

"Well...I'm no expert...but they'll certainly get leave to appeal - George against his sentence and Peter against his conviction. Incredibly, all parties want the same outcome...so hopefully it won't take too long Ben. Depends on the backlog of cases I suppose. A bit of wheel-oiling might speed it up...who knows?"

"And as soon as the appeal goes through we arrest the Solents for murder?"

"'Fraid so Ben."

"How do you feel about all this anyhow Ma'am? I mean Bruno was an evil bastard...hospitalising people...Jesus...and probably even worse for all we know. Ruining lives by the dozen...and here we are pushing for a murder conviction against a pair of guys like these. Christ, they could hardly be more upright."

"Yes, it's a tough one. He was a vicious monster. And I don't doubt that his methods caused more than one premature death, but I guess murder's murder ...it's not an eye for an eye these days Ben...they shouldn't have taken the law into their own hands."

"Hm. That may be true but the law hadn't done much to help them though, had it?...they had reported him twice remember. The law hadn't helped the rest of Bruno's victims either for that matter. It'd done bugger all in fact."

"No, you're right Ben. Witness intimidation and disposable underlings saw to that. The brothers have my total sympathy, they really do. Not only that, I actually like the pair of them. They are undoubtedly decent men, but unfortunately I have no option but to press for a conviction. And nor do you Ben. It's our job as law enforcement officers. Damn it."

"Anyhow, Ma'am, if, as is now pretty clear, they didn't steal Slighman's toaster...then who the hell did?"

"Who indeed Ben. I certainly don't know...and we'll probably never know."

Chapter 28

Inspector Slighman sat looking confident, but feeling far from it, as the recruitment panel took their seats. The Toaster nightmare and the Och Aye Murder had consumed him completely. Instead of weeks of measured preparation, he had been reduced to some frantic mugging-up of interview skills the previous evening on the train coming down to Manchester, and then in his hotel room throughout the entire night. Never had he drunk so much coffee. His head buzzed. And, over and above all that, what if they'd been monitoring his work in Auchtergarry? What if one of his many enemies had enlightened them to the truth regarding his less than glorious role in the theft of the damn toaster?...or the constant leaks to the press when he was supposed to be in charge of security?...or his absolute certainty regarding the about-to-be-overturned guilt of the Toasters...?...what if?...what if? Impossible to tell anything from the faces in front of him. Remember...meaningful but not overdone eye contact; don't gabble, don't fidget, don't slouch...not too rigid though; repeat the question if you need time to think; ask for clarification if you don't understand the question; don't repeat memorised answers parrot-fashion; you're a mature and intelligent law officer...don't forget it...oh shit...

"Good morning Inspector Slighman, and...er...welcome. As you know, I'm Chief Superintendent Theodore Greenside and I am the...ah... senior officer on this panel. As you know, this is the final stage before selection for the post of Chief Inspector." CS Greenside was a large man with a red bespectacled face, thick white hair, and a slight air of absent-mindedness.

"Good morning Sir, and thank you."

"I must warn you, however..." he paused, agonisingly for Inspector Slighman, leaned back and gazed briefly at the ceiling, "...that there are, as I'm sure you're aware, four other applicants for this post, and that although we will make our selection within the next few weeks...erm...that decision will be not announced, to you or to anyone else, for...erm...a considerable number of weeks. Red-tape unfortunately Inspector...we're having to wait for the new rules governing Subsection Eight paragraph four of our practices and processes...er manual...thing...erm...to be ratified. I'm sure you understand Inspector."

"Of course...yes...perfectly," replied the inspector, baffled. He had hoped to be in his new post before the murder trial began. Ah well, courage Slighman, courage.

"The thing is..." continued CS Greenside, once more leaning back and focusing on a light-fitting almost directly over his head, "...we put the advert in a couple of months too early really...but...well...you know..."

"Indeed Sir."

"Anyhow, let's get on with it." The Chief Superintendent returned to a more upright sitting position and introduced the other members of the panel; Chief Inspector Maxwell Latterby – Traffic Department; Detective Chief Inspector Freda Frobisher – Specialist Organised and Economic Crime; Detective Chief Inspector Robert McPrint - Homicide and Serious Crime Section; and Sergeant Mahalia Abimbola from the Federation who was there to ensure adherence to correct protocol.

"Chief Inspector Latterby, would you like to kick off?"

"Yes Sir, thank you. Er...Inspector Slighman...nice to meet you." CI Latterby had an aura of slight superiority about him.

"Thank you Sir."

"Erm...clearly Inspector Slighman, as a Chief Inspector you would expect to have a team to manage. Yes?" Slighman nodded an intelligent nod. "Right, give us a rundown, if you would, Inspector, of how you would set realistic, specific, measurable, achievable, and time-targeted goals for your team."

"Er...yes..." began Inspector Slighman, his mind a hopeless blank, "...I'd...erm.." he pulled his face into a mature and erudite expression, and was about repeat an 'erm' and a 'yes', when CS Greenside, in the act of straightening up once more, caught his sleeve on the edge of his chair and sent his pen spinning across the top of the table and on to the floor. CI Latterby and DCI McPrint, bending over simultaneously to retrieve it cracked their heads together with a dull shuddering clunk.

"Oh dear...you chaps all right? Not hurt are you?" enquired a concerned CS Greenside.

"Eh?...what?...hurt?...eh...no   no, not at all," said CI Latterby tenderly holding a closed eye.

"No no. Fine." Said DCI McPrint now sporting a slightly swollen lip.

"Good...good...er...what was your question again Max...er Chief Inspector Latterby?" asked CS Greenside.

"Erm...er...what   was   it?...ah...yes...erm...goals   Inspector Slighman. Goals."

"Right...er...well, first and foremost...ah...I'd make sure they were...erm...achievable,   realistic...erm...specific...measurable, and er...time-targeted. Definitely time-targeted. And certainly specific. Sir."

"Very good...yes excellent. Thank you Inspector," said the temporarily one-eyed and utterly disorientated Chief Inspector.

"DCI McPrint? Your question?" The Chief Superintendent, having facilitated continuity, leaned back and studied the egg-and-dart frieze running round the top of the walls.

"Yeth, thank you," said the somewhat dazed DCI gingerly fingering his now very swollen lip with one hand and groping for his question sheet with the other. "Yeth. Right. Er... Inthpector, could you give uth an idea of what your role ith within your current team, what egthact input you perthonally have made to improve ith functionality, and how you thee thith tranthferring to the potht here ath detailed in the job dethcription?"

Ah, this was more like it. A question he understood. A question he had managed some preparation for. Deep breath…and onwards.

"Yes of course. Thank you Sir. I have two…er…connected…roles at present in our major ongoing investigation into the murder of John Bair. I'm in charge of internal security - keeping a lid on leaks mostly, and I'm also press officer. As you can no doubt imagine media interest has been worldwide and intense throughout the case …." The Inspector answered the question at some length, although he was aware that the Chief Superintendent remained absorbed with the intricacies of the egg-and-dart frieze and that Latterby and McPrint were both clearly still in a state of some shock and no little pain. "…And…" he finished, eventually, "…I fully believe I can bring this professionalism, and these strengths, building on them even further, to the post…to the challenge indeed… of Chief Inspector here in this Division."

There was a brief silence till Chief Superintendent Greenside awoke to fact that he was required yet again.

"Er yes…very good. Excellent in fact Inspector. Ehrm…who's next? Ah…yes..DCI Frobisher…could we have a question from you please?"

DCI Freda Frobisher was a dedicated, hard-working, and efficient police officer but she was precisely eight working days away from retirement and had four days annual leave still due…so, effectively she had another four working days left as a police officer. She had been drafted on to this promotion panel at the last minute to stand in for a sick colleague and, quite frankly, as a life-long Italophile her head was firmly in Italy. Bergamo, Milan, Rome, Naples and then, possibly, the whole of Sicily. Oh yes yes yes. Starting next week…a leisurely tour - two months…three months…maybe forever…who knew? And best of all…meeting up with Sophia…ah Sophia…her *nuovo amante segreto*…her new secret Italian lover. Heaven.

"Er..Inspector Slighman…good morning."

"Good morning Ma'am."

"Inspector…"

"Yes…"

"…We all have weaknesses Inspector. What would you say your greatest weakness is…in a professional sense?" True, she had yanked the question off Google a mere twenty minutes earlier, but it would have to do.

"Ah yes…of course..." Manna! Clara had told him, in a tiny window of some mutual near-congeniality, that this was a potential question. Now, which answer to choose? Being too much of a perfectionist?…being over-conscientious?...being perhaps a little too popular with those under him?...right…here goes…

"…Well Ma'am, I would regard my inability, on occasion, to switch off from work…you know…being over-conscientious and working too hard really, to be my …" On he droned. Nobody listened. Freda Frobisher was miles away…Tuscany, Chianti, Frascati, Prosecco, Bruschetta, Tortelloni alla zucca –Sophia - aaahhh. Latterby and McPrint were both in dire need of paracetemol or stronger and had zero interest in Slighman's weaknesses. The Chief Superintendent was re-planning his allotment, and Sergeant Abimbola recognised a prat when she saw one and had switched off some time back.

"…so I would say…" said Slighman, drawing his rather lengthy soliloquy to a conclusion "…that in this way I have turned around the weakness of perhaps being a little too…er….shall we say 'popular' with my team…into a strength." Oh shit! He had started with the 'over-conscientious' weakness, babbled brainlessly for five minutes, and somehow managed to end up with the 'over-popular' one! Imbecile! He looked frantically from face to face. Everyone was now looking at him.

"Thank you Inspector Slighman," said DCI Frobisher snapping off from a balmy evening at the opera in Verona, "thank you very much indeed. A good answer, I thought. Yes. Thanks again." She smiled encouragingly.

The other faces round the table were nodding together in wise agreement. Slighman relaxed his knotted stomach and took a long slow breath. Whew.

Another round of questions...another round of completely ignored rambling answers. The Inspector was nearing exhaustion.

CS Greenside realised that he hadn't actually asked a question himself yet but felt sure he ought to have asked at least one. He could only think of two of his pre-rehearsed questions – one about attention to detail – the other about using humour in the workplace.

"Erm...one final question, Inspector, give us an example of ...erm...ah...your attention to detail."

Slighman's overworked and over-caffeined brain shut down. Eh? What? Attention to detail? Merde. Nothing there. Say something for God's sake Jonathan. Anything. Now.

"Er...well...I always...er...blow my nose....umm...before...um... weighing myself, Sir."

The Chief Superintendent gaped briefly, and then broke into a proper Santa Clause of a laugh.

"Oh ha ha! Wonderful...well Inspector you certainly answered any concerns about a sense of humour eh? A wonderful reply! So quick...so witty! Ho ho!"

Inspector Slighman's returning smile had a bewildered edge to it. What was that all about?

"Right, everyone..." said CS Greenside now under control, "...that's about it. Erm...Sergeant Abimbola? Would you like to have an input at this stage?"

"Thank you Sir. Only to comment that all protocols have been correctly observed...except that the applicant hasn't been offered the opportunity to ask the panel questions himself."

"Of course, of course...sorry Inspector. Do you...ah...have anything you would like to ask the panel?"

One last effort, and thankfully he was primed to respond. Good old Carla.

"Er...yes thanks. What would you say was the most challenging aspect of the post...if I were to I be appointed?"

Chief Superintendent Greenside looked round the table.

"Bob?...er...DCI McPrint...would you like to answer that...you'll probably be working fairly closely with the new post-holder."

"Thertainly Thir. Er...yeth, Inthpector Thlighman, I should shink the motht challenging athpect of the posht ith probably dealing with the preth. Thpeaking on the hoof...unrehearthed, tho to thpeak. That thort of thing...er ethpeschially when dealing with theriouth ischueth." concluded the DCI.

Theriouth ischueth? Inspector Slighman tried not to look puzzled.

CS Greenside, gathered up his papers, "Right...thankth...er...thanks Bob. That's fine. If nobody has anything else to add, then I guess that's it. We'll let you know our decision in the fullness of time Inspector Slighman. And thankth again."

Chapter 29

The brothers' appeals breezed through the appeal court, meaning they were now declared innocent of the crime of toaster theft. With their alibi of being elsewhere at the time of Big Bruno's demise now carefully removed, DI Blackthorn was free, somewhat against her better judgment, to arrest them and charge them both with his murder. This rather pleased Superintendent Smart who had his force's reputation to think about; absolutely delighted Inspector Slighman who had his career to think about; energised Billy Bootle who had circulation figures to think about; and somewhat saddened everyone else...except for the brothers themselves who appeared to be neither up nor down about the whole thing.

The nation, at least as it was reflected in the pages of the Daily Post, was outraged that these two men, now regarded as national treasures, should be facing possible long-term imprisonment for what was, in the Daily Post's eyes, an act of outstanding bravery and public service. Billy Bootle, as he had promised to DI Blackthorn, started a 'Free the Toasters' campaign which occupied at least part of the Post's front page every day. He unearthed dozens of Big Bruno's erstwhile victims and ran half a dozen of their heart-rending stories in every edition. The Post's online petition was under constant threat of collapse due to the sheer number of people trying to sign it. The nation had been mobilised.

...

The crowd outside Edinburgh's High Court had started to gather at five in the morning. Spaces in the public gallery were going to be at a premium and anyone turning up after six o'clock had no chance. But the crowd grew on. Some enterprising souls were loudly selling pin badges depicting a slice of toast sporting the words 'Free Them Now'. Others were selling wristbands and posters, sandwiches and pies, umbrellas and plastic macs, the Record, the Herald, and the Socialist Worker...the atmosphere was truly carnival. Cafés in the neighbourhood couldn't produce slices of toast fast enough to keep up with demand. The High Street buzzed from the Tron Kirk to the Lawn Market, and a dozen students had been hired to mingle with the crowd and had out free copies of the Daily Post which had **'Och Aye' Murder Trial – Day One** emblazoned across its front page.

A police cordon allowed access to the courthouse. The main protagonists, as they arrived, were greeted either with cheers and whistles, or boos and whistles, depending on whether they were trying to convict or free the brothers. The loudest boos were reserved for the man appointed advocate depute – the prosecutor. He was a very large, jutting-jawed, rather hunched-over man with thick brown hair and bushy eyebrows, who went by the name of Darquan Strong. No shrinking violet he, as he strode, nay, swept, glowering happily through the jeering throng.

The loudest cheers, of course, were for the Defence Counsel. His name was Milton Wilkie of Wilkie and Thinne WS. His attempt to emulate the majestic sweep of Darquan Strong failed somewhat as he had neither the stature, the jaw, the hair, nor the chutzpah for it, but the people were on his side, and although he tripped a little, he didn't actually fall. Police witnesses were roundly booed as a matter of course, except Bonnie, naturally. Her consideration for the brothers seemed to have made itself known to the populace at large and somehow, although she was the chief investigative officer, she was regarded as a friend in the enemy's camp. And quite a dishy friend at that.

...

And so day one of the trial began: the forensic details; the questioning of witnesses; the accusations; the denials; the overblown theatrics from prosecution and defence; the occasionally suffocating hide-bound traditions of procedure; the moments of high drama... the hours of low drama...the occasional lapses into snoozeville.

By the end of the day, everyone was a little more informed, and perhaps a little wiser.

Chapter 30

The tables at La Grande Assiette had all been booked weeks in advance. It had always been advisable to reserve a table here, but since the brothers' rise to icon status, demand had rocketed and places were at a premium. With the added attraction of the trial, the clamour for tables had gone through the roof. For the next few days at least, this was where the movers and shakers of the land were to be found. And, where there were movers and shakers to be found...there in their midst was Carla Slighman, poised and ready to network. Husband Jonathan sat with her, but he was far from poised, and networking was the last thing he wanted to do.

"I can't believe I let you talk me in to coming here," said he.

"Oh Jonathan do be quiet. Sit up properly...and please, please, take off those ridiculous glasses."

"I daren't. I shouldn't even be here."

"Oh for God's sake stop speaking tosh. Who cares if you're here or not – and nobody here is going to know who you are anyhow."

"Eh? I'm a major figure in this trial you know...of course people know me. And I shouldn't be here."

"God, you're so deluded! And trying to look like Hank Marvin isn't going to help."

"Look like whom?"

"Hank Mar...oh never mind. Who's that man over there? He keeps looking over and smiling...the one at the table under the Baroque mirror?"

"The what?"

"The Baroque mirr...oh never mind...the sleazy looking bloke with the bow-tie."

Jonathan turned his head and groaned. "Oh no. Anyone but him. It's Billy bloody Bootle. God Almighty...why why why did I let you talk me into coming here. Oh Jesus - and that's his photographer sitting with him. I must be insane."

"Bloody hell Jonathan calm down. He's not going to be writing about you now is he? He has more important fish to fry. Actually...I might just pop over and have a word with him at some point...he could prove useful."

"Eh?! You'll do no such thing! He's a monster."

"Jonathan, I'll do precisely as I please thank you very much. Monster or no monster...he might prove useful at some point. For information...contacts...that sort of thing."

"Carla, it's only a few weeks ago that you wanted me to punch him."

"You have to learn to move on Jonathan. Dynamics change."

"Really? Well do tell..." he was brought to halt by a sudden hush in the restaurant and a gasp of surprise from Carla who was staring past him towards the restaurant door. He turned to determine the cause, and there, smiling calm benevolent smiles, were the Toaster brothers threading their way through the food and drink-laden tables of their beautiful restaurant, commanding the focus of every eye. Jonathan immediately raised his hand to his brow and tried to hide behind it. To no avail.

"Inspector Slighman! How wonderful!" exclaimed George as he approached their table.

"Yes, how delightful!" agreed Peter.

"What a pleasure to have you in our restaurant!" they said in near unison. Every eye had now switched to Jonathan who tried to minimise himself behind the pepper-grinder. He offered a frail smile. Carla offered an intercontinental-roomdazzler.

"And this must be..."

"Er, my wife, Carla."

"How marvelous to meet you Mrs Slighman," said George bowing a little, "and may I wish you the warmest of welcomes to La Grande Assiette. I'm so glad you've chosen to eat here tonight – we are honoured by your presence…and whatever you choose this evening will of course be on the house."

"It will indeed," added Peter, "and I'll have a bottle of our very best Chateau de Neuvvy le Barrois sent over immediately…you like champagne Mrs Slighman?"

"Oh thank you so much! Yes of course…but you must call me Carla!"

"Well, thank you Carla…I'm Peter, and this is George. If you haven't chosen yet, I can fully recommend the Soupe à l'Oignon Gratinée – with perhaps the Poulet Chasseur…or le Filet de Saumon au Beurre Rouge to follow. But whatever you choose – I think you will enjoy it." He smiled and bowed a friendly bow.

"Why, thank you so much Peter…and George. How terribly kind." Carla hit them again with the full global radiance. "Isn't that wonderful Jonathan?"

"Er…yes…of course," said the incredibly shrinking police inspector desperately forcing a smile, "thank you, gentlemen."

"No no, Inspector, thank you!"

With this the brothers took their leave and headed for the kitchens. The eyes of the diners slowly peeled away from the Slighman's table and the conversation re-assumed normal levels.

"Oh Jonathan, how wonderful," Carla whispered, still in a euphoric state, "but I can't believe they're not in custody…I thought everyone facing a murder…"

"…No no no, they got bail. But they'll be banged up for good at the end of this trial though. That should wipe the silly smiles off their faces."

"Jonathan! How could you?...they're lovely! Two nicer men I've never met…delightful… charming. Oh I do hope they get off."

"Carla! They stole our toaster remember!"

"Oh who cares about a silly toaster Jonathan. Borrow a step-ladder…get over it."

"What!? They're evil Carla…and they may have derailed my application for Chief Inspector."

"Oh really…well, Jonathan…that's more like it…how evil can you get? They definitely deserve a life sentence for that. Idiot. If anyone's screwed that up it's you yourself."

"They're murderers Carla."

"The man they killed, Jonathan, in case you hadn't noticed, was extreme low-life. A vicious, nasty, thug. An act of public service…that's what it was…done purely out of compassion for his victims. The whole nation is behind them…and quite rightly so. They're darlings Jonathan. Absolute darlings. And in any case…if, as you say, they nicked our toaster…they can't have murdered Bruno…now can they?"

Jonathan fumed impotently in the face of such unshakeable logic.

"Anyhow, everybody in the whole damned place knows who I am now. And they know that I've received a free meal…that could come back and bite me you know…I'm compromised now."

"Oh do stop talking rot Jonathan, nobody's even remotely interested in you. And stop writhing! Mmm…this champagne is divine."

Their meal was unquestionably the most delicious Carla had ever eaten – she floated on a cloud throughout. Five stars – unquestionably - from start to finish. Jonathan would have awarded one star…on the basis that it was free.

After a leisurely delicious, scrumptious, light and yummy dessert, a waiter appeared with a glass of Cointreau for Carla and a Drambuie for Jonathan.

"Compliments of Mr Bootle."

Carla turned and raised her glass at Billy Bootle, giving him the full benefit of her amazingly white even teeth and her dancing eyes. "Thank you," she mouthed. Jonathan glowered.

"How does that bastard know our favourite liqueurs?"

"Oh don't be such a conspiracy theorist Jonathan. Just enjoy it. Probably just guessed."

"Guessed my arse. He has ways of uncovering things...underhand, that's what he is. Devious. Oh God, he's coming over. Damn."

"Billy Bootle of the Daily Post....at your service Ma'am...you must be the lovely Carla. How awfully nice to meet you."

Carla beamed at him. "Why thank you Mr Bootle. Such a wonderful restaurant don't you think?"

"It certainly is Carla. And such a delight to see the brothers looking so well."

"Yes, they look marvellous don't they.

"I say, Jonners, old thing," said Bootle looking downwards, "those socks your mum knits for you are actually rather super. I like them."

Carla found this hilariously funny. Not so Jonathan.

"Bootle...how in Hell's name do you know my mother knits my socks?"

"Oh, Felix must have mentioned it I suppose."

"Felix!? You've been speaking to our son?!"

"Oh hasn't he told you?...he phoned me up...he's going to do his school work-experience with me for a week at the Post. Such a talented lad – unbounded energy too – he'll certainly go far."

Carla's smile widened markedly. "Oh how terribly kind of you Billy! No, he hadn't got round to mentioning it. That's wonderful."

Bootle smiled, giving a rare display of his gold-fillings, and took his leave.

"Kind!? Wonderful?! Are you mad Carla? The Daily Post's a nasty evil rag. The very lowest of the tabloids."

"Mm...well maybe," replied Carla, calmly sipping her Cointreau "but it's jolly successful. He'll get an excellent insight into the cut and thrust of business life there."

What an evening she was having. The best ever. She felt an overwhelming sense of well-being, and the look of sullen tantrum on Jonathan's face made everything just that little bit more toothsome.

Chapter 31

The trial progressed. Days came and went. The brothers duly testified...as did everyone else connected with the case. Every detail was weighed and examined; every observation dissected; every recollection quizzed and queried; every nuance prodded. For six full days the hearing of evidence advanced painstakingly, until, on the afternoon of the seventh, came the closing statements by the defence, the prosecution, and the judge:

Mr Milton Wilkie, defence advocate, ambled over to the jury-box to give his final statement, and, in spite of thoughts to the contrary, gave it an earnest 'Ah good, I'm dealing with intelligent people' look. He rested his notes on the jury-box rail, clasped the lapels of his gown, and, in a high squeak, began his oration.

"Your Honour, ladies and gentlemen of the jury, we have now heard all of the evidence, and I put it to you that it is severely...nay...hopelessly, inconclusive. Everything we have seen and heard with regard to the murder of John Bair is...er...open to question. Wide open. We have before us two men accused of murder. Two men of immense character...two men whose probity is unquestioned...two men who have contributed hugely to their community and to society at large...two men who have become in the eyes of the nation, beacons of honour and integrity. Two men...who absolutely deny the crime of which they have been accused."

He stopped briefly to grab at his notes which had started to slide off the rail.

"If we...er... look at the evidence with a clear eye and an open mind, we see smoke and we see mirrors, ladies and gentlemen...we see nothing concrete upon which to convict such men."

He paused and gestured to the main exhibit with his small yellow pencil.

"As you know, the murder weapon...is a banjo. It is a banjo, it cannot be denied, which has the fingerprints of both of the accused upon it. But it also has the fingerprints of twenty-three other people on it, sixteen sets of which remain unidentified. Sixteen sets! How conclusive is that? Let me tell you, ladies and gentlemen, how conclusive it is - it isn't conclusive at all. It certainly isn't evidence enough to commit two decent men to life imprisonment. It's a wreath of smoke, that's all it is. A wreath of smoke.

"And this photograph. What are we to make of this photograph ladies and gentlemen? Can you identify the three people in this photograph? Of course you can't. And nor can I. Nobody can. So, somebody has orange trousers on...and somebody else is wearing a hat which, conceivably, could be a deerstalker. Is that conclusive? Of course it isn't. Damien Gridning, the young man who took the photograph happily recounts that he himself was wearing orange trousers on the day he took the photograph...chosen from a popular range of hiking gear, seemingly. Conclusive? I think not."

Mr Wilkie gave the jury a thoughtful gaze, twirled his small yellow pencil and walked back and forth a little - stopping once or twice to retrieve the pencil from the floor.

"And as for the nonsense of Big Bruno's mobile phone...well, that's just what it is isn't it? It's nonsense. *Och aye the noo mon?* Are we supposed to take this seriously? Surely not. Anyhow, nothing..." Milton Wilkie shook his head slowly in mock disbelief, "...and I repeat, nothing, can link the messages on that mobile telephone to these men in the dock.

"The same goes for the van with the whisky in it. No hint of a link there either. Smoke and mirrors ladies and..." drops pencil, picks pencil up, "...er...gentlemen...smoke and mirrors."

He paused, assumed what he believed to be a look of utter conviction in what he was about to say, and dropped his little yellow pencil again.

"Now, ladies and gentlemen, we must address the strange case of the theft of the toasting machine...a crime committed at precisely the same time as the murder...a crime perpetrated by someone who readily admits to it as a once-in-a-lifetime-aberration...a never-to-be-repeated moment of uncharacteristic impulsiveness....well, ladies and gentlemen of the jury, I put it to you that George Solent did indeed steal that toaster...probably with some assistance from Peter Solent...who..er... unfortunately...cannot remember where he was at the time of the crime..."

This prompted some laughter and subdued cheers from members of the public gallery, but they died a quick death as the Honourable Lady Gladys Brown mercilessly strafed them with some furious rapid eye movements.

"...And therefore they cannot possibly have been in the shadow of Ben Dorain murdering Big Bruno."

A few brave souls in the public gallery risked expulsion by muttering 'hear, hear'.

He paused again, put his pencil in his top pocket after only two attempts, took a deep breath and continued, looking just a little like a man who felt he still had a little mountain to climb.

"And now, ladies and gentlemen of the jury, what shall we make of the motive being cited for their imputed crime? The motive upon which the entire case rests. We are told that somehow, two men of previously impeccable character felt strongly enough about someone...felt hatred enough for someone...to plan and execute his cold blooded murder in broad daylight. Really? I think not. Yes, undoubtedly they had reason aplenty to dislike John Bair. We know from the evidence put before us over the last few days that John Bair was not a likeable man...far from it...but murder is not the answer to a problem like John Bair. No. And it certainly is not the answer that two such upright members of society as we have here before us, would arrive at. The answer they would arrive at would involve recourse to the law…an involvement of the police…not murder. And indeed, as the evidence told us, they did in fact twice report John Bair's behaviour to the police in Manchester. They did the right thing by doing that, ladies and gentlemen, and we have absolutely no reason…and certainly no evidence…to believe that they would ever do the very wrong thing…the ultimate wrong thing, namely, murder.

"In closing, ladies and gentlemen, let me reiterate that the evidence at no point, and I repeat, at no point, is remotely conclusive. Is there reasonable doubt?...of course there is. There is not one single piece of evidence which categorically and irrefutably links George and Peter Solent to the murder of John Bair. Not-one-single-shred. They are wisps of smoke ladies and gentlemen, wisps of smoke. And to convict such men as these…" he turned and gestured fulsomely to the men in the dock, "…these gentlemen…on wisps of smoke, would be a travesty. A terrible travesty. Thank you."

He sat down. Stood up again, removed his reading glasses from his chair, checked they weren't broken, and sat down once more.

A low hubbub of conversation broke out and was briefly tolerated by Lady Brown while everyone rearranged themselves, coughed, scratched, and searched for sweeties. The brothers could be seen exchanging whispers and smiling their gentle, imperturbable smiles.

"Thank you Mr Milkie…er Wilkie," said the Honourable Lady Brown. She then called upon the advocate depute to give the prosecution's closing remarks.

Up stood the imposing bulk of Darquan Strong, and the courtroom was immediately filled with his presence. He crossed the floor to assume his position in front of the jury and gave them a slow, relaxed, once-over which told them they needed guidance and enlightenment and that he was the very man to provide it.

"Your Honour, ladies and gentlemen of the jury…good afternoon." His rich deep voice carried effortlessly throughout the room.

"Let me begin, ladies and gentlemen, at the beginning. Please let me take you back to that bright morning in early June when, on Scotland's magnificent West Highland Way, a man, John Bair, known as Big Bruno, was murdered by being hit with a banjo. Coincidentally, at the same time a mere thirty-odd miles away as the crow flies, in the village of Lochain, a toaster, we hear, was being stolen by a man…or perhaps two men…whose fingerprints just happen to be, by pure coincidence on that very banjo. Hmm.

"Now, this toaster theft…ladies and gentlemen…it really had to be very well organised didn't it? The telephone call…the fore-knowledge of the police inspector's movements…the layout of the house…all had to be known in advance. And yet, we are asked to believe that George Solent, an upstanding member of the community, just happened to be passing, and on a wholly uncharacteristic whim, he nipped in and swiped the thing. Oh really? Don't you suspect, ladies and gentlemen, that as part of a grand plan carefully orchestrated by the two men here before you…" he gestured towards the dock, "…that the toaster was stolen by an as yet unidentified third party, or parties, freeing up the brothers to…er…shall we say…be elsewhere? And we all know where that elsewhere was…don't we? I certainly suspect that that's what happened…and if you're honest with yourselves…you must suspect it too."

The silence in the courtroom was profound. Prosecutor Strong flowed mellifluously on.

"We also now know, ladies and gentlemen, that on that morning in June a young man climbing the sweeping slopes of Ben Dorain happened to capture the murder scene on camera

256

mere seconds before the actual slaying took place. The photograph he took has been fully authenticated for both time and place, and everyone seems to be agreed that the big man in the centre dressed in black is indeed John Bair. But we are told that although the other two men in the picture happen to be of similar build to the Solent brothers, and are wearing clothes – orange trousers, and what looks mightily like a deerstalker hat – which have become the signature attire of George and Peter Solent...we are told that, once again, it's pure coincidence. And I say once again, oh really?"

Darquan Strong moved slowly to the other end of the jury box, rested his right elbow on its rail, and loosely clasped his left lapel with his left hand. He looked as if he owned the place.

"The mobile phone, ladies and gentlemen, and the van. Red herrings. Distractions. *Och aye the noo mon...?* Oh come on...a comic interlude, no more.

"But what is very far from comic, ladies and gentlemen, very far from comic indeed, is the motive behind the deed. As we have heard, John Bair and his father devastated the young lives of George and Peter Solent...their brother and their father both suffered terrible beatings at the hands of the Bairs, their parents split up because of it, and the young Solent brothers were torn away from their father, their brother, and their adored and loving sister. Oh yes, they had every reason to hate John Bair. Every reason to despise him.

"But more was to come. Many years later, they were to discover that their niece, their darling niece, their young and beautiful niece, had fallen into the nasty clutches of John Bair – and that she too had received a beating from him...such a beating that she still cannot fully open her left eye.

"What could they do? Well the right thing would be to report what they knew about John Bair to the police...which of course, they did. Twice, in fact, as we have heard. And what happened? Nothing happened. Absolutely nothing. Mr Bair continued precisely as before - completely unmolested and unhindered by the forces of the law. Why? Because...ladies and gentlemen...because the police were hamstrung. Oh yes, they were well aware of John Bair's vicious criminality. Well aware of the wretchedness and desolation he left in his unspeakable wake. They could have taken you to meet his countless, hapless victims...but these hapless victims, ladies and gentlemen, would say naught against John Bair.

"Fear, ladies and gentlemen. Fear and intimidation. The principles upon which John Bair based his terrible fiefdom. The principles which kept the police at bay.

"So what to do...ladies and gentlemen? How do two intelligent, morally upstanding men rid the world of a brutal, inhuman monster who has caused them and their loved ones untold misery?...a monster who they know is continuing to sow pain, despair, and woe throughout his realm as he savages his way through life. A man who has proved himself immune to the forces of law and justice. Well, we know what they did...don't we? Oh yes...we all know exactly what they did.

"These brothers...George and Peter Solent...the Toasters, if you like, are heroes throughout the land. Throughout Scotland...throughout the whole of the UK...and beyond. They are revered...venerated even. Why so? Why are they held in such esteem? Is it because they reported John Bair's crimes to the police? No, of course not. Is it because they *didn't* murder John Bair? No no no. No, ladies and gentlemen, that's not why they are heroes throughout the land. You know, as well as I do, that, rightly or wrongly, they are heroes throughout the land precisely because they *did* murder John Bair."

Darquan Strong stepped back and fixed the jury in a gaze which each of them felt was directed exclusively in their direction.

"You *must* return a guilty verdict ladies and gentlemen. We have their fingerprints on the murder weapon; a photograph of them at the time and place of the murder; and an overwhelmingly powerful motive: to rid the world of the brute that was John Bair. Is it beyond all reasonable doubt? Well...you know they did it ...I know they did it...we all know they did it. End of story. Thank you.

He sat down to a deafening silence.

The Honourable Lady Gladys Brown then addressed the jury with a brief overview of the evidence given and ended by directing them thus:

"Ladies and gentlemen, both prosecution and defence have stated plainly that John Bair ran a criminal empire with absolute ruthlessness. You may well believe that he fully deserved what he got...but you must not...and I repeat...*you must not*...let that belief influence, in any way whatsoever, your decision regarding the innocence or guilt of the two accused men."

Lady Brown paused, made a slight adjustment to her wig, straightened the great red crosses on her robe, and took a sip of water.

"Thank you, ladies and gentlemen of the jury. Please go now and begin your deliberations."

...

Meanwhile, back in the Highlands, in a wet and windswept Auchtergarry, gathered around Superintendent Smart's desk were Detective Inspector Bonnie Blackthorn, Inspector Jonathan Slighman, Detective Sergeant Ben Munro, Detective Sergeant Bob Silver, Doctor Alistair Probe, and of course Superintendent John Smart himself. All of them were on edge. What was happening back in Edinburgh? Everyone expected a verdict today...but which way was this baby going to fall? Nerves were taut. Tempers touchy.

"...What's the problem?" demanded Inspector Slighman, "please please please tell me what the problem is. They're murderers. Murder is against the law. Find them guilty, bang them up, melt down the key...simple."

"Well I dunno..." offered Bob Silver.

"No...it's not that simple..." tried Sergeant Munro.

"Of course it's simple. Jesus Christ...murder is the worst crime in the book. These are bad guys. Absolutely deserve whatever's coming to them."

Alistair Probe shook his head sadly. "But these are decent men Jonathan...bloody hell...they were provoked beyond endurance."

"Provoked!? Cold blooded murder, that's what it was...premeditated...malice aforethought ...whatever...not a single fucking leg to stand on."

"Right calm down everyone..." said Superintendent Smart, "things are getting rather..."

"Er...that's your phone Sir," interjected Bonnie.

"...I beg your pardon?"

"Your phone Sir, it's ringing."

"Ah...eh...hello Superintendent Smart here. Eh...right. Really? Okay, thanks."

He put the phone down and looked round the room.

"Right everyone...the news from Edinburgh is that the jury is out. Damn nerve-racking this. What d'ye think Bonnie? Eh? Give us your thoughts."

"Well Sir...the evidence certainly points to their guilt..."

"Hear hear..."

"...er...thanks Jonathan...but it's the strangest case ever. These are intelligent men...why leave their fingerprints on the banjo? Why leave the banjo at all? Why wear such outlandish...well maybe not outlandish exactly...but such noticeable clothes...?"

"Eh? Oh come on Bonnie...they made basic mistakes that's all...they're not great criminal minds you know..."

"Maybe so Jonathan..but..."

And so the arguments raged back and forth. The long wet afternoon passed slowly and fractiously. Tempers were frayed and temperatures raised.

It seemed an age before the superintendent's phone finally rang again.

"Hello   Superintendent   Smart   here.   Oh…okay…well well…right…yes…thank you."

He looked round the table once more.

"That   was   Edinburgh   everyone…the   jury   has   reached   a verdict…erm…they're guilty."

Chapter 32

The 'Och Aye' Denouement

"Yes! Yes yes yes!" Inspector Slighman punched the air. "You beauty! We did it! We got the buggers." He jumped up and performed a somewhat uncharacteristic celebratory jig. Nobody else in the room felt like celebrating. Even Superintendent Smart, who felt relief that the case was finally over without further embarrassment to his division felt no real elation. The others were positively subdued. The Solent brothers had made an impression on each of them and although they all had been pretty sure from the start what the verdict would be, they still felt a sense of sadness at the outcome.

"Oh well," mused Sergeant Silver, "I know it's life for murder, but I suppose they'll get out after six or seven years...good behaviour and all that."

"Yeah they'll get treated leniently...mitigating circumstances...extreme provocation etcetera etcetera," said Ben Munro as he gazed unseeing out of the window.

"At least, Bonnie, you'll get credit for a good case well handled," said Alistair Probe morosely, "that's something I suppose."

"I've never been happy about this case Alistair, you know that. There are too many...I dunno...weird bits...unexplained bits..."

Superintendent Smart felt the need to bring some closure to the case.

"Right folks...at least we can all get back to normal now...back to the day-to-day stuff...that's the excitement over, thank God."

As if to emphasise his point a desk sergeant came in and placed the day's action folder on his desk. The minutiae of everyday

262

policing...life without the Toasters and the Och Aye case...was already returning to normal. A brief skim through it revealed the reassuring dullness of traffic reports, duty rosters, disciplinary reviews, training programmes, and budget statements. There was even a couple of photographs of the superintendent at breakfast with his wife at the Chesterlake Hotel in London. The superintendent smiled a rueful little smile and shook his head at the bygone-ness of the whole thing.

"One wonders," mused Alistair Probe, "what the tabloids will make of all this tomorrow."

Superintendent Smart had little doubt. "The Post, unquestionably, will continue to champion the brothers and froth at the mouth with faux outrage about the justice system in this country. Accursed rag."

"Accursed rag indeed. Bootle's a rogue..." growled Slighman, "...would print any damn lie...defame any person alive... if he thought it might boost circulation."

"Well," said Bonnie, "I guess every tabloid in the land...and probably some broadsheets too...will be demanding clemency. A pardon even...though there's no chance of that..."

"No...unfortunately..." added Ben Munro wistfully.

"Yes...it's all very sad..."

"...Mmm.."

The conversation, already desultory, slowly petered out.

"Right everyone..." said Superintendent Smart after a prolonged pause, "...is that it? Anybody got anything else to add?"

Heads shook around the table

"Right, many thanks everyone...a job well done...we'll call it a day at that. Now..." he smiled a gently sardonic smile,"...let's return to the daily grind of normality."

Everyone quietly gathered their bits and pieces, pushed their chairs back, stood up, and headed for the door. Except Bonnie, who appeared, thought Sergeant Munro, to be lost in a reverie...a wide-eyed reverie. Then he realised she was staring at something on the desk. Without looking up she addressed a question to the superintendent.

"Er…Sir…erm, when exactly was that conference in London?…this breakfast in the photograph?"

"Eh…oh…er…oh yes…well, believe it or not it was the morning of the toaster theft… and of course the murder. We flew up to Glasgow later that morning. Was at my desk by three in the afternoon."

Bonnie stood up slowly.

"Oh my God. Oh…my…sweet…."

Everyone looked at her.

"What is it Ma'am?" asked Ben.

"…Oh help. Help help help."

"Whatever's the matter Bonnie?" asked the superintendent.

Bonnie continued to stare at the photograph, her face a picture of shocked incredulity.

"Take a closer look at your photograph Sir…especially take a closer look at who's sitting at the table behind you…"

The five men in the room crowded behind her and peered at the photograph. One by one they gasped.

"Oh Jesus."

"Holy moly!"

"Hell's bells…"

"What in the name…"

"Flamin' Ada…!"

"It's him, isn't it…?" asked Bonnie rhetorically, "….it's Peter Solent."

"It certainly looks like him!"

"It's him all right…that's definitely Peter bloody Solent."

"It most assuredly is him."

"Staring right at the camera."

"Nonsense," interjected Inspector Slighman, "it's a look-alike. Can't possibly be him."

"Oh yes it can Jonathan…" responded DI Blackthorn shaking her head with disbelief and admiration, "…oh yes it can. Planned to perfection...couldn't remember where he was eh? I bet he remembers well enough now. Well well well...that's certainly got him off the hook."

"Good God...I knew I'd seen him before." said Superintendent Smart slumping wearily into his chair.

"Brilliant...absolutely brilliant..." breathed DS Munro, enrapt.

"I'm so glad..." began Alistair Probe.

The superintendent's phone rang. Still somewhat dazed, he picked it up. "Er hello...Superintendent Smart here. Who?...eh?...Bootle?...Bootle of the Post?....dreadful man...what the hell does he want? Not exactly the best moment...okay okay put him through...hello?...hello, yes...yes Mr Bootle, I'm fine thank you...yes...yes and you too...now how can I help you? A what?...a mobile phone?...on your desk?...really?....eh?...the one George Solent lost...no, me neither...a photograph of *what*? Say that again...oh good God. Yes yes...yes...fine...send the thing on. Thank you."

The superintendent closed his eyes and delicately replaced the receiver.

"That," he said, "as I'm sure you all gathered, was Billy-damn-his-soul-to-hell-Bootle from the Post." He tentatively opened his eyes again. "A mobile phone has turned up on his desk...out of the blue...allegedly...and, as I'm sure you all heard, it's the one lost by George Solent...I didn't even know he had lost his damn phone for God's sake. Anyhow, there's a photograph on it we must see, seemingly, so he's just emailed it to me. I guess it should be here by now," he said, firing his computer into life.

Everyone gathered with some apprehension around his laptop. He tapped his mail icon, opened the email and tapped the attachment icon. A photograph filled the screen.

Again, stunned gasps filled the room.

There, smiling a gentle, apologetic smile, standing in the kitchen belonging to Carla and Jonathan Slighman, with a copy of that morning's Daily Post under one arm, and a toaster under the other, was George Solent. He had taken a selfie. A selfie which, once it was ruled authentic...which nobody doubted it would be...would prove him guilty of the theft of a toaster, but innocent of the murder of John 'Big Bruno' Bair.

"Well, gentlemen," said Bonnie once everyone had stopped gasping and things had calmed down a little, "it seems we have been well bested by the Toasters. Everything timed to perfection...all the bits of evidence...the banjo, the motorbike, the phones...strewn all over the Way. The guilty verdict can't stand of course and the case'll have to be re-opened..."
"Oh God," groaned Superintendent Smart.
"...But," continued DI Blackthorn, "the waters have been so muddied, so hopelessly churned-up, that bringing anyone to justice now for Big Bruno's murder will be beyond the powers of any police force. The case is now utterly impossible – there's not a prosecutor in the land who'd look at it, and not a jury in the land who'd convict."
"So who the hell did bump the scumbag off?" asked Sergeant Munro.
"My guess would be either Jessica's brothers or Peter and George's sons...Douglas's son maybe...her cousins. That's a team of at least seven...I certainly think they could all have been involved in the planning...as of course were the Toasters themselves. Though I doubt that Jessica knew anything about it."
Alistair Probe laughed self-mockingly. "So, a couple of their nephews...or sons or whatever...dressed in orange bloody chords and a deerstalker...just in case anybody should spot them from a distance...whacked the horrible man, in perfect synchronicity with the toaster misdemeanour in Lochain and a particular breakfast in London. Exquisite."
"I always knew he'd stolen our toaster..." complained Slighman bitterly.
His mobile rang.
"Hello?"

"Inspector Slighman?"

"Yes."

"It's Chief Superintendent Theodore Greenside here from Greater Manchester Police. I'm delighted to be able to tell you that we're offering you the post of Chief Inspector...starting as soon as you're available." And so, to Inspector Slighman's rapturous joy, the world-wide ineptitude of recruitment panels manifested itself once more. He smiled beatifically. He floated. He had escaped.

"And, of course," continued Bonnie, "we have not a shred of evidence against any of them. Not a shred."

"No," agreed Sergeant Munro, "and nor are we likely to find any."

"So, we'll never know whodunit?" asked Alistair Probe

"Nope, I don't believe we ever will Alistair."

"Good," said Bob Silver, Ben Munro, and Alistair Probe in unison.

Inspector Slighman's phone poinged to tell him he'd received a text. He read it and gave out a low heart-rending moan.

"What is it old man...whatever's wrong?" asked Alistair Probe.

"It's Carla — she's just received two free vouchers for La Grande Assiette."

DS Munro's mobile poinged too. Text from Becky:
Fancy doing the WHW together? Xxx

The Daily Post

Toasters Innocent!

Exclusive

Billy Bootle Reporting

In a dramatic turn of events in the Och Aye murder case, the Post has uncovered photographic evidence which proves beyond any doubt that the Toaster brothers are innocent! They remained in custody last night but...

...The End